POETIC JUSTICE

R.C. Bridgestock

THE
DOME
PRESS

Published by The Dome Press, 2019
Copyright © R.C. Bridgestock
The moral right of R.C. Bridgestock to be recognised as the author
of this work has been asserted in accordance with the
Copyright, Designs and Patents Act 1988.

This is a work of fiction. All characters, organisations and events portrayed in
this novel are either products of the author's imagination or are used
fictitiously.

A CIP catalogue record for this book is available from the British Library

ISBN: 9781912534159

The Dome Press
23 Cecil Court
London WC2N 4EZ

www.thedomepress.com

Printed and bound in Great Britain by Clays Ltd, Elcograf S.p.A.

Typeset in Garamond by Elaine Sharples

Praise for *Poetic Justice*

'*Poetic Justice* is a dark tale that intertwines high stakes mystery with personal tragedy. Detective Jack Dylan manages to retain his humanity in the face of terrible adversity in a story that brims with authenticity.' **Adam Hamdy**

'Rings with a sure touch of insider authenticity' **Adrian Magson**

'A multi-faceted page turner. The perfect way to meet Jack Dylan' **Alison Bruce**

'*Poetic Justice* combines gritty realism with great heart.' **Ashley Dyer**

'*Poetic Justice* is crime fiction gold, with secrets, lies and tragic consequences. This is the authentic voice of the police procedural; crime fiction written by experts, who have lived through the real thing. R.C. Bridgestock books always deliver a cracking story with an expert's insight.' **Howard Linskey**

Poetic Justice is a terrific read. The Bridgestock's are an authentic voice in crime literature and have created a compelling character in DI Jack Dylan.' **J.D. Fennell**

'Jack's back – and this time it's personal. His wife is dead, his daughter is in danger and now two local teenagers have gone missing. But DI Jack Dylan is no ordinary detective. The ninth novel in the series is actually a prequel to the previous eight, and has all the elements you expect from crime writing duo Bob and Carol Bridgestock. The writing is smart and sharp, with plenty of insider knowledge and lashings of local Yorkshire colour. The plot grips from the start and doesn't let up. A fast-paced, high-octane read.' **Paul Burston**

'A cracking read – fantastic story embedded in authentic police procedure' **Helen Pepper**, Forensic specialist

'Draws you in from the first page – one of the best crime novels I've read in years' **Adam Croft**

POETIC JUSTICE

R.C. Bridgestock

To our family who lived with us through the real
crime and support us in fiction.

For law enforcement officers – the true heroes – who strive
for justice for the victims and their families.

You reap what you sow.

Be not deceived.
God is not mocked: for whatever man soweth,
that shall he also reap.

Galatians 6:7

Chapter One

Frank Bland's hand trembled as he fumbled for the phone. The receiver felt too heavy as he lifted it. His heart was pounding in his chest; his shoulders heaved with the effort of running; his legs felt like jelly. When he breathed in, the cold air froze his throat and lungs. Leaning heavily against the door, Frank dialled 999 and, while he waited for someone to answer, he closed his eyes and left a prayer on God's answering machine. An angel in the mortal guise of a BT operator answered.

'Emergency, which service please?'

Shock, it appeared, had rendered him dumb. The controller sought to get him to speak, listening all the while for background noises, ruling out a kid's prank. Frank licked his lips; his tongue felt like sandpaper.

'Can you tell me your name? Where are you ringing from?'

When the line remained soundless the operator persisted. 'Can you cough or make another audible sign to let me know that you are in need of assistance?' she said.

He could see his breath spiral upwards out of his mouth. He tried, and tried again, but he couldn't make a noise. A rush of adrenalin caused a burning sensation to run through his veins and, as his panic loomed larger, he could feel the perspiration run the length of his spine.

The operator persisted. 'Dial 55 if you are in danger.'

Fleetingly, Frank looked at his right hand, the skin pale grey in the moonlight that shone through the window of the call box. He was shaking, and not from the cold; sweat stuck his shirt to his back. He extended his quivering fingers and, as quickly as they'd allow, dialled 55.

The call was immediately transferred to the police operator. His voice was deep, calm and soothing, but at the same time authoritative, just what Frank needed at that moment. He felt the blood rush back to his brain and control come sliding in.

'If you're in danger please dial a number,' said the police operator.

Frank forced his voice out through his lips. His throat felt so constricted, he marvelled that he could breathe. His words came out in a rush, as if they'd been suppressed in a bubble.

'There's been an accident. The car in front of me, it went off the road and vanished down the ravine.'

His frantic, breathless words, as the only witness on the road at the time heading in the same direction towards Harrowfield Town, were recorded.

When the police operator ended the call, Frank slammed the receiver down and, backing away, pushed the heavy red door open and went out into the darkness. As advised, he returned to the scene.

He followed the reflective road studs that lined the sweeping highway, which weaved and stretched for miles ahead across the Pennines. The sky was clear and the moonlight softened the darkness. The mild, dry conditions were a complete contrast to the previous weekend, when winter had arrived overnight, as it often did in the north of England. It seemed too calm for what he had seen to be real.

Hands in his pockets, and still trembling from shock, he watched the hazard lights on his car flashing rhythmically. With only a little light from the sky, he stood on the grass verge, still struggling to believe what he had seen, and peered down into the blackness of the ravine. All was quiet and still. His heart was beating painfully fast in his chest, after the exertion of the uphill hike. He struggled to catch the tight, hard breaths inside him and forced them out slowly instead, to make himself calm down.

He looked about him. The lights of the M62 were behind him, but neither they nor the reflective road studs were any use in his attempt to follow the numerous sheep tracks that led down into the abyss. If only he were younger and fitter, he'd have been down like a flash. He looked up to see a swirling shape appear, shimmering like the folds of a curtain in the sky, stirred by the wind in an eerie silence. But this was no divine intervention come to help those in the crash; it was smoke rising from the vehicle – a sign, he feared, of worse to come.

Frank looked from left to right, unsure from which way the emergency services would come, straining to hear the sirens approaching, hoping and willing another vehicle to come along to bring him support on the isolated stretch of moorland road. He felt useless, he felt vulnerable, he felt extremely scared.

In the stillness, and with little else he could do, he berated himself for not listening to his daughter, who had begged him, on the death of his wife, to get a mobile phone. 'What if the telephone box had been vandalised?' he could hear her say. He shuddered to think what he would have done then.

After what seemed like an eternity, and to his utmost relief, in the distance he saw a convoy of blue lights traversing the valley below and coming in his direction. Their lights brightened up the sky immediately above them in a continuous blue streak.

Frank knew only too well that people had differing views about the use of the blues and twos during the hours of darkness, especially when the roads were generally quiet. He'd sat in on enough discussions, with arguments both for and against. The objectors didn't see the need for the emergency services disturbing them in their homes at night and thought that they should show restraint ; he'd said as much himself. However, he now understood that, for those awaiting the assistance of emergency services, the sound of a siren or the sight of a blue light was a reassurance like no other.

The old man watched the convoy pass through the village of Marsden. The blue flashing line moved at speed against the blackened backdrop. Now they turned up toward Standedge.

The sirens got louder and louder and, hopping from one foot to another, Frank anxiously waited to greet them. Shivering, he watched their final approach. It was nine-fifteen in the evening on this February night and in the valley a swirling mist could now be seen creeping from the moorland in the path of the headlights. Was this nature's attempt to hide the devastation beneath?

As the police, ambulance, fire brigade and the mountain-rescue vehicles came together their sirens silenced in unison. They parked in an orderly fashion near where the vehicle had left the road, just below where Frank stood.

'Down there.' The jittery old man pointed.

Taking instruction from Frank, the crews began to assemble their equipment. Within minutes, dark bodies, not unlike seals in high-vis jackets, began scrambling down the unwelcoming terrain, slithering into the unknown towards where the vehicle had disappeared into the forest, with shouts of, 'Hold on, help is on its way!'

Initially, the flashlights shone in every direction, showing the rescuers their steep descent into the dense, dark wood below. But, minutes later, the team came together in an illuminated line. The site of the upturned wreckage had been located. A rescuer's shout appeared to come from the bowels of the earth.

'The vehicle's caught on pine trees approximately fifty metres down the slope, so in my estimation there's still a further drop of around fifty metres to the river below.'

A uniformed police officer approached Frank.

'Mr Bland?'

'Frank,' he nodded enthusiastically.

'PC Pamela Clare, although everyone calls me PC.' Her warm smile was comforting. 'I believe you telephoned the incident in on three nines?'

'Yes, from the telephone box down the road,' Frank said. Trying to anticipate the next question, he called upon his memory to recollect some useful information. He closed his eyes for a moment, concentration making him frown. 'I was on my way from my daughter's in Bury. I go every week since my wife ... Anyway, as you're aware, this road has just re-opened after the snow and ice and, well, I don't "do" motorways – especially the M62 with all the heavy goods vehicles constantly on your tail. This road is fast enough for me. The only downside is,' he hung his head, 'it means I have to pass the infamous Saddleworth moors. That bit of the journey always sends a chill down my spine, no matter what time of day. Hindley and Brady and the five children they killed – you're probably too young to remember ...'

PC Clare's body language and facial expression told him to return to the accident. 'Can you tell me what you saw tonight, Frank?'

Frank shook himself. 'Sorry, I'm rambling, aren't I?'

PC's gentle smile and professional manner encouraged him to continue.

'The road was quiet, in fact, I'd not seen another car except the Saab in front, as I came down. It was travelling at about forty miles an hour, I would guess. The driver didn't appear to be in any sort of rush. Then, suddenly, for no reason that I could see, it was as if the wheel had been grabbed from the driver's hand. The Saab suddenly swerved into the concrete posts on the left side of the road. The passenger, if there is one, would have taken a real whack. It gave me one hell of a shock. The next thing I knew the car was being driven normally again. I wondered if the driver had been drinking, or if they'd fallen asleep. Then, lo and behold, it happens again, and again. By this time, I'm dropping back, wondering what the hell is going on.'

'So, in your view, this was no accident?'

Frank shook his head despondently. 'I don't see how it could be.'

'And, when the car left the road? You think that was intentional too?'

Frank pulled a face. 'I don't know. After the car had hit the third post it didn't recover as easily, it hit the crash barrier, then rocked from side to side before heading towards the opposite side of the road towards the ravine. I knew there was an almighty drop over the edge. I admit to closing my eyes. Only when I opened them did I see the brake lights come on. You wouldn't bother braking if you intended to do it, would you?' Frank spoke quickly, anticipating her question. 'God, it gave me one hell of a shock to see it flip over and spin out of control down the ravine. There's no way I could get down there with my bad hip, but I know this road well enough to know there's a telephone box near the next lay-by, so I got to it as quick as I could, praying it hadn't been vandalised.'

PC Clare gave him a quick nod of agreement. 'And, rang three nines.'

'I feel bad that I couldn't do any more.' He nodded down towards the hillside. 'I hope they will be all right.'

Frank paled suddenly and his shaking became uncontrollable. It was clear to the seasoned police officer that the old man was in shock. Mentally noting what he had told her, she caught the attention of one of the medics and called them over.

'Can you make sure he's okay when you get the chance?' she said in a whisper. She saw Frank's eyes narrow, his deliberate intake of a deep breath. She reassured him that he had done the best that anyone could have done in the circumstances. The medic arrived with a blanket to wrap around his shoulders, but his eyes could not be drawn from the activity down the ravine.

'It looks very overgrown and pretty inaccessible to me. Can you imagine if you'd attempted to get to them and injured yourself?' PC Clare nodded slowly. 'No, you did the right thing, Mr Bland.'

He turned to her. 'Frank, please,' he said, running a bony hand through his white, wire-brush hair. Suddenly he yawned, and she offered him a seat in the police car. He declined.

A burst of frenzied voices told them that the rescue teams had reached the upturned vehicle. There was a rush of people at the road surface then quick, fleeting glimpses of equipment being lowered down to those requesting it. The shouting, although controlled, held great urgency.

'Is he alive?' A strong, incisive voice asked.

A shrill reply came. 'I have a pulse.'

The pause wasn't long enough to prepare Frank for the disembodied whisper that followed this news. It was quieter and seemed slower to reach the onlookers, as if it had been suppressed along the way. 'She's not breathing ...'

The Saab had a personalised number plate: JDYN 1. The vehicle was now a mangled, contorted heap of metal, and even though some paintwork still showed signs of the cosmic-blue colour in places, collectively it looked like it belonged in a scrapper's yard. There was the gut-wrenching smell of blood; but the underlying smell of petrol was more of a worry to the rescuers.

Chapter Two

The shattered glass of the windows was scattered about them, among the blood and what was probably flesh and bone. One of the first things visible, before artificial light gave them more clarity, was the tiny flames licking around the driver's head and his pendulous arm. The driver was trapped by his seatbelt, which was almost strangling him. The strange sounds emanating from his motionless body told them he was breathing, if only shallowly. His shirt sleeve was all but ripped off, and the light beam revealed horrendous damage to his arm, which was horribly twisted, the flesh torn.

Once the flames were extinguished, the rescuers were able to work safely, although thick smoke still encircled the area around them, making it difficult for them to breathe. Everyone there worked quietly and diligently, in no doubt that an unintended spark could cause an explosion; their lives were most definitely still at risk.

There had been two people in the car and, as one emergency team dealt with the driver, the passenger was seen to by another. They had to decide who needed their attention more urgently; neither was moving. The seatbelt of the female was detached and her airbag hadn't activated. Her body lay some metres away from the vehicle, crumpled and twisted, more like a rubber model of a person than a human being. Only the blood around her head, and the guts that spilled from her side, indicated that this body had once been alive.

The paramedics quickly checked for vital signs. Her face was hidden by her long dark hair. There was no pulse. Pushing her hair to the side off her face revealed a large, sunken head wound on her left side, oozing quantities of blood.

In the unforgiving location, with nothing to lose but everything to gain by working on the badly wounded victim, the team frantically carried out CPR. Unresponsive, the woman was pronounced dead at the scene, and as the rescuers hung their heads, sweating profusely from their exertion, her body was covered with a blanket and placed on a stretcher, ready to be taken back up the hillside and into the waiting ambulance.

On the opposite side of the vehicle, the driver had been rescued from his bat-like position and hauled through the open driver's door onto a stretcher. His airbag had deployed but was severely scorched. Adding to his injuries were several burns to his face, lower arms and hands.

The paramedics stabilised the driver, dealing with his burns as best they could and continuing to check his vital signs. His pulse was very weak and, with him still unconscious, they started the long climb up the ravine. Only then did their concentration turn to getting the two to hospital. It was a far from easy task to manoeuvre the stretchers up the steep and uneven slope, but with all the emergency crews working together, the ascent was managed with as little stress on the injured as possible. Once the two were on board, the ambulance hurriedly left the scene, its blue light whirring under the dark sky. The wailing sirens could be heard breaking the silence of the night, as the emergency vehicles re-traced their journey.

'There's no point in upsetting the witness more tonight,' whispered a rescuer in PC Clare's ear.

'I'll tell Frank that they're unconscious, shall I?' she whispered.

The rescuer nodded in agreement.

Having been examined by a paramedic, Frank made his way over to PC Clare. He could see one of the rescuers speaking with her. He felt a lot calmer now and the paramedics had deemed him fit enough to continue his journey home.

'My daughter will be very anxious until she hears I've arrived safely,' he said. 'If she's heard about the crash, she'll no doubt be panicking.' It was a weak attempt to raise a smile that focused two sets of concerned eyes upon him.

'That's what daughters do,' smiled PC.

The verbal account Frank had given to PC Clare about what he had witnessed meant that the police would need to catch up with him for a written statement within the next twenty-four hours, and she told him she would update him then on the condition of the car's occupants.

Frank Bland drove slowly home, willing himself to remember every last detail in order to be of as much use as possible to the emergency services. He was used to their procedures, having dealt with them as a mortuary assistant all his working life, although the young 'uns wouldn't remember him now. The events were still swirling around in his mind ten minutes later when he pulled up outside his house. It was in darkness. All he wanted was to get inside and to hear his daughter's voice, even if that meant she'd reprimand him – and, yes, he would agree to get a mobile phone now.

The long hours the emergency service teams spent practising rescues had proved invaluable. This may have been a fatal road accident, and might yet prove to be a double fatal, but the rescue itself had gone like clockwork; it had been faultless and was therefore deemed a success by the emergency services commanders.

The police supervisor from the Road Traffic department was called to the scene as soon as he got home after a ten-hour shift. When he arrived, he was pleased to see that the immediate area had been coned off for security and to enable investigations. Photographs had been taken. The road conditions, just as the witness, Frank Bland, had said, were confirmed by the investigators as 'good'. There was nothing obvious to the trained eye that should concern a driver. Cat's eyes illuminated the centre of the road and defined the lanes. The officer noted that the full moon gave a much better light than would normally be expected at this time of year. There were no sheep or other livestock in the area that could have caused an obstruction to distract a driver, or made him swerve suddenly not once, not twice, but three times, as had been reported. It was immediately apparent that there was considerable damage to a number of concrete posts at the side of the road – he counted one, two, three – and to the crash barrier at the hairpin bend. Bits of concrete and parts of a wing mirror, wheel trim and other debris had scattered at the points of contact and were strewn over the roadway, giving him a sense of the force of the vehicle's impact.

He bent down and touched the tarmac. The road surface was dry. *Could a mechanical failure be at fault?* he wondered. *Or was it human error?*

The police had a duty to investigate how someone had died and that was exactly what he would ensure was done: checking every bit of information carefully, using every technique and all the equipment he had at his disposal. The vehicle needed to be recovered, searched and examined in detail. That, by itself, wasn't going to be an easy task. To lift the metal, plastic and rubber mass of a car weighing over a tonne, a winch would be required at the very least, and maybe a crane. No matter what it took, it was, however, totally necessary in order to understand exactly what had taken place. He needed to find out precisely what had caused the vehicle to leave the road, ultimately leading to the loss of life.

Both driver and passenger, he had been told by the medics, were approximately mid-thirties. With no suggestion from the witness that the car had been travelling at excessive speed prior to the accident, the reported actions of the driver of the Saab puzzled him.

The traffic sergeant heard soft footsteps creeping up behind him, but he chose to keep studying the scene before him, systematically processing his next move.

'Where the hell to start?' asked PC. She sighed heavily.

He didn't look at her. His attention was on the edge of the ravine and, beyond it, on the wreck of the vehicle.

'You know as well as I do, PC, that dead men talk; a dead body affords us so much evidence of the life lived. But we'll have to wait for the results of DNA, or a report of missing people, to get a result on their identity – unless he wakes up and talks to us beforehand.'

'Do you think they're husband and wife?'

He shrugged his shoulders. 'God knows. Apparently, she's wearing a wedding ring, he isn't.'

Pamela Clare grimaced. 'I heard visual identification's impossible due to their injuries.'

He stood up and turned. 'He's heavily sedated, I've been reliably informed; his face, shoulders and arms covered in bandages.'

PC's face darkened. 'Critical?'

'Stable.'

'The next twenty-four hours are crucial.'

'Yep, and then with some luck he'll be brought out of his induced coma and be able to enlighten us.'

'If he can remember what happened, that is.'

'Well, he'll certainly be interviewed, and challenged about his account, if what he tells us doesn't fit what we already know.'

'I wonder, if there is no identification, whether we might find something in the car that would help?'

'We'll have to wait for daylight to recover and search the vehicle.'

'The recovery vehicle has been called out?'

'It has, and I guess when we both drive home from this we'll drive a little bit slower. Life's fragile, isn't it?'

The registered owner of the vehicle, according to the Police National Computer was a Mr Jack Dylan of 37 High Villas, Ripponden, Halifax, West Yorkshire. This area was covered by the neighbouring police division of Calderdale and so the traffic sergeant liaised with colleagues there and made them aware of the situation. A local police officer would visit the address and find out if Mr Dylan was the current owner and, if so, glean what information they could about who had been driving the car at the time of the accident. It was always possible that he was the injured man.

The unit dispatched was made up of a rookie and his mentor.

'When I was in the Traffic department, fatal RTAs were dealt with differently,' said Harry Leach.

The young rookie rolled his eyes and stared out of the vehicle's window. He felt sick to his stomach, sort of like the way he did when he had to speak in public but much worse. How could the old fella be so calm when he may be about to deliver the worst news in the world to a family?

The old timer glanced at Sultan Alam Mohammed. 'You okay, Sam?'

Sam nodded. He felt a lump in his throat.

'Back then a force photographer would take photographs of the scene and send us copies through the internal mail a few weeks later. We'd get a written report from the vehicle examiner, who would take a close look at any mechanical defects on the vehicle that might be a contributory factor to the crash. Oh, and an accident investigator would draw us a detailed plan of the scene and give some calculations on the speed and braking efficiency of the vehicles. His report could take two or three months.'

Arriving at the address, the pair found the detached house in darkness. Harry knocked loudly on the door and they stood and waited patiently on the doorstep. Sam noticed his breathing was so heavy he could feel and hear every breath he took and he wondered if the old timer could too. He tried to calm down.

'The basic rule of thumb is to get in there, give them the death notice without dilly-dallying and get the hell out, okay?' said Harry, out of the corner of his mouth.

Sam nodded emphatically.

'If you want to be a police officer you'll have to learn to become a sponge: able to soak up large amounts of emotional trauma, but not be affected by it too much. You're lucky, our welfare is now at the top of the force's concerns. Pfff – that never happened before; I don't know why it has now. I guess all the new rules mean it's mapped out now that they are responsible for our welfare.'

When there was no response at the door, Sam followed Harry to the back of the house. Security lights came on, illuminating the path. There was no answer to their knocking at the back door either. Harry looked through the patio windows. The rookie expelled the long breath of air he had been holding unintentionally. He was relieved that he didn't have to be the bearer of sad, life-changing news quite yet.

The knocking and the tell-tale sight of the security lights had caused one of the neighbours to come out to see what all the commotion was about. Mr Anderson, in his grey and red striped pyjamas, dressing gown and sheepskin slippers walked down the path towards the officers. He and his wife Janice were friends of the Dylans and he invited the officers inside and confirmed that the blue Saab they were enquiring about still belonged to his neighbours.

'I waved to Kay – Dylan's wife – as she was leaving home in the car.' He looked thoughtful. 'It'd be about five o'clock.'

'Was she alone?' asked Harry.

'Yes, I think so,' he said. He cocked his head to one side, his eyes narrowed and his face turned grave. 'Before you say any more, you do know her husband Jack Dylan is a senior police officer, don't you?'

There was a long pause as Harry stared at Tony Anderson, a blank expression masking his internal struggle. Sam had never seen his mentor quiet for so long, and he felt compelled to say something. 'Do you think she might have been going to pick Mr Dylan up from somewhere?' he asked.

'I don't know,' Tony replied. 'Maybe. I haven't seen Jack around for a couple of days. I just thought he was on a job. He's in and out at all hours of the day and night.' Tony looked a little embarrassed. 'Well, as you guys know. It's the job.'

The information was passed back to headquarter's control room, where the operator contacted the divisional commander to inform him that Jack Dylan's vehicle had been involved in a fatal road accident.

'Owing to the nature of the survivor's injuries, visual identification is not possible at this time,' the operator said.

'What about the casualty's fingerprints? Can't these be checked against force records?'

'Again, due to extensive burns to the driver's hands, I am reliably informed, sir, that it's not possible.'

'I see. And the passenger was pronounced dead at the scene?'

'Yes, sir, and the passenger was a female.'

As senior detective covering the station in Dylan's absence, DS Banks was made aware of the crash, the injuries of the male driver and the death of the female passenger early the following morning. The moment he put the phone down, Larry Banks reached for the bottle hidden in his desk drawer. He had been given news like this before but this was different. He took several swigs from the bottle and, after a few minutes, managed to calm himself down a little. 'Never assume,' he heard Dylan's voice saying in his ear, as plain as if he was there beside him. With a flicker of hope, he began to think more clearly. It looked bad, that much was true. Someone had died and another person was seriously injured and lying in intensive care. But was it possible the two people weren't actually Dylan and Kay?

Larry ran a hand distractedly through his hair. *What could he do?* He spun the cap on the whisky and paused for a moment before removing it, taking another swig and throwing the empty bottle in the bin. He rested his head against the back of his chair and closed his eyes. *What would Dylan do at a time like this?* he asked himself.

And then it came to him. Larry reached across the desk and pulled Dylan's tray towards him. He searched through it until he finally found the copy of the letter that confirmed the details of Dylan's residential course. The two-day course was south of Sheffield, so Dylan had needed to stay over for at least one night and had elected to stay for two because of the early morning meetings. He'd also taken one of the CID cars … Larry jumped out of the chair as if it were on fire, leapt to the window and searched the police station's backyard. There was no sign of the CID car. He widened his search to the illuminated streets beyond. As far as he could see, the CID car was not there either. The question remained: had Dylan returned early?

Back at his desk, Larry picked up the phone and rang the porter at Dylan's hotel, giving him the details of the vehicle Dylan was using. Disappointment overwhelmed the DS when he was told that his boss's room keys had been returned to reception. Larry explained why he was calling and the porter immediately agreed to check Dylan's room and the register in which Dylan would have signed in and out.

As he waited for the return call, Larry noticed his hands trembling. He silently prayed his friend would be okay. Detective Inspector Jack Dylan was the best boss he'd ever had, his colleague, his mentor and his friend. Thirty-five, six feet tall and born in Yorkshire, Jack was known for his hard exterior – much needed in the job that he did – but Larry knew him to be kind-hearted underneath. Jack had a good sense of humour and had covered Larry's back, and those of others under his command, on many occasions. He was known by the hierarchy as a safe pair of hands.

When the call came it was not with the news that Larry had hoped for. It appeared that Dylan had left the hotel in the CID car, but the porter could not tell him exactly when. It seemed very possible that he might be the casualty lying in intensive care, fighting for his life.

The night report for the chief's log read as follows: *A female passenger was pronounced dead at the scene of a car accident on the A62. She is believed to be the wife of Detective Inspector Jack Dylan. The driver, who is unable to be identified at this time owing to his injuries, is believed to be Mr Jack Dylan. The driver is in a critical condition, currently in an induced coma at the hospital.*

Chapter Three

Ten days earlier

Detective Inspector Jack Dylan was in the City of London where he had just finished an intense, two-week residential development course for negotiators. Threat levels had risen to 'severe' due to ricin having been discovered in the north of the capital, an indication that this could be the most worrying terrorist threat to Britain since 9/11, the previous year. Though the intelligence reports named Heathrow, where some of Dylan's hostage training had taken place, the thought was that terrorists might refocus their efforts away from the airport and the hope was to deter them by increasing the number of uniformed officers in the city. Uniformed police were being assisted by the deployment of troops following a tip-off from MI5 to Scotland Yard. Downing Street had stressed the need not to overreact and 'do the terrorists job for them' and encouraged everyone to continue to live a normal life.

Dylan made his way to a telephone kiosk at King's Cross Station, swept along with the crowd, at a seasoned city dweller's pace. So tired was he from the schedule – kept awake for hours on end by interrogations, woken up from his sleep, undergoing long, arduous hours of negotiation – that when he and his colleagues had been able to let their hair down on the last night, they all opted for their beds and an early night. As soon as he'd put his head on the pillow he'd gone out like a light, forgetting to plug his mobile into its charger.

Berating himself for the second time that morning for being disorganised, Dylan squeezed into the telephone booth. Shuffling sideways, he looked down around his feet for a clean spot to put his holdall down. The concrete floor was littered with the stuff that people leave when they wait around a lot: cigarette butts, gum wrappers and crisp papers. Dylan put his change on the little shelf under the phone, picked up the receiver and wiped it with his coat sleeve. He dialled his home number. Facing the kiosk wall, he saw an adornment of cards and phone numbers, some written in lipstick, advertising personal services, massages and all types of unrestrained immoral self-indulgence. Alongside these was a selection of abusive graffiti. Dylan's eyes settled wearily on one: *ACAB* – All Coppers Are Bastards.

Outside, two uniformed police officers were cuffing a scruffy individual. At his feet lay a handbag, its contents strewn over the floor. Dylan caught the eye of the young rookie who was covering his partner's back while he dealt with the prisoner. His eyes spoke volumes to Dylan. *Why am I doing this?* Dylan felt his frustration. Then he looked beyond and saw another officer on his knees comforting an old lady. 'That's why we're doing this, mate,' he said in a whisper.

There was no answer at home. He sighed heavily and put the phone down. Dylan looked at his watch, slightly puzzled. Kay should be home now. He waited.

When Kay didn't answer a second time, he tried her mobile. It went to her answer service.

'What is the point of having a mobile, if …?' he fumed, and then thought immediately about his own situation. *She could be driving*, he thought. He left a message, not knowing what else he could do. He hoped that she would be there to greet him off the train at Harrowfield train station at six-thirty. As he came out of the phone box, the announcement came over the tannoy: the Leeds train was boarding on platform 8.

Striding onto the platform, he was more than grateful that his forward journey was above ground. Travelling on the Northern Line into the City earlier in the day had not been an experience he wished to repeat often. Strangers squashed in stale air, the only respite coming when the doors opened. And he'd nearly missed his station. Oh, how he admired those who used the underground daily as their mode of transport. His musing was broken by the announcement that his train was about to leave. Safely tucked away in a seat by the window, he was pleased to see there was no one sitting next to him and for this he was grateful too.

The whistle blew and the train pulled out on schedule.

With the end of winter near, the ground was wet and slushy, the sky grey and dismal. As the train chugged slowly out of the station the half-empty carriage clattered over uneven tracks and battered points. Dylan took in the graffiti and wondered what kind of person risked their life to display their art in that way. The industrial buildings, once a hive of activity, would now seem so dull and lifeless without it.

Gradually the train picked up speed and the world whizzed past his window. He hardly noticed the time pass as the gentle rocking lulled him into a state of relaxation. He reflected, in a dreamlike state, on the hostage negotiators' course at Hendon Police College. It had been by far the most intensive in his police service. There had been very little respite from the round-the-clock scenarios and constant, continual pressure. He knew the role of a negotiator required a high level of self-control: to be able to remain calm even under immense pressure, possess extraordinary interpersonal skills, be able to use active listening and be able to work well within a team. He had to admit to feeling a little bit terrified of holding what might be someone's last moments in his hands when they were at their most vulnerable.

In the past two weeks he had worked alongside strangers, some of whom had a very limited command of the English language and little knowledge of life in the UK. Negotiation, he had learnt, was not on the agenda everywhere. Should hostages be taken in some countries, the approach was lay siege to wherever they were held and plan an armed assault in which, hopefully, only the kidnappers would be killed. The course had, no doubt, given the police officers from those countries food for thought.

Dylan was pretty certain he had been kept going by adrenalin in the last couple of days; his energy levels were truly drained. It was nice to sit quiet, still, and not be expected to talk continuously. Having passed the course, he would immediately be an 'on-call' negotiator, back in the Yorkshire force, for serious life-threatening incidents including kidnap, extortion, terrorism and suicide; the latter being undoubtedly the most common.

'And, what do you get for it?'

He heard Kay's angry voice in his ear. It startled him. He opened his eyes and sat up. Looking to the seat next to him, he half expected her to be there. He turned and looked through the window and instinctively lifted his face up to the rays from the sun, that had emerged from between two clouds. 'Nothing,' he answered in his head.

He imagined her scoffing, 'So, you choose to spend time your time away from me for no extra money?' He saw himself nodding at her, in the kitchen of their salubrious home, his eyes still resting on his newspaper.

'I'm doing it because I think I can make a difference.'

Kay's wrinkled nose lifted her glasses. 'Who do you think you are? God?'

Dylan felt a little nostalgic when the train pulled into Penistone railway station, because it reminded him of his dad, who had worked on the railways. In his mind's eye, he could see his father talking to a colleague on the platform, his mother looking hot and bothered and him and his siblings in the carriage in their Sunday best with their holiday trunk. Dylan's stomach would have been jittery, feeling his mother's anxiety that Dad might not make it on board to join them. But he always did.

The train picked up more passengers. With hardly a spare seat to be had Dylan put his head down and thumbed his way through the pages of his newspaper. Having not had the opportunity to speak to anyone in the real world for two weeks, he was interested to see what had happened while he'd been locked in the Hendon bubble. He was distracted by a disturbance futher down the aisle. An elderly lady stumbled. She looked around as she swayed to and fro with the rhythm of the train, trying to find somewhere to sit. Dylan half stood, raised his hand and pointed to the seat next to him. Those behind her gratefully ushered her on. In silence she sat down and gathered her things around her. Turning her head away from him, she blotted her eye with a handkerchief from up her sleeve. She wore leather gloves and was dressed a little more finely than their carriage companions and she smelled of fresh roses. He turned to the window to allow her a moment and briefly closed his eyes. She reminded him of his mother.

Dylan didn't normally feel the need to converse with his fellow passengers, but for some reason he wanted to reassure the old lady. When he turned towards her, his eye was caught by an angry-looking man who was walking down the carriage in their direction. They eyeballed each other. Dylan knew that look; he knew that face; he knew that man – but where did he know him from? His mind searched frantically for a name, which would not come.

Suddenly, the carriage was plunged into a darkness that seemed to go on for ever, before the train dramatically twisted and turned, to spill out into daylight on a high path surrounded by the gnarled roots of immense trees. The angry man had disappeared, Dylan guessed through the electric doors into the next carriage. The old lady turned and asked where Dylan was heading and told him she was going to church. Dylan was momentarily taken aback. She noted his surprise and went on to explain that she was going to a funeral. She lived near the train station; the train was easier, and more reliable, than the bus.

He should go to church – he hadn't been in a while.

He was still curious about the man. He had to remember who he was. As much as he tried to remain focused on what the old lady was saying, his mind played games attempting to remember the man's name.

The next signpost announced that they were in 'God's Own Country' – and boy, was he glad to be nearly home.

Dylan stood in the gangway with his suit carrier and holdall, eagerly waiting for the train to halt and the doors to open. A short walk to the next platform and the waiting shuttle and in twenty minutes he'd be in Harrowfield.

As he sat on the bone-shaker, he thought about the times he'd had to close this line, the times he'd walked the railway line to recover the limbs of those who had taken their own lives so that they could be laid to rest, whole again, for their family and friends to grieve and ask themselves why they hadn't seen this coming.

It felt good to stretch his legs as he walked the station platform, after having sat for so long. He carried his bags up the single flight of stairs from the platform to the concourse immediately outside the station. It was raining, the sky was scarred with dark clouds and a mist swirled towards him across the busy car park. Pedestrians jostled him. He listened to the sound their footwear made as they splashed in the running water. He stood just outside the cover of the station's stairs and, in the downpour, stretched out his spine, bending down to place his bags on the floor at his feet while he waited. He breathed in the cool, fresh, clean air, and it felt good to be alive, to be free of the courses and the watchful eyes monitoring his every move. Dylan was looking forward to seeing his wife and hearing her news. A fortnight was far too long to be out of the loop.

As he waited in the now light rain, the clouds thinned to a pale grey and the sun peeped through, its rays glistening off the water as it slowly ran down the gutters. He waited, and he watched, but neither Kay nor the Saab were anywhere to be seen.

Then a car horn sounded and he looked up hopefully. A taxi pulled up on double yellow lines beside him. He reached for the warrant card in his inside pocket. The driver was an Asian male of about twenty years old, he guessed, his passenger a young, white male, no more than sixteen. He didn't see where they had come from, but two young girls aged around thirteen or fourteen were suddenly at the open passenger window. They giggled, they laughed, they both jumped in the back seat of the car and the taxi took off at speed. Dylan slid his warrant card back in his pocket and smiled to himself. He'd not been back on home turf for five minutes and he was in work mode. Or was it just an in-built instinct he'd developed for sensing trouble, he wondered?

The traffic flow had reduced significantly and would-be travellers strolled around the entrance with their cases on wheels in tow, no longer hurrying.

It seemed strange, opening the door of the red, iconic telephone box, having had the use of his mobile for a while. He stopped short. The telephone had been ripped from the wall, the coin box smashed open and the vandals had cut through the wire that had once attached the handset.

'Bastards,' Dylan muttered under his breath.

With heavy legs, he walked in the direction from which Kay would arrive, so familiar with the route that he barely paid any attention to it. Dylan stepped down onto the banking of the canal to avoid the town's one-way system and headed towards the bridge that crossed the canal. Usually he'd take the time for a quiet, relaxing reverie. But this time he was agitated, and muttered to himself, angry with Kay. His thoughts were splintered by a sudden scurry of footsteps behind him and his heart skipped a beat just as a tree branch bounced off his shoulder and caught the side of his head. As he stumbled from the blow, he retained enough of his survival instinct to glimpse the tall, dark shadow of a man. Silently, he dropped to his knees. His hands hit cold mud that slipped through his fingers, which was the last thing he remembered before a blow to the back of his head saw him sprawled, face down, in a gritty puddle.

Chapter Four

She was late. For the past two weeks she'd been late. She hated being late and it was all Kenny Fisher's fault. Kay also hated being home alone and with daughter Isla being a residential university student – something Kay had fought against from the day she had expressed a wish to spread her wings – what else was she supposed to have done to relieve her boredom but take part-time work? If Jack had worked nine-to-five, it would never have happened. Yes, it was Jack's fault she had turned elsewhere for entertainment and the excitement she craved. How selfish to encourage Isla to pursue the university course and to abandon his wife too.

Thinking about Kenny gave Kay a headache. A headache that promised to turn into more. She felt sick. Was it a migraine coming on?

Jack would be upset if she was late, but in his own, quiet way. She sometimes wished he would scream and shout at her until he was blue in the face. The pin-drop silence was the worst. She knew him well enough though to know he'd be happy to see her when she did eventually get there. Being late was awful. Dylan was never late.

Kay considered the truth. She hadn't actually ended up hating being left alone as much as she'd thought she would. In fact, she'd revelled in the freedom as Kenny, her boss, had pursued her relentlessly, making her feel vibrant, sexy and young again. She'd loved the attention.

Kay drummed her fingers on the steering wheel impatiently. She disliked traffic congestion at the best of times. With nothing else to do but wait for the vehicles ahead to move, she tilted her head upwards to look in the mirror, examining the bruise Kenny had caused when he'd grabbed her face to make her look at him. 'If you won't tell him, I will,' he'd growled through gritted teeth.

She'd answered him back, guessing by his reaction that he wasn't used to it, saying, 'I can't leave him and I won't leave him, not for you or anyone else. This is just a bit of fun, right?'

When she'd eventually got away, after promising him it wouldn't be the last time, he had followed her to the isolated lay-by where she stopped to change out of her sexy clothing and slip into her 'comfies'. He had followed her for a while … it made her feel uneasy. Was he going to follow her to the train station, to confront Dylan?

She smoothed her hair back from her face and scraped it into a ponytail. Her make-up had been removed. She pinched her pale cheeks in an effort to make them rosy, biting her lips slightly to redden them. Turning her attention to the static traffic ahead, she felt the heat of anxiety run through her. Suddenly, spray from the adjacent car's windscreen wiper hit hers; she turned and saw the young man in the car smiling at her. She smiled back flirtatiously.

But it had to stop! She had managed to keep her furtive secret for long enough, but as quickly as she had tired of the affair, Kenny had become more obsessed with her. She was only late because she had been arguing with him. Did her lover *want* her husband to find out about them? In truth, she feared he probably did.

'What if something happened to Dylan?' Kenny had said.

'You know that would be different, but let's not go there, eh?' Kay had said. She'd closed her eyes, laid her head back on the leather seat, breathed in deeply through her nose, counted to six and breathed out slowly through her mouth.

'I'm serious,' he'd said. 'You need to understand that. I want to spend the rest of my life with you.'

The past two weeks had been idyllic, in a juvenile, furtive kind of way. But it had become obvious to Kay that, for her, happiness wasn't about getting what she wanted all of the time, it was about knowing what she had and being grateful for it.

When she'd got Jack's message she had been in Kenny's Mercedes, parked in a secluded spot on the Yorkshire moors, where the silver-tongued Kenny had taken her after a spot of lunch. Kenny didn't need to be in the office any more. He'd demanded sex and as usual she had found him hard to resist. The wealthy, ruthless businessman, well connected in the community, always put her first. He could afford to dress stylishly and buy anything that his heart desired, or that he desired for her. His designer clothes, precision haircut and pampered body never had the lingering smell of the mortuary, in contrast to her husband. But leave Jack Dylan? Really?

Kay's car came to a screeching halt outside the railway station. She took some deep breaths to try to calm herself. Kenny had begged her to leave Jack, promising her she'd never want for anything. His parting comment had been, 'Dylan doesn't deserve you, yet I feel like I'm waiting for something that's never going to happen.'

Kay looked around, scanning the station car park, but Dylan was nowhere to be seen. She got out and ran the whole length of the platform, dodging the occasional passenger and stacks of luggage along the way. She peered through the windows of the waiting room. No joy. She rushed over the railway bridge, pausing once or twice to catch her breath. Eyeing the mountain of metal stairs in front of her she wished she was a bit fitter. Nevertheless, she ran up the steps two at a time. Kay stood at the top, blinking against the cold, damp air that blew in her face, so she could see if there were any trains waiting on the sidelines to pull into the station. There was another station exit at the far end of the platform which led onto the canal path, but she couldn't see anyone at the opening. Could it be that the London train had been delayed and her mad rush had been for nothing? Had Dylan jumped into a taxi? Fumbling around in her pocket for her mobile to call home, she was approached by a station official.

'Can I help you?' he asked 'You look a little, er … stressed.'

Kay pulled a tissue from her pocket and dabbed her eyes. 'It's only the wind,' she said. 'I'm not crying. It's just that I was a bit late to collect my husband from the London train and now I'm trying to find him.'

The old man looked away towards the railway line. 'The London train was on time,' he said. His face looked drawn, as if troubled by some private thought. 'I don't wish to alarm you, but I've just been informed of an incident outside. Apparently, a man has been taken to hospital by ambulance. It may not be connected …'

She didn't wait for more before she started running. Kay knew one thing about her husband, if there had been an incident Dylan would definitely be involved. He wasn't programmed to side-step issues, no matter how dangerous.

The words she had just used to Kenny rang in her ears. 'I don't want to hurt him.'

'Hurt him? And how are you going to avoid that when he finds

31

out about us? Anyway, what sort of a detective is he if he doesn't know his wife is being fucked by someone else, right under his nose?'

Kenny's words had stung. She'd never seen him so angry before. When had their meetings stopped being fun, passionate and exciting? He'd frightened her.

'Don't spoil things, Kenny,' she'd begged. 'I don't like it when you talk like that. Dylan has done nothing wrong. I guess, like they say, what he doesn't know won't hurt him.'

Arriving at the hospital, she frantically sought a place to park and followed the signs to the emergency entrance. The automatic double doors opened as she neared. At the brightly lit reception desk she told a nurse that she needed to find the person who had been blue-lighted from the train station, 'Because,' Kay's voice faltered, 'it might be my husband.'

Suddenly, she spotted Dylan slumped in a wheelchair down the corridor. He looked broken, his doubled-over figure couldn't hide his blood-stained clothing and there was a gaping wound at the side of his head. A temporary gauze the size of a lady's handkerchief had been placed over it.

'Will it need stitches?' she whispered.

The nurse nodded her head. 'I imagine so.'

Kay made her way to Dylan's side and bent down in front of him. Tears were rolling down her cheeks. 'What happened?' she said. Jack looked disorientated and in pain. She grabbed his hand. His fingers did not curl around hers, but remained limp. His eyes beseeched her.

'Where were you?'

'I was out jogging. I lost track of the time. I'm so sorry, it would never have happened if I'd got your voicemail earlier ... My phone ...'

Dylan gave her a tight smile. 'It was turned off.' His eyes looked over her head at the nurse who had silently crept up behind his wife. Kay looked up.

'He's given me his personal details,' the nurse said.

Kay turned back to Dylan. 'Did you see who did this to you?'

Dylan shook his head jerkily, then slowly and briefly closed his eyes.

'The doctor has prescribed something for the pain, Mr Dylan,' said the nurse. 'Once that's kicked in we'll clean you up and put some sutures in the wound.'

Dylan put his hand to his forehead and gave a low, deep groan. 'Thanks,' he said.

'The doctor has asked for a CT scan: we need to make sure there is nothing else going on in there.'

Dylan looked up and attempted to stand, but by the way the nurse said, 'Sit!' Kay knew she would be obeyed.

'We don't want you collapsing again, do we?' she said in a softer tone. She turned to Kay. 'He'll be staying with us tonight for observation, just routine – better to be safe than sorry.'

When Dylan didn't object Kay knew that he must be feeling bad.

Since Dylan had fallen asleep from the injections they'd given him, the doctor suggested that Kay return home and come back the next morning. Kay kissed Jack's forehead as he slept.

Driving home, she suddenly felt exhausted. Her nerves were jittery and a sense of foreboding engulfed her as she recalled Kenny's last words. A cold chill ran down her spine.

'Remember this: I love you and I will do whatever it takes to have you to myself.'

She drove on, telling herself that her lover's talk had just been bravado. Kenny Fisher was known for not getting his hands dirty. Anyway, it was impossible for him to have reached the train station before her ... Would he have gone to the lengths of arranging for someone else to do his dirty work for him, risking prison as a result? She shook her head emphatically. No, he wasn't stupid.

Arriving home, Kay rang Isla and told her what had happened. Isla's voice sounded strange and she was breathing heavily. She said that she had been at the library, doing research for her degree, and had just run up the stairs.

'Should I come home?' she asked, her voice full of concern.

'No, especially not with your exams being so close,' replied her mother.

Isla's silence took Kay aback. Had she detected a sigh of relief to hear that she wasn't required?

That night Kay turned and tossed in her bed. In her spiralling state of mind, doubt, worry, misgivings and fear all circled round her head, haunting her dreams again and again. She'd always had dreams and, as time had gone by, she'd come to believe they held signficance. Usually, things didn't happen in the real world in the way they did in her subconscious, but occasionally they did. She hated the bad dreams. As she fell into a deep sleep she became engulfed by an ominous darkness closing in on her. She reached upwards for the full moon, flapping her arms helplessly towards the night sky. She could see the light of the moon shining over a grassy vale from the depths of blackness, yet she could not reach the summit. A feeling of necessity overcame her, but nothing was discernible. It was then that it became obvious to her that her attempts were failing. She flapped her arms faster, but to no avail. Quickly, breathlessly, she turned and screamed.

Her sudden movement and the loudness of her voice woke her and she sat up in bed, gasping for air.

Lying back on damp pillows, her eyes filled with tears. What did it mean? Was the darkness her sin, or the payment sought by the universe?

Chapter Five

The rundown taxi office was on a corner plot, the main door slightly ajar and hidden at an angle to the road. Two teenage girls stood giggling on the doorstep of the takeaway opposite, Rosie grasping the £50 note Tariq, the nephew of the taxi office owner, had given her from the battered old cashbox.

Slouched in the heavily soiled, threadbare armchair, Tariq tugged at the grimy net curtain that was draped limply at the window, whose dark green paint was peeling from the frame. Seeing the girls look his way, he waved a couple of vague fingers to them. They watched his head fall back as he took a drag of his spliff and, when he passed it to his younger companion, Wayne, the lad swapped it for a flowery mug that contained vodka. Wayne pressed his nose against the glass, clouding the window pane. Tariq ran his hand over the clouded window, clearing the glass, keeping his beady eye on the pair, on the off-chance they fled with the cash.

Entering the office half an hour later, after taking a fare, pot-bellied Mohammed Farooq's bloodshot eyes immediately fixed on the empty boxes strewn across the office and his lips set tight, in the way mouths do when they are angry. Rosie Clarke and Tanya King had returned with their food but were too much under the influence to care. Tariq had suffered the wrath of his displeasure previously. He was wary of his foul mood.

'Tell me,' said Mohammed, his false, fixed smile displayed across his lumpy face, showing them his front teeth were missing. 'Who will be taking these young ladies home now that you've been drinking?'

'I've only had a couple,' Tariq said, with a challenging look. He put the mug to his lips and drained it. When he tried to stand his chair toppled from under him.

Mr Farooq pushed him back into the chair with ease, using the palm of his hand. He bent down, his nose to Tariq's. 'That's as may be, but just the one – as you well know my boy – is one too many.' His voice filled with authority as he stood. 'What are you trying to do, lose me my licence? You stay here and look after the office. And you,' he said, pointing to Wayne, 'clean up this mess.' He turned, glaring at Tariq. 'I'll speak to you later.' He looked at the girls and pointed to the door. 'Right, ladies, your taxi awaits. I think it's time for home, don't you?'

The girls had to be pushed out of the door by Tariq. 'Go, go, go!' he scolded in a half-hearted way.

Rosie took the lead and, once they were both safely through the door, Mohammed turned, a bunch of keys dangling from a raised finger. 'I'll be back shortly, Tariq. Don't you dare go anywhere, do you hear?'

Mr Farooq turned the ignition in his taxi and the strains of a fast, twanging sitar, along with a high-pitched voice singing along in a language that the girls were unfamiliar with, filled the car.

Tanya bobbed her head along with the rhythm. 'Nice tunes, mister,' she said.

Mr Farooq's elbow rested on the door's arm-rest. Nodding his head to the music, smiling, singing and tapping his fingers on the steering wheel, he drove out of the small town and along the gentle curving road before the precipitous incline, which featured several hairpin bends, snaked upwards. He appeared too wrapped up in the music to have heard Tanya.

A sign for Field Colt Children's Home popped into view with the suddenness of the hare that had run in front of the cab earlier. Mr Farooq slammed on the brakes, uttered a few choice expletives in his native tongue and pulled off the road, through big, rusty gates onto a long driveway. The headlights picked out deep potholes to avoid. The taxi lurched from side to side as the wheels bounced in and out of the ruts. Finally, he steered the vehicle gracefully around the circular pond – which had once been full of water lilies, goldfish and koi and was now filled in, no doubt for health and safety reasons – pulling to a stop in front of the large Georgian house that was the girls' home. Looking into the back of the cab he saw that Rosie was fast asleep on Tanya's shoulder. Tanya was still somewhat the worse for wear, the expression on her pale face blank.

'Do they treat you nicely here?' Mr Farooq asked.

'No. It's shit,' she answered. Her eyes were vacant.

'Where do you go to school? Harrowfield High?'

Tanya scoffed. 'Supposed to, but once we've done registration we don't hang about.'

Mohammed Farooq pondered a moment and pulled a face in the rear-view mirror. He nodded slowly. 'Guess what?' he said, in an upbeat way. 'I've just been given the contract to ferry students from here to Harrowfield. I'll be sure to make certain you get there and stay there!'

He watched Tanya help Rosie stagger up the three wide stone steps. She rested her against a pillar, one of two that stood either side of the front door. The house looked as sad and uncared for as the girls. When he saw the door shut behind them, Farooq drove away thinking how much others could learn from his culture's family values.

On Saturday morning Kay was at the hospital early, hopeful that she would be able to take Jack home. Under her arm she carried a plastic bag containing Jack's clothes.

Less than twenty-four hours since he'd been immobilised by a whack on the head from someone unknown, Dylan was examining the damage in the bathroom mirror. Half of his face was a red and blue mess. He had eight stitches in his head, he'd been told, and had suffered a haemorrhage in his right eye, but he was pleased to see the swelling to his ear had subsided dramatically. His knees and wrists and the palms of his hands were chafed and his shoulder bruised from the fall.

'You're lucky your teeth are still intact,' said the doctor, when Kay arrived, looking at Dylan over the top of his half-rimmed glasses. 'And the good news is that the CT scan shows no evidence of a fracture.'

'Can I take him home, please?' asked Kay eagerly.

The two men's eyes met. Dylan didn't want to clash with his doctor's authority, but if he had to, he would. There was no way he was going to spend another night listening to old men who were gasping their final breaths; it did nothing for his confidence.

The doctor gave Dylan a half smile before he turned to Kay. 'In all honesty Mrs Dylan, I do think your husband will recover a lot better in his home environment.'

Kay beamed at Dylan, but her heart sank like a lead weight when she saw him look away the minute she'd handed him his clothes. He'd asked the nurse to help him to get dressed.

They were waiting in silence for the nurse to bring Dylan a prescription for painkillers and his medical notes for his GP, when Dawn and Larry walked in. Dylan's face lit up immediately.

'Ouch! Who the hell have you upset, boss?' asked Detective Sergeant Dawn Farren.

'That's what I'd like to know,' he said. 'I'll feel a darn sight better when we find out who did this to me – and, more importantly, why.'

Dawn walked towards the window, opened the brown paper bag she was carrying and plucked some juicy red grapes from their stalks.

'Those for me, by any chance?' Dylan asked.

Dawn looked from the bag to Dylan and back again. She grinned.

Kay turned to Larry, looking for support. 'Tell him, will you, how lucky he's been? Next time you might not be so fortunate,' she said, turning to Dylan. 'You could have ended up with life-changing injuries or, God forbid, dead.' Her voice rose hysterically. 'I could be planning your funeral right now!'

Dawn raised her eyebrows at Dylan. 'Yeah, but I know you hate grapes, so I might as well eat them. You know me, waste not, want not.'

Dylan smiled, then grimaced at his DS.

There was a look of bewilderment on Kay's face. 'I don't know how on earth you two can laugh. Haven't you learned anything from yesterday, Jack? How many more times are you going to put yourself in danger because of the damn job? You could have been killed!'

'And I could have been knocked down crossing the road,' said Dylan flatly. His gaze turned from Dawn towards his wife. 'I hate to burst your bubble, Kay. It's called life.'

Larry turned to Kay. 'Who's to say it's anything to do with the job?' he asked.

'Don't worry, the life insurance policy is up to date,' Dylan said.

Kay practically spat at her husband. 'Don't even joke about it. I'm serious.'

'And so am I. Deadly serious.'

Kay shook Dylan gently. It was already the next morning and, as he woke, the conversation they'd had on their way home from the hospital about her lateness began whirring round Dylan's head again.

'I'm sorry,' Kay had said.

'Sorry for what?'

'Sorry for what's happened,' she'd said.

The ice was broken.

'You've got nothing to be sorry for, have you? It wasn't your fault that someone decided to take a swing at me.'

'But if I'd been at the station, waiting for you, this would never have happened.'

'What I don't understand,' Dylan had ventured, 'is why would you go out jogging, and have your mobile turned off, when you were expecting the call? You knew I was coming home.'

'I've already told you. I'm sorry. I did have my mobile with me. It just wasn't fully charged when I set off and I somehow lost track of time. I didn't check it till I got home.' There had been tears in her eyes when he'd glanced across at her from where he sat in the passenger seat, but he couldn't bring himself to forgive her, not yet.

Kay had sighed. 'Anyway, how was the course? You haven't even mentioned it. That's unusual for you.'

'It was challenging. Every scenario was filmed and critiqued by observers, experienced negotiators. Courses are usually nine-to-five, not this one. The end of the day didn't mean the end of our shift; we worked through the night with different instructors.'

Kay's voice rose an octave. 'You passed though, didn't you?'

'Yeah, but not everyone did. It wasn't that sort of course.'

Dylan was sitting at the kitchen table. The heating was on, but he felt a cold chill deep within. His hands were wrapped tightly around a mug of coffee, warming them. Rain splattered on the kitchen window and the sky suddenly turned dark and menacing. The whole scene reflected Dylan's mood. He closed his eyes for a moment and inhaled slowly, then exhaled just as slowly.

'So,' he began, in a tone that made Kay flinch. She raised her eyes from the newspaper she had been quietly reading. He'd found a way to hide his anxiety and paint cheerfulness on his face, but the smile didn't reach his eyes. 'Tell me, what have you been up to while I've been away?'

'Me?' she looked surprised. 'Well ...' she started, pondering the question for a minute. 'Er, well ... I ... gosh,' Kay raised her hand and put her fingers to her mouth, as her thoughts floated through her mind. He saw her lip quiver as her face reddened. 'I can't remember everything.'

Dylan lifted his chin slightly and laughed out loud. Then his face turned serious as he placed his mug down on the table in front of him. 'What do you mean, you can't remember everything?'

'Nothing!' Beads of sweat appeared on the top of her lip. Her eyes left his face and went to look directly up at the ceiling, her hands dropping into her lap where she squeezed them tightly. 'Oh, let me think now.' When her eyes finally met his she'd apparently remembered, reciting, 'Housework, cleaning, ironing, shopping, work. Just the usual boring stuff.'

The puzzled look on his face deepened as he saw her trembling, the beginning of tears welling up in her eyes. 'Surely there can't have been that much housework, what with both me and Isla being away?'

Kay took the opportunity to try to change the subject. She slid his empty mug towards her and took it to the sink. As she ran the water she spoke to Dylan over her shoulder. 'Talking of Isla, I rang her to let her know you were in hospital.'

Dylan's head was still so full of questions for her that he thought it would explode, but they remained unspoken. 'You shouldn't have bothered telling her. I don't want her to be worried about anything; she's got enough on her plate with her exams.'

'She would have been annoyed if I hadn't told her. Mind you, by the sound of it now you're going to be doing this negotiating lark, I could be on the phone to her constantly if I have to call her every time someone takes a swipe at you. At least this time I was able to tell her you were okay.' Dylan saw a flash of the old Kay when she stopped talking and turned away from the pots she'd been drying. 'It was lovely to hear her voice. She sounded tired, but she's okay,' she said.

The pot washing seemed to take much longer than usual. Then Kay moved on to start wiping the kitchen worktops. Dylan remained silent, but Kay was more than aware that his eyes were still fixed on her.

'Any post come for me while I've been away?' he said at last.

'Just a couple of letters: one letting us know the car insurance is due for renewal and a statement for the mortgage. Other than that, just junk mail. They're on the coffee table in the lounge.'

Dylan put the palms of his hands on the table and, pushing down, rose carefully from his chair. He moaned from the exertion. 'That reminds me, I've not seen any bills for your mobile phone for a couple of months,' he said.

'Have you not?' she replied, as she reached up to clean a cupboard door. 'I wouldn't worry about it. They're probably sending them via email, to save on paper. Lots of bigger companies are doing that now.'

Dylan walked tentatively to the lounge door and slowly opened it. The answer-phone was bleeping: a message waiting.

Hearing it, Kay rushed through the dining room, through the hall door and into the lounge. Dylan's outstretched finger hovered over the 'Play' button. She watched as his finger hit the button, a look of angst on her face. 'Were you expecting a call?' Dylan asked.

Her heart was pounding so hard and fast in her chest that she feared Dylan would see it through her blouse. Was this Kenny's doing? Suddenly, Kay feared that her whole world was about to come crashing down around her.

Chapter Six

The female voice on the answering machine brought a level of relief Kay had never previously experienced. However, it was short-lived when she heard Isla's tutor, sounding concerned, asking them to contact her as soon as possible: Isla was facing immediate suspension.

Kay and Dylan stared at each other in disbelief as they considered the significance of what they had just heard. Kay didn't know what to say, so she said nothing, leaving it up to Dylan to pick up the telephone to return the call. Her heart pounded.

'God, please let Isla be all right,' she whispered fervently.

Dylan listened to the phone ringing out, then heard a click followed by the voice of the professor.

'Doctor Feather, Sheffield University.'

Kay's ears strained to hear the muffled words in the background. She struggled to read Dylan's facial expressions and work out what the professor was saying to afford such stilted replies from him. When he put the phone down his face was solemn.

'What's happened?' Kay faltered. 'Tell me ...' she asked.

'We've got to go. Straight away,' he answered, reaching for the car keys. 'Isla's been found in possession of drugs.'

'Drugs? What drugs?'

'She didn't say.'

'But she's okay?'

'They're extremely worried about her welfare.'

'What does that mean?'

'Doctor Feather thinks she might be depressed: she's lost weight and this morning she threatened suicide.'

'But ... I only spoke to her the other day ... She sounded okay ...'

'Yes, so you said. But did you actually have a proper conversation with her, or just talk at her, like you usually do?'

Kay swallowed visibly.

'She's not a child, Kay. She's a grown woman.'

'Well, she's certainly not acting like it if she's threatening to kill herself. It sounds more like attention-seeking to me.'

From time-to-time Dylan looked sideways at Kay as she drove, offering her directions now and again. He knew she was upset, anxious. Now was certainly not the time to get into an argument.

Being summoned to the head's office had the same effect on Dylan as it'd had twenty year's previously. However, Dr Glenda Feather was nothing like the ermine-fur-gowned head of year of his day. Dr Feather was, Dylan guessed, in her late forties, petite and pretty, with enigmatic soft blue eyes. Her voice, although authoritative, had an air of calm about it; she wore her professional mask well. Her dark green, roll-neck dress clung snugly to her body and she wore a slim black leather belt tight round her waist and glasses dangling on a silver chain around her neck. After standing up to shake their hands, she offered them two chairs placed in front of the big, antique oak desk. Her colleague remained seated in the fourth chair between the bookshelf and her desk and nodded his greeting when he was introduced as Mr Paul, student welfare officer. A decade younger than Glenda Feather, Dylan guessed, and distinctly athletic-looking, David Paul was as dark as she was blonde.

'I'm pleased that you could come so quickly, Mr and Mrs Dylan,' said Dr Feather. She put on her glasses. Her concentration was strictly on the file in front of her. Opening it, she took a moment or two to consider it before speaking. Although her cheeks were flushed, when she looked up her face was grave.

'Earlier today we were made aware by some of Isla's friends that she has been, let's say, living student life to the full. Her friends were concerned enough to speak to Mr Paul about her eating habits and weight loss. I've been reliably informed that she is binge drinking and is a regular user of recreational drugs. Uncharacteristically, she has recently shown signs of aggressive behaviour. And aggression and addiction, as we are well aware, are intertwined in many ways. She has, she tells me, been prescribed antidepressants by her general practitioner. When searching her room for the drugs, we also found evidence that she has been hoarding food and keeping a highly unusual quantity of laxatives.

'Having found her in possession of illegal drugs, I'm afraid, I have no other option than to suspend your daughter with immediate effect. As I mentioned in our telephone conversation earlier Mr Dylan, the university has a duty of care to Isla and, although she is eighteen, we' – Dr Feather nodded her head towards Mr Paul – 'took the decision not to tell her that we were sending her home until you arrived. We have told her that you have been asked to come over to discuss these latest developments. Her response to that was to threaten suicide.'

Dylan heard Kay gasp and sniffle and, out of the corner of his eye, saw her wipe away a tear. He reached into his pocket and pulled out a handkerchief which she gratefully accepted. In his own distressed state, it was as much comfort as he was able to offer.

'Have you called the doctor?' asked Dylan.

'No,' answered Dr Feather. 'We think it best that she sees her GP at home. In my opinion, Isla needs long-term assistance and, as much as we'd like to help, this is beyond our capabilities on campus.'

'With all due respect, I think we know our own daughter better than you,' Kay said sharply. 'My husband is a police officer, a negotiator no less, and I promise you that if we'd had an inkling that my daughter was involved with drugs, or needed any professional help, then I would have been the first to seek help for her.' She turned to Dylan for support.

'This is where confusion has set in ...' Mr Paul said, scratching his head. 'You see, this is the first time that I've heard your daughter's name mentioned. She has never exhibited any sort of aggressive behaviour here, to my knowledge, until now. Our previous experience has shown that if anger issues do manifest themselves, they are often the key to deeper and more longstanding problems which will need proper and thorough investigation.'

There was an awkward pause, followed by a loud tap at the door. All heads turned. Slowly, the door brushed across the woollen carpet and in stepped a gaunt, waif-like figure which Dylan hardly recognised as his beautiful Isla. The woman who followed her inside proffered a faint smile as she placed a guiding hand at the base of Isla's bony back for encouragement. A smell of sweat and talcum powder wafted around the oak-panelled room.

Dylan stared down at the hand of his daughter, clasped tenderly in his own, running his finger over her calloused knuckles. Her cracked skin felt dry and the blood drying at the base of her nails made him wince.

How could she have changed so much physically in such a short space of time? Flakes of dry skin were sprinkled across the shoulders and sleeves of her scruffy black jumper. Her jeans were far too big for her tiny frame. Crossing her legs as she slouched in the chair, a tatty, stained plimsoll dangled precariously from a trembling foot.

Isla stared down at the floor while the conversation between her mother, Glenda Feather and David Paul continued around her. Dylan thought that her hair had thinned and was falling out. He willed her to look up at him and, when she finally did, he winked at her. 'It's going to be okay,' he whispered soothingly, at the same time instinctively squeezing her hand. She flinched and his eyes silently apologised for causing her pain.

'I'm sorry,' she mouthed to him. A lone tear trickled down her cheek and Dylan brushed it away gently with the tip of his finger.

They went to Isla's room and Dylan's eyes were drawn to the family photos displayed on the dressing table, a poignant reminder of happier times. Discarded clothes lay strewn in every available space. Her precious record collection, accumulated since her early teens and formerly her pride and joy, was scattered across the floor, some records still in their sleeves, most uncovered and tossed aside. He glanced down at the turntable of the portable player they'd given her last Christmas. Soul diva Aretha Franklin's 'Respect' stared ironically back up at him.

Most of all, he was sad to see her favourite childhood companion Pooh Bear, battered and bruised, lying abandoned in the farthest corner of the room. He picked him up and tucked him safely under one arm.

Quietly, Isla's flatmates gathered her personal belongings together and helped Dylan carry them to the car. He thanked them, then he thanked Dr Feather, Mr Paul and the members of staff who had helped her, before joining Isla and Kay and escorting them back to their car.

It was apparent to Dylan that Kay was in no fit state to drive. He held out his hand for the keys and, for once, she gave them to him without any fuss. He looked in his rearview mirror to see the two of them staring blankly out of the side windows in silence, each lost in their own thoughts, no doubt still attempting to digest what had happened.

Pausing at the junction of the university entrance and the open road, he waited patiently for the oncoming traffic to pass. He checked his rearview mirror again, studying his daughter's face for a moment or two: she looked desperately fragile, vulnerable and lost. Their eyes met briefly and he saw hers harden. Then the look of wilfulness that had crossed her face swiftly disappeared. Had he imagined that look in her eyes? He sincerely hoped so, because he'd seen eyes like that many times before: they held the emptiness of a 'dead man walking'.

Instinctively, and without the others' knowledge, he flipped on the child locks – a precautionary measure, but with Isla's state of mind so much in question, travelling on the motorway without the lock on was not an option for the seasoned detective. Besides, he would be naïve not to put every precautionary measure that he had recently learned at Hendon into practice. Isla was in a dark place and he needed to concentrate on the road ahead while staying one step ahead of his daughter should she decide to attempt jumping out of the car.

The silence was suddenly broken by rushed outpourings from Isla.

'For God's sake, will someone say something? You don't need to punish me with the silent treatment. I already know I'm a disappointment to you … But,' she shrugged her shoulders, 'if you want to tip me over the edge, you just carry on … You're doing a great job, because you're both doing my fuckin' head in now.'

Her words tugged at Dylan's heart strings, but it was Kay who spoke. 'I don't know what to say …'

Isla leaned towards her mother as if she was about to share a secret. 'I'd have thought you'd want to reassure me that you didn't take a blind bit of notice of Ma Fluff and her Casanova!'

Kay raised her eyebrows. 'What do you mean?'

Isla sucked in her breath and widened her eyes. 'Come on! Tell me, why on earth would the doctor come in on a Saturday to deal with insignificant little me, if she wasn't hoping to get a bit on the side? Come on, Dad, you're not stupid! You couldn't miss those furtive looks and those puppy-dog eyes?' She sniggered. 'Bloody barefaced liars, the lot of 'em.' Her eyes narrowed. 'Ask yourself why they haven't suspended Boo Boo then.' Isla's eyes glistened.

Kay's eyebrows knitted together. 'Boo Boo?' she asked.

'The drug dealer, I guess?' said Dylan.

Isla lips were tight when she nodded to her mother. 'Because Boo Boo knows ... and they know he knows.' She drew back, tilted her head and looked again. 'Hey, Kay, come to think of it you've got a bit of a shifty look, too ...' She leaned forward towards Dylan. 'Don't you think she looks shifty, Dad? What you trying to hide, Mother?' she said, putting a finger to her lips and chuckling to herself.

Kay reached out for Isla's hand, which was swiftly snapped away. One of her daughter's eyebrows rose and she stopped laughing and leaned forward. 'Once a cheat, always a cheat, eh, Dad?' she said.

Dylan's eyes were fixed on the road as he manoeuvred the car onto the slip road at the next exit. He specifically steered clear of looking in the rear-view mirror, hoping to avoid the look on his wife's face, until the moment passed.

'Always trust your gut instincts,' Isla spoke softly. 'Isn't that right, Dad? If something feels wrong, it usually is.'

Slowly, Isla unclenched her fingers. A trickle of blood ran down her right palm.

Dylan handed her a tissue. 'Do you feel like talking yet?' he asked as they sat side by side together on the plush sofa.

'Later maybe,' she said, dabbing at her puncture wound. She sniffed, as if a bad smell had wafted under her nose. 'Would it be okay if I went up for a bath?'

'Of course.' Dylan forced a smile. 'Just remember we're here for you whenever you do feel like talking.'

Dylan watched Isla drag herself to the top of the stairs. At times the exertion seemed too much. 'I'm going to make us something to eat. Shall I call you when it's ready?' he called after her.

Isla turned and looked down at him. Her voice was shaky. 'No, but thanks anyway,' she said. 'I'll get something later.'

Isla's room was just as she had left it and for that, at least, she was very grateful.

'Why did you let her go up without any dinner?' asked Kay, when he joined her in the kitchen. With her head stuck in a black bag, she was sorting out Isla's dirty clothes. She pulled a face, pulled the drawstring, opened the bin and dropped the bag inside.

'Do you think that's wise?' questioned Dylan, sitting down and picking a newspaper up off the table.

The sound of a door banging upstairs and another one opening signified to Dylan and Kay that Isla had gone straight to her room and before long they could hear steady, laboured sobbing. Dylan's head rose from the newspaper. Finally, he looked at his wife, who rolled her eyes.

'What did you want me to do, tell her she couldn't go upstairs in her own home?'

After a while Kay glanced up at the ceiling. 'It's all your fault,' she hissed. 'You're too damn soft with her – always have been. What she needs now is a slap around the head, just like you've had. It'd knock a bit of common sense into her.'

'Right now, all she needs is our love and support,' said Dylan.

Kay shook her head. 'Unbelievable. I mean, just look at the way she spoke to me in the car and you never said a word!'

There was a pause. Dylan stared at his wife. 'What did you want me to say? Did you really think I'd be your knight in shining armour and defend your honour? Tell me, Kay, how could I, when I'm being forced to question it myself?'

'I don't know what you mean. You actually think what she suggested is true?' Kay's face flushed. 'How could you?' she snapped. Leaping up, she towered over him. 'I'm going to put a stop to this self-serving, indulgent behaviour once and for all.'

'You really don't give a damn about anyone but yourself, do you?'

Kay moved quickly, but Dylan was quicker to reach up and catch her hand. 'Not now, eh? Shouting at her isn't going to do any good.' When she looked down at him with her huge brown eyes he pulled his hand away, the ache in his heart simply too much to bear. His eyes reverted to his newspaper. 'When she's ready to talk to us, she will.'

Kay slumped into the chair opposite him. Her voice wobbled. 'But she says she wants to kill herself. Don't you care?' she said softly. Again, she paused.

'She's only just got home. Do you think I like her talking about ending it all? We need to get her professional help and we will do that first thing tomorrow.'

Kay scoffed. 'She doesn't need professional help, that's just silly talk. She's just attention-seeking; isn't that what they tell you on those courses of yours? Have they brainwashed you too? Being treated with kid gloves hasn't worked in the past, so what's so different now? We need to be strict with her from now on, and you have to stop letting her wrap you around her little finger.'

Kay waited for a reaction, any reaction, but Dylan wouldn't be drawn.

'Let's agree to differ, shall we? I've dealt with people who are depressed and desperate – so desperate that they act out of character and often take their lives without a second thought. This "attention-seeking", as you like to call it, is not going to change overnight. She can't help how she feels. She's ill, Kay, and you've got to understand that, although you're her mother, she may never talk to us about it.'

'Isla's not like that. She's always talked to me, told me everything ...'

'I truly hope you're right.' Dylan's stomach rumbled. He went to the fridge and opened the door. He held a milk carton up and looked at the date. He frowned. 'This is over a week old!' He looked for something else. On the shelves there was a lump of yellowing cheese that looked as if it had been there for some time and a small box of chocolates. Inside the door sat a lonely bottle of Cava. He groaned and ransacked the cupboards, to discover nothing more than a few tins of beans, a tub of dried milk they kept for emergencies, a crumpled box of cereals, half a bottle of vodka and a box of tea bags. Two stale bread crusts sat in the bread bin. His eyes looked questioningly at Kay.

'Er, yes,' she said. 'I meant to call at the supermarket, but I didn't have the time.'

Dylan sighed heavily and, putting the kettle on for a much-needed coffee, retrieved a loaf from the freezer. *What a day!*

Chapter Seven

Kay slept soundly on the other side of the bed. Head on the pillow, Dylan faced her. Sleep usually came easily, born from years of shift work, but not tonight. Tonight he was held in the iron grip of insomnia. He could smell Kay's perfume over the scent of their sheets. Was it a new one? He frowned as he caught the faint aroma of something else ...

As he gazed at her, the waxing moon shone through a break in the clouds to lend a brief glimpse of light that illuminated Kay's contented smile. It brought about a sadness deep within him. Then, just as quickly as they had parted, the clouds once again covered the moon, putting her face deep in shadow. He wondered what, or who, she could be dreaming of to make her look like that.

A few damp strands of hair clung to her skin on the shoulder nearest to him, but although he desperately wanted to, he simply couldn't bring himself to touch her. It was imperative that he wait for the right time to challenge her about his fears and this was most definitely not it. A ray of hope shone through with the moonlight as it came to rest on her face again. She looked beautiful, a picture of serenity and innocence. What if he was wrong? He tried to picture himself asking her whether she was having an affair. He'd spotted enough signs. The delicate lacy underwear hidden away in her bottom drawer, which she'd never yet worn for him; her sudden interest in dieting; her expensive new gym membership. Over and over again, he imagined confronting her about it, but each time he ran through the scenario he couldn't predict her reply – and that frightened the hell out of him.

He lay awake until the hallway clock struck three and his thoughts shifted to how he could help Isla and then to being worried that, should he close his eyes, she might do something stupid while he slept. Fighting slumber now, he perched on the edge of the bed, and stifled a yawn. He looked back at his wife and yet again considered whether he should just come right out and ask her.

As he stood at the bottom of the stairs Dylan silently prayed that his movements hadn't woken the others. His ears strained for the slightest noise. When he was sure there was none, he cautiously tiptoed to the kitchen, carefully closing the door behind him. While the kettle boiled, his eyes were drawn to the window ledge and a big, beautiful bouquet of hand-picked flowers tumbling over the sides of its vase, a colourful spectacle that almost covered the windowsill. A bold statement if ever he'd seen one.

Staring beyond the flowers into the darkness of the night, he sought answers to new questions. Where had the bouquet come from? Was what Kay had said true: that he was so wrapped up in his job that he had taken his eye off the ball as far as his family was concerned? It *was* true that he didn't seem to know them any more – their hopes, their dreams, or their fears – and maybe that had been the case for longer than he cared to admit. But that was because he was always at work. When it came down to it, he was only working the long hours he was to provide for them, to give them a better life.

Or was he?

It wasn't unusual for him to be up at this time on his own, getting ready to go out on a call, but this was different. This time he had nowhere to run to, no emergency to help him out. Although he wasn't occupied with the job, for once, his brain was still working overtime.

He brewed a cup of coffee, automatically opening the fridge door to get some milk, before remembering, as he stared at the empty shelves, that there wasn't any. His jaw clenched so hard it ached. In his sleep-deprived state, a feeling of intense anger gripped him and it took all his strength not to throw the bottle of Cava against the wall. Instead he poured the contents down the sink, watching as the effervescent liquid swirled rapidly down the plughole.

The bottle fell softly onto the bag of Isla's clothes lying in the bin. Stuffing the flowers on top relieved some of Dylan's tension, but he wasn't finished yet. He took the box of Kay's favourite chocolates from the fridge and, as he sat at the kitchen table drinking his coffee, crushed the soft centres one by one between his fingers. As he reached the bottom layer he wondered, *was he going mad?*

Isla woke with a start. She stared at the ceiling for a moment or two. She was hot, she was terribly hot. A wave of nausea washed over her and she rolled over onto her side and groaned. A brilliant streak of light flashed from the foot of her bed and she sat up, drew up her legs and hugged her arms around them, trying to protect herself. Strips of flames leapt up the bedclothes towards her face. The heat was so intense she could actually feel her skin shrivelling. She was going to be roasted alive. The smell made her vomit. Seizing her pillow, she beat out the flames. She couldn't breathe, the smoke stung her eyes.

'Dad! Help me!' she screamed as she rolled off the bed to the floor. Crawling on her hands and knees, she collapsed at the door.

Dylan placed his hand on her forehead. 'You're okay, darling,' he soothed. He picked her up with ease, cradling her gently in his arms. His voice cracked. 'It was just a bad dream.' He stroked her thin hair and noticed a knotted mess at the back of her head.

'More like she's coming down from the drugs,' snapped Kay, standing at the door in her dressing gown, shaking her head at the mess and covering her nose to mask the smell.

Dylan looked up at his wife and held her stare. He spoke through gritted teeth. 'Just leave us be.'

Isla could feel the thump of Dylan's heart against her cheek as he held her and it comforted her.

From time to time, while he was cleaning the room the next morning, Dylan went downstairs and checked that Isla was breathing as she lay on the sofa. He sat next to her, stroking her head and making soothing noises.

Kay had been to the supermarket when he finally finished and went back downstairs. It appeared her mood hadn't changed one bit. Isla was sitting quietly on the sofa nibbling, rabbit-like, on a piece of toast. Kay marched in from the kitchen and sighed.

'Haven't you had a shower yet?' she snapped at her daughter.

'Yes, I have,' Isla said without taking her eyes off the TV, as she flicked her way through the channels with the remote control.

'Then why are you still in your PJs?' Kay went back to the kitchen saying to Dylan, 'She should be up and dressed and tidying her room by now.'

Dylan, however, was optimistic. 'She's resting, and that's her second slice of toast you know.'

'And?'

'And she's admitted that she's got herself into a mess and accepted that she does need help.'

'That it?'

'Well, it's a start.'

Later that day, while a nurse took Isla's bloods, the doctor spoke to her parents in her office.

'If Isla is being honest with me, and there is no reason for me to think otherwise as she's quite an intelligent young woman, I think we have a long journey ahead of us.'

Kay stood up and hugged her daughter when she came back into the doctor's office. Isla instantly pulled away. The doctor's eye caught Dylan's; they clearly shared some deep concerns.

Back home, Dylan opened the front door, stepping aside to allow Isla to go in before them. Together they watched her inch herself up the stone steps, using the wrought-iron railings for support. The exertion of the trip to the surgery had clearly taken it out of her. It was a pitiful sight.

The phone started ringing. Isla, already halfway inside, looked back at Dylan; he urged her to go on. 'If it's important they'll leave a message,' he said, 'or ring back later.'

A sense of foreboding welled up in Kay when the phone continued to ring. Once Isla was clear of the door, Kay pushed past her daughter into the narrow hallway. Although it had only been a small shove, it was enough to cause Isla to lose her balance. Kay was already in the lounge, frantically searching for the cordless phone, when Isla answered it.

Dylan fixed Kay with an icy stare as she came back into the hallway. Her breathing was as rapid as her racing pulse, her face ashen. 'The phone was on the hall table,' he said, 'where it always is.'

'You look as if you've just seen a ghost,' Isla said to Kay, passing the phone to Dylan. 'It's Dawn from work for you. She wants to know if you're up for a night out.'

'You're sure you don't mind me going?' Dylan asked Isla for the umpteenth time.

Isla's lips curled up at one side. 'Of course not. You don't have to keep an eye on me twenty-four seven you know. What time is she picking you up? Eight? I'll be off up to bed by then. I won't even know you're gone.'

'Well, your mum will be here and I'll only be at the police bar.'

Kay and Isla sat at either end of the sofa. Dylan straightened his tie in the mirror over the fireplace and smoothed his hair with his hands. He winced as he accidentally pressed on the bruises surrounding his head wound. There was no doubt in his mind that his injuries would raise lots of questions tonight and cause some mickey taking. The team were used to having battle scars now and again and, though he was the boss, it would be taken in good spirit.

Isla wolf-whistled through her teeth as Dylan turned. 'I'd forgotten how well you scrub up for an oldie.'

'Thank you!' He smiled. 'I just wish I didn't have to leave you.'

'He doesn't *have* to go,' interrupted Kay. 'He wants to go ...'

Dylan raised his eyebrows. 'Yes, that's true. After all, it's not very important to me to say farewell to a colleague who has spent the last thirty years of his life loyally serving his Queen and country.'

Kay scoffed. 'If his wife's there, buy her a drink from me. In my opinion it's her who deserves a bloody medal.'

'Mum, that's awful!' Isla rolled her eyes at Dylan. 'How on earth do you put up with her, Dad?' Isla's hands were visibly shaking as he leaned over to kiss her goodnight and the pained look in her eyes told him just how hard she was trying. She ran her tongue over dry, cracked lips before putting the glass of water to them and he heard it vibrate against her chattering teeth.

'Well, I hope you manage to get a good night's sleep,' he said sincerely, his hand resting briefly on her head.

'I promise I won't be late,' he said, turning to Kay, his terse nod acknowledging the large glass of red wine clutched in her hand. 'I doubt your mum's going to have any trouble dropping off.'

As soon as the door had slammed behind him and she'd heard the key turning in the lock, Kay took a huge gulp of wine, threw her head back against the cushion, closed her eyes and inhaled deeply. After a few minutes she looked accusingly up at Isla. 'Did you ever stop to think exactly what the consequences would be before you took those tablets?' Kay pursed her lips, her eyes welling up with tears.

'Of course, but my friend's been taking them for ages and he's fine. He told me they helped him feel better.'

'And do you?'

'Do I what?'

'Feel better?'

Isla shuffled her feet uneasily.

'What you need my girl is some early nights. That's all you need.'

'What you're really saying is that you want me out of your sight, isn't it?'

Kay stared straight ahead at the TV, struggling to hold back the tears.

'Why are you trying to get rid of me?'

Kay appeared to ignore her and reached instead for her mobile phone. With a shaking hand, she started typing. It instantly 'pinged' a reply.

The comfortable sofa was not easy for the frail Isla to get up from, but she eventually achieved it. At the door, she turned and opened her mouth as if to speak, but Kay was typing away furiously. Quietly, Isla opened the door and closed it behind her. In the kitchen her search for alcohol began. The first sip of vodka brought the contents of her stomach back up into her mouth and her anxiety rose. She stopped and listened to see if her mother had heard anything. The television was blaring away in the next room. It sounded like a soap opera argument, either that, or Kay was talking to someone on the phone. The next sip went down nicely and Isla tucked the bottle into the pocket of her dressing gown and sneaked back upstairs.

In her room, Isla began rooting through her drawers, desperately seeking a cigarette, and she was soon rewarded with a packet of ten. She looked up to the ceiling, thanking her younger, more organised – and much richer – self for buying them in bulk. She lay on her bed, smoking, drinking and thinking about her mother. Thoughts ran randomly through her head: black thoughts. Her heart raced. She wanted to run, to fight, to die or to get fucked; to go blind and dumb and have no heart – anything but feel. Then the blackness sucked her slowly down into the abyss …

Detective Sergeant Larry Banks pulled up outside the door of the local off-licence. He looked at his reflection in the rearview mirror and ran his hand through his wet hair, stroking his chin and checking the whiteness of his teeth as he spoke on his mobile, confirming to Dawn Farren that he wouldn't be long.

'You'd better not be, they're almost ready to do the speeches.'

'What does the old guy drink anyway? Do you think whisky will be okay?'

Dawn growled in dissatisfaction at her colleague. 'How can you be so bloody disorganised? You've known for months about Terry's retirement do. God, he's been crossing off the days on his desk calendar for long enough!'

Tanya King spied Larry Banks from where she was skulking behind the racks of groceries in the shop. Her heart sank. There was no getting away with her stolen stash now. One by one, with her beady eye on the detective, she pulled the tins of lager from up her jumper and put them carefully back on the shelves. Faz, the young shopkeeper, was watching the in-house CCTV and, just as Larry Banks went to pay for his bottle, all hell broke loose. Much to his pregnant wife's surprise, Faz leapt over the counter and promptly sat on the squealing young girl. Tanya's verbal abuse painted the air blue. Sharmin continued to serve Larry, wrapping his purchase up in a neat little package.

'Gerrof me! Gerrof!' Tanya shouted. 'I didn't nick anything, Mr Banks, honest I didn't. I can show you. I've got money to pay!'

'That's only because I didn't give you the chance to nick 'owt,' Faz said.

Larry went over to them and, smelling the alcohol on Tanya's breath, asked, 'How many have you already had?'

With Faz's hand still grasping her by the scruff of her neck, Tanya gave Larry a sickly smile that immediately indicated to the detective that she was drunk. 'Come on, Mr Banks, look, here's the money,' she said, her hand thrusting a twenty-pound note towards him. 'If uniform takes me back again, they'll move me on to another home. I've already had a yellow card.'

'I'll take her,' Larry said to the shopkeeper. 'Unless you want me to call uniform to come and lock her up that is?'

Faz looked at his wife; she shook her head. 'I might have been mistaken,' he said, releasing Tanya from his grasp. 'If you say you'll take her home, then that's good enough for me.' He turned to Tanya. 'But you just keep away from here from now on, do you hear me? I don't want to see you again until you're eighteen.'

Out by the car, Tanya stood with her hands on her hips, waiting for Larry to open the passenger door. She shivered and wiped a few spots of rain from her face.

'He's a right twat is that Faz. He doesn't really mean it you know. He's only being nasty to me because *she's* there. Him and his brother give me plenty of free booze when they want a grope or a shag. I got given a bottle of plonk off of him yesterday for a hand job.'

Larry walked round to the driver's side of the car. 'I've heard enough. Look, you can either behave yourself and I'll take you home, or you can spend the night in the cells – your choice.'

Her compliance without any argument surprised him. She slid into the passenger seat and clicked her seatbelt. Larry turned on the ignition, flicking on the headlamps and windscreen wipers. Sleeting rain beat diagonally across his light beams. Navigating his way to the children's home on the unlit road in total silence was a revelation where Tanya King was concerned. She was normally quite vocal. A car passed by them at great speed and the wail of a police siren on his tail didn't surprise him. In the rearview mirror he could see flashing blue lights. The car came level with him, then glided past with ease. A chase was on.

Tanya turned to Larry. 'Cor, that's a bit exciting, isn't it?' she said. 'Shouldn't we follow them? I want to be a copper one day, just like you.'

Larry gave her a sideways glance.

She giggled. 'Can I have a swig of that whisky you bought, Mr Banks?'

'No, definitely not!'

'Pretty please, just a little one? Whoever it is you're trying to impress, I'm sure there'll be plenty to go round.'

'I'm not trying to impress anyone. It's a special present for a colleague who's retiring, if you must know.'

Tanya was quiet for a while. As they turned into the driveway she found her voice again.

'Do you still fancy me, Mr Banks?'

'Have a bit of self-respect, Tanya.'

The teenager reclined in the passenger seat and put both feet up on the dashboard. The belt she wore as a skirt rode up, revealing bare legs right up to her bottom.

Larry put his foot on the brake. 'Get your feet down now!'

Tanya pulled a face. 'Why are you being like that, Mr Banks? You never used to tell me off for putting my feet on the dashboard. You used to say that I had nice legs when you were stroking them.' Tanya ran her hand slowly up her thigh, provocatively. 'Don't you like me any more?'

'You never used to smoke or drink or, worse, sleep around.'

Tanya sat bolt upright. Larry pulled onto the side of the road, just short of the security lights. 'I've got myself a boyfriend now, you know. He's called Tariq and him and his friend are very good to me and my friends. I was supposed to be meeting him tonight.' She pulled a face. 'He's going to go ape when I don't turn up for the party. If I told him what that Faz, his brother, and the others did to me he'd kill 'em. I think Tariq loves me, Mr Banks.'

'How old is this Tariq, Tanya?'

'Not as old as you, Mr Banks.' Tanya opened the door. 'I can walk from here.'

'And you promise me you're going straight home, right?'

'Aw, don't be a spoilsport, Mr Banks. You're going to have your little bit of fun, aren't you?' she said, winking an eye. As she got out of the car she said, 'Thank you for the ride, Mr Banks. I know you're only being protective, but I'm okay, really I am. I do what I have to do. You know, just like you.'

Larry scowled at her.

'Do you want me to kiss you, or do you want something else? I'll do anything you want for you, you know – just like old times.'

'Get lost,' Larry said. 'I'm afraid you're a lost cause, Tanya King.'

Chapter Eight

Tall, heavy set and bronzed, Terry Spence had recently completed thirty years in the force, having avoided dismissal by the skin of his teeth. Twenty-six of those years had been spent in the Traffic department. If Dylan had expected the typical mundane retirement ceremony that came together with the usual hollow accolades from the hierarchy and the customary goodbye speeches, then he couldn't have been more wrong; but then Inspector Spence had survived the good ol' boy system in the days when being a cop with a working two-way radio meant that you ruled the streets of Harrowfield.

Still only fifty years of age, Terry had a love of travel and, he told them in his speech, that was precisely what he intended to do for the rest of his time on this mortal sphere – use the skills he had gained in the force to inspect the rest of the world, with his beloved wife travelling alongside him in their newly purchased mobile home.

After he had spoken, various colleagues and family members stood up to say something. Their speeches all tended to include tales of various fixes the man who'd been nicknamed Teflon Terry had found himself in.

Throughout the speeches, the inspector appeared emotional, showing a side to his personality Dylan had never seen before. It seemed that he was yet another who had worn his professional mask well. Terry shook his head in denial when he received recognition for his ability and leadership and applauded those around him for their help in making his career all that it had been, often saving his neck.

During his wife's short speech, she spoke of how much she loved and respected Terry, not only as her husband, but as a man and as her best friend.

During his own speech, broken up with raw emotion and near to tears, Terry had held his wife's hand, gazing lovingly into her eyes as he spoke of his gratitude for her commitment, love and undying devotion to him and not least for her comradeship.

'After the sights I've seen and the hefty workload we all endure, I'm not ashamed to say that I've often been driven to the depths of despair but, petite as she is, she has always managed to pick me up … No, I couldn't have done any of it without this lady's love and support.'

After the speeches, Terry stood up to hug his comrades in the same way that he hugged the members of his family. Finally, he looked about the room and wished his colleagues well, obviously aware that his life would never be the same again.

'I'm one of the lucky ones,' he said to Dylan afterwards. 'I have been given the precious gift of being able to leave it all behind and to live my life as I choose from now on. Not everyone has that privilege. There's only so much trauma, sadness and inhumanity that one person can digest. You know it, I know it, everyone knows it; but there comes a time when we are forced to admit it to ourselves. And now the time has come for me to leave everything in the capable hands of the next generation and just hope that I've managed to teach my brood enough to be able to cope with whatever life throws at them.' Terry nodded towards his young team congregated round the bar and smiled the smile of a proud man.

What Dylan had heard in Terry's speech had stuck a chord. He felt a twinge of something he couldn't quite put his finger on. Was it envy? And, if so, what exactly was he envious of? Was it that Terry had done his time? Retirement sounded fun. Or was it the way in which he and his wife behaved together?

The DJ stopped the music and announced a request for a record. Terry searched the room for his wife. Dylan watched him go to her, take her by the hand and lead her to the dance floor where he put his arms around her and whispered in her ear. She looked down, a little coy. Then he put one hand on the back of her head and gently laid it on his shoulder. There was no doubt, like Frank Sinatra sang, Terry did it 'My Way'.

What Dylan could see in front of him was real, longstanding love and what he had with Kay, at home, was far from it. He didn't want to live that way any more ...

Jennifer Jones had been delighted to be asked to Teflon's retirement do. Although she was quiet and unassuming, she felt as if she was beginning to be an accepted part of the social scene of the police family. It hadn't been easy for her to relocate, moving three hundred miles from her birthplace – a little village on the slow-paced Isle of Wight where she'd had the most idyllic childhood – to live in a multicultural town which was very different from what she'd been used to. But, as she saw it, she'd had no choice. The further away she was from the island the better. Either Shaun needed to move away when he ended their relationship (and that was never going to happen with a new woman in his sights), or she did.

'How are you coping with our Northern climate? I hear it's ten degrees colder up here than where you come from,' Dawn asked the tall blonde, who was standing alongside their colleague, the even taller, highly efficient and experienced CID administrative assistant, Rita Murray. After spending twenty-five years in police admin, what Reet didn't know about the job, or about the officers who confided in her, was nobody's business. One of the lads, Rita could knock up any file from an officer's pocket book and make it fit for court purposes and for that reason alone, the officers would have loved and respected her above many of their superiors.

Jen smiled. 'It's certainly different from what I'm used to. But I remembered to bring my woollies.'

Rita put an arm around her shoulders. 'She's already joined the aerobics class. And I've told her, if she moves fast enough, she'll not catch her death.'

Jen looked around the room, running her eyes along the line of dark wooden four-legged stools with their red velvet seats lined up in front of the bar. To the right of the bar mirror was an assortment of spirit bottles and different sized drinking glasses placed on two glass shelves. A fire door stood at the top of the steps, which lead to the gym, changing rooms and viewing balcony. Surrounded by her new colleagues, Jen felt safe in a way she hadn't done for a long while, secure in the knowledge that her new police family would protect her. So secure, in fact, that as she listened to their banter in the happy and supportive environment, she could finally visualise having the courage to tell Martin it was over.

Starting a relationship so soon after the break-up of another, especially a long-standing relationship, had never been a good idea, she had to admit – but she'd been lonely. Martin had helped her through the loneliness and then, like others before her she now knew, she had been well and truly won over by Martin's mask of bonhomie and charm.

Her new role in the police had opened her eyes in many ways and, one day, as she typed up some files on cases involving victims of domestic abuse, she had started to recognise her own situation in them. She became aware that Martin was luring her into a dangerous cycle, one in which idealisation sat alongside a cruel devaluation of her self-worth. It was a comfort-punishment dynamic which would end up destroying her if she allowed it to continue. To have been given these files to work on seemed like serendipity.

She had already questioned several times the stupidity of his behaviour, having come up against his seemingly boundless jealousy. She had discovered first-hand that his ex-partner wasn't crazy, as he'd delighted in telling her when they'd first got together. Jen had worked with her in the last few days of the temporary employment where she'd first met Martin, and she and Jo had got along just fine. And, although she had refused point blank Jo's offer of help and support to get away from him, Jo had confided in Jen her reasons for finally having the courage to end the relationship.

Now Jen had come to her senses at long last, realising that Martin was a malignant narcissist whose actions had depleted and drained her. He tried to make her question her own actions simply because he feared she was growing in courage and strength. The truth was she had only stayed with Martin so long because she couldn't bear to think she had failed again already, and so soon after leaving the Isle of Wight. She'd been with Shaun since she was a schoolgirl. What would her parents say if they knew she'd already had a failed relationship in the North.

Earlier in the evening, though, Martin had thrown another tantrum when she had announced she was going out with her colleagues, threatening that he might not be at home when she returned. Fortunately for her, her new post as a police civilian had given her the courage to stand up for herself and her own happiness. Never again would she allow anyone to dominate her. From now on she would be her own person.

Leaving one group of people to talk to another, Larry Banks fleetingly grabbed Dylan's arm as he passed. It broke Dylan's reverie. 'I'll be back in just a second. I'll just get us a refill,' he said after devouring everything on his heavily laden plate and swilling it down with the remainder of his pint.

At the bar Larry bought a glass of red wine too and, on his way back to Dylan, after gently placing his hand on Jennifer Jones's shoulder and smiling into her upturned face, he put it down on the table in front of her. The music was extremely loud. 'Welcome to the Division,' he whispered in her ear.

Jen, who had her back to where Larry had gone to stand back with Dylan, looked bemusedly at Rita.

'Detective Sergeant Larry Banks,' Rita said. 'He should really have been called Reynard, it would have been far more suitable.'

'Reynard?' Jen looked puzzled.

'He's as crafty as an old fox. You want the run-down? Spends more time on the sun bed,' she nodded towards the gym, 'than any woman I know. Chases anything in a skirt.' She raised an eyebrow. 'Sorry, kiddo.'

Jen drew back. 'Oh, God no, don't be. Please go on.'

'He's been married twice, no kids. He's a charmer.' Rita's face turned serious. 'Look, you're the new girl on the block. First few weeks, they'll all be like bees around a honey pot, and rest assured, that sort, they're all bad news. Most of 'em carry a lot of baggage and their latest conquests soon become common knowledge. You mark my words, girl. He's after one thing and one thing only. Don't be fooled by the charm.'

Dylan shook his head at Larry. 'You never give up, do you?'

Larry's eyes were still on Jen and Rita. 'Have you met the new member of admin? I copped her in the gym. I think I'm in there ...' he said with a wink.

Chubby Ned Granger was within earshot. 'She's way out of your league, boss. More my type, I think,' he said, nodding his curly head and giving Larry one of his greasy smiles.

Dylan looked at Larry and slowly shook his head. 'Have you ever thought that she might be married, or already have a partner?'

Larry's eagerness would not be dampened. 'Ah, but that doesn't necessarily mean she's happy, though, does it? She might just fancy a taste of the finer things in life.'

'And maybe she's intelligent enough to know that all that sparkles is not golden, in your case.' Dylan laughed. 'You're like a dog on heat. Do you think of nothing else but getting your leg over?'

'Hey, I don't force them, you know.' Larry raised his glass. 'It's going down a treat tonight,' he said. His voice rose. 'Your very good health everyone.' He toasted them all, raising his glass higher. A cheer went up and Jen looked round.

'Look at her. She looks as if she needs a little bit of care and attention so, let's face it, she may as well try the best first.' Larry sniggered. 'That's all I'm saying, boss, all I'm saying.'

'Seems it's anything with a pulse in your world, Larry,' said Ned. 'When you gonna grow up and not be led by your dick?'

'At least, for me, they have to have a pulse,' Larry said, rewarding himself with a head-thrown-back laugh. 'I think it's your round.'

Ned looked a little embarrassed as he turned the coins over in his pocket. Dylan sensed his unease and took both his glass and Larry's to the bar, apologising to those he had to sidestep as he wove his way through the crowd, dodging tables and chairs.

Jen turned as he walked by on his way back from the bar, her smile lingering until his eyes fell on her. He passed by without stopping, heading towards Dawn who, with her bobbed dark hair, bore a striking resemblance to her namesake, Dawn French, Jen thought.

'Isn't she the lucky one to have a husband who's a chef?' said Rita.

The two watched Dawn join the men and Jen stood in awe of any woman who could hold her own with those formidable characters.

'You're drinking too much these days, Larry,' Dawn said.

'Who are you, my mother? I only drink until I fall over and start spilling it.'

'That's not funny. You need to be more careful.'

'I am careful. I hardly spill any!' Again, he threw back his head and laughed raucously.

'I've told him, women and booze will be his downfall, but will he listen?' said Dylan.

'Hey, I'm not hitched like you two. I don't have to answer to anyone.' He lifted an unsteady head and counted off his fingers one by one. 'Sex, booze and money to buy other nice things,' he said, 'and in that order. Grab it while you can, that's my motto. Live, and let live!' Larry leaned in towards Dawn. 'Have you heard those bastards at headquarters are trying to close down this bar?'

'Being chased down the street by a knife-wielding husband or receiving death threats from another is not my idea of fun, but whatever floats your boat,' said Dawn.

'Ah …' he said, as he tried to focus on the beautifully embroidered hankie she had taken from up her sleeve to wipe her mouth. 'I'm more careful these days. I've taken to not wearing socks so I can get away quicker when the chase is on.' Larry wobbled on one foot in an attempt to show her his feet. He tittered as he grabbed her arm to steady himself. 'I have to use all the tricks of the trade nowadays. I can't run as fast as I used to.'

Didn't Dawn know it well, the way the demon drink innocently crept up on people and, before they knew it, they had a problem: a massive problem.

Larry excused himself and headed for the toilet.

'Sadly, you can't teach an old dog new tricks,' said Dylan.

'At least he'll die happy,' said Dawn.

Terry's wife had planned the tribute painstakingly, right down to the last detail. Her choice of song was from his favourite artist, Matt Monro, and soon the DJ announced the last dance. When the tune to 'Softly As I Leave You' filled the room the lyrics were apt in more ways than one and brought a tear to the most hardened of hearts as they waved goodbye, leading Dylan to wonder whether he would ever be loved in the same way as Terry's wife loved him.

He sincerely hoped so ...

Chapter Nine

By the time Kenny Fisher had found a good spot from which to view the house, the sun had nearly set and, although the moon was almost full, he chose to remain in its shadows.

Kay woke up alone and in almost complete darkness, her face mashed into her favourite cushion. The only light was from the flashing of the TV. Tentatively, she lifted her head very slightly and, with a plaintive moan, immediately dropped it back down. Her neck ached and the pink velvet cushion felt soggy, thoroughly dampened by her drool. As she was shocked back into reality, a warm fuzziness began to pound inside her brain, swelling to a crescendo in time with the beat, it seemed, of the loud banging at the door.

'For God's sake,' she groaned between gritted teeth as she propped herself up on one elbow. 'Why'd you not take your key?' Sitting up sharply, and grimacing from the resultant pain, she slowly rubbed her jaw, turning to look towards the door. Had she only imagined it? Then it came again: bang … Bang … BANG!

No, there was nothing wrong with her hearing. Kay rolled off the sofa.

'Do you want to wake …?' she began, as she unlocked the front door. When she saw who was there, her stomach lurched and her heart began to race. 'What the hell are you doing here?' she said to Kenny. Instinctively, she wrapped her robe tightly around her. She stepped out into the darkness, goosebumps covering her bare arms. 'I thought we had an understanding?' She pulled the door to behind her, in the hope that Isla wouldn't hear them. 'You know the house is off limits now that he's back.'

Kay's eyes darted over Kenny's shoulder, across the lawn to the Anderson's house, looking for any twitching curtains. She scanned the house, studying every window for signs of Tony or Janice Anderson, as Kenny began to speak in hushed tones. When she appeared not to be listening, he reached out for her hand, clasping her warm one in his cold one. Kay's frightened eyes immediately told him that his efforts were futile.

'What are you afraid of?' he asked.

'You don't understand,' she said, with more than a touch of panic in her voice. 'You must go, now!'

For a moment the set of his face terrified her. But his face softened and he continued to talk excitedly. 'I'm not afraid of your husband, and you don't need to be either, not with me by your side.'

'Why would I need to be afraid of Dylan?' She was confused at the conclusion he had come to, from unfounded accusations she hadn't even made.

'Come with me now and I promise you I'll make you the happiest woman in the world.'

'Kenny, please leave. This is neither the time nor the place for that.'

He could see his dream dying before his eyes and his desperation showed. 'Please,' he pleaded.

'Isla's upstairs,' Kay explained calmly. 'She's been suspended from university. She needs my help. She needs her mother ... And Jack has been attacked. This really isn't a good time.'

Kenny raised his eyebrows. 'Serious, I hope?'

Kay looked at him quizzically.

'Pity,' he said with a snarl.

Kay turned away and opened the door.

Kenny caught her hand. 'I'm sorry. Meet me tomorrow and we'll talk.' He paused, while he touched her face with a trembling finger. 'You can't love him, otherwise you wouldn't be with me, would you? Why can't you just face up to it? You and Dylan are finished. You just need to admit it and move on.'

Kay turned back towards him. 'Like I said before, you don't understand. I really can't come with you now. Isla has threatened suicide.'

Kenny stared at her, shaking his head from side to side, in small, controlled, rhythmical movements. 'Will you please stop making excuses. She's an adult, for goodness' sake! The way I see it, you've a choice, Kay. Meet me tomorrow or, I swear to God, this time I will tell him about us.' He pulled her roughly towards him, and she stumbled into his big, powerful arms. 'It's you who doesn't understand. Just the *thought* of you sleeping with him turns my stomach,' he whispered in her ear. 'I will do anything – absolutely anything – for us to be together.'

There was the rumble of a car in the distance. It was getting closer and Kay knew that meant only one thing. Her heart leapt up into her throat; she felt sick. There were only two places the car could be heading now. She reached up onto her tiptoes to see the bright yellow security lights appear on each side of the Anderson's garage. She pulled Kenny further into the shadows. With his head to her chest she watched as her neighbours' garage door automatically opened and their car disappeared inside.

'Go! Go now!' she hissed, pushing Kenny away.

'Okay, I will. But only if you promise to meet me tomorrow,' he said, a wide grin spreading across his face.

There was movement upstairs. Kay's eyes darted up to see a bright light shining through the vines from Isla's bedroom window. Kenny blew her a kiss as he walked back along the border of the lawn, traversing the gravel softly and tiptoeing back to his car. He left his words trailing behind him on the breeze. 'Till tomorrow, my darling ...'

Kay locked the front door and stood with her back against it, breathless. The light at the end of the hallway beckoned her. She needed a drink, and she needed it right now.

Isla stumbled down the stairs, went into the living room and flopped onto the settee. She rolled onto her back, put her hand to her forehead and closed her eyes. Kay could smell smoke.

'Who was at the door?' Isla asked, curling her feet up underneath her. Isla clenched her fists. Sweat ran down her chest and arms, trickling down the back of her legs. She could hear her mother talking, but from what seemed like a long distance away.

'Have you been smoking?' Kay accused her with trepidation as she leaned over the back of the sofa. She watched as Isla rolled onto her side, groaned and suddenly started to heave. Kay dashed into the kitchen, returning with a bowl.

'Do you still feel nauseous?' Kay asked, as she stroked Isla's back soothingly. Isla, who now sat upright beside her, shook her head. She patted her puffy, grey face with a damp cloth. Her lips were bleach-white, and her pallid skin felt hot to the touch, although she was shivering uncontrollably. Sitting backwards, she leaned her head heavily against the cushions, groaning now and then. She opened her eyes to see a large bug in the corner of the room. Instantly, she closed her eyes tight.

'What is it?' Kay asked, seeing her daughter recoil in horror.

'The bugs!'

Kay looked at the wall but saw nothing there.

Isla tried again, but the walls were closing in, then expanding outwards. She'd seen it all before. If she just sat for a while it would soon pass.

Kay covered her with a throw. 'What have you been taking?' she demanded.

'The vodka from the kitchen cupboard ...'

'What, the whole lot?'

Isla nodded and the nausea washed over her again; cramps gripped her stomach. Doubled over in pain and crying, she tried to stand. Kay held out her hand to steady her, but it wasn't enough and she watched helplessly as her daughter fell to the floor.

Shocking images and scenes ran through Isla's head and Kay watched on in horror to see the distorted look on her beautiful face. Isla covered her ears. Intermittently, her eyes flashed open and she cowered at the ceiling, the door, the sofa and the chair as if they were all closing in on her from every angle. All Kay could do was look on.

'Get off, get off,' Isla screamed at something unknown, trying to knock it off her body. She clawed furiously at her skin.

Kay picked up her mobile to ring Dylan as she watched her daughter wet herself, and then she was finally still.

'Oh my God, don't leave me. Don't leave me!' Isla's cries reverberated through the house.

Chapter Ten

Jennifer Jones was very grateful for the offer of a lift home. The slight amount of alcohol she had consumed was far from rendering her over the limit, but she never had been one to take risks; that is, until now, she concluded, as she looked up at the bright square of the bedroom window in the old, end-terrace house.

With tired eyes and one hand on the iron gate she waved a hand to Rita, proffered a smile and watched the tail lights on the vehicle disappear as Rita continued on her way towards Tandem Bridge.

Jen stood for a moment, her back to the closed gate, allowing her eyes to adjust to the dark. Gradually, the long back garden and the high fence came into view, a black slab against the sky. There were street lamps beyond high conifers at the end of the garden, casting a dim light. She edged her way up the uneven path. The biting cold pressed against her face and clawed at her hands. It streamed into her ears and round the back of her neck, penetrating her flimsy, billowing silk jacket. Her teeth chattering, she put her hand in her pocket and stopped, her smile slipping from her face as she began to fear she had lost Martin's spare key. It was then that the darkness wrapped around her tenfold. Fists clenched, she stood anxiously at the door. Without a shadow of doubt, he'd be waiting for her and her only hope of escaping a showdown was to sneak past his slumbering figure as he slept in the chair in a drunken stupor, like he had last time; in fact, *every* time they had been invited out with their colleagues and he had refused to go.

The lower floor of the house was in darkness and no sound came from within. She reached for the leather bag that hung on her shoulder and, with trembling fingers, unfastened the zip. Fumbling around, she felt a long, thin cardboard box. She hesitated, looking up at the sprinkling of stars in the sky, and began to pray fervently. *Please, God, let there be some pills left. Just one to soothe my nerves.* But, the thought was gone as soon as it came, like the wisp of cloud that glided past the moon. She didn't need anxiety drugs. What she did need was to grow some balls and face life's challenges head-on, just like she'd told Shaun he should do when she'd left the island.

Her feet had begun to go numb when her fingers finally touched on cold metal. Her heart leapt with joy: the key. 'Thank the Lord,' she said, but her voice floated away, up into the night sky. A shiver ran down her back, as she felt a furry warmth brush against her leg. A scream caught in her throat. If Martin hadn't let Harry in, that meant he wasn't in bed.

In truth, Martin had seen her come home and was watching her from behind the curtain where he'd been waiting for some time.

Jen opened the door. The rustle of fabric was loud to her ears as she bent down to slip off her shoes. Carefully and quietly, she placed them neatly by the doorjamb next to Martin's, just where he liked them to be. Martin didn't like anyone wearing shoes in the house. The hallway was pitch black. The only noises were the tick of the clock and Max, her golden retriever, bounding up at the door of the utility room where he slept. She frowned and paused for a moment; his cries were unusually muffled.

At that very same moment there was a flash of white fur, followed by a hysterical meow as Harry streaked up the side of the pine dresser. But before she had time to consider why the heavy front door had slammed violently behind her, a clammy hand came from nowhere to cover her mouth and bring her to her knees. The sickly taste of aftershave made her retch. Jen struggled, writhing under a heavy weight when suddenly she felt something cold pressed against her throat. She swallowed hard, choking down her sobs, breathless and sweating. She lay still, blinking tears from her terrified eyes, silently begging Martin not to use the knife.

'You disgust me,' Martin hissed, his breathing strong and hard.

With every ounce of strength she could muster she reached up with trembling fingers to touch his face. Immediately, the pressure that held the knife down disappeared.

Martin's head tipped to one side. 'Do you still love me?' he asked. 'Say it!' he demanded. 'Say you love me and that there isn't anyone else.'

Jen's voice faltered. 'I ... love you.'

'Again. Tell me again.'

'I love you,' she said, her voice much stronger this time.

'One more chance,' he said, through narrowed eyes. 'Just one more chance ...'

Martin rolled off her and lay on the hardwood floor next to her. Jen's face crumpled, and tears rolled down her cheeks. Her sobbing made him reach out and pull her towards him. He wrapped his arms around her, pressing her face to his chest.

'Don't cry. You're okay. It'll be fine and dandy when it's just you and me and nobody else sticking their two penn'orth in,' he said, patting her soothingly, like a parent would a child.

Although much of Isla's night had been lost in an alcohol-induced blackout, the last thing she remembered was stepping back from her open bedroom window through which she had been wafting the smoke of her cigarette because a posh car was crawling past the house in the street below. The occupant appeared to be taking a great interest in the place. It wasn't long afterwards that she had seen the visitor approaching the front door from the shadows and heard him knock enthusiastically. He and her mother had stood under the vines, the muffled excitement of their voices loud enough to keep her awake.

She assumed her mother had kept him outside because she was ashamed of her daughter. *Who was he?* she wondered when she woke from her alcohol-induced oblivion; or had he also been a figment of her imagination?

'Welcome back,' said Detective Sergeant Dawn Farren, nodding at Dylan's overflowing in-tray and scowling at Larry Banks who sat with one elbow resting on the chair arm and one hand to his brow. A white plastic bag hung from Dawn's wrist and three cups of strong coffee sat on the tray she was carrying.

'Hmm, something smells good,' Dylan said, eager to see what was in the bag. He tossed his head in Larry's direction. 'I hope that coffee's strong enough to waken the dead!'

'It'll sure scare some of the fuzziness out of his brain.' Dawn chuckled, her shoulders bouncing up and down.

Dylan grimaced. 'You mean he's actually got one? He put himself down for eleven till seven today.' Dylan pulled up his shirt sleeve at the cuff and looked at his watch. 'So, my guess is that it's probably not worth going home and he'll be working at least three hours for Queen and country today.'

Larry looked up at Dylan, his bleary red eyes widening in horror. 'You are joking?' he said.

Dylan shook his head.

Dawn laughed out loud.

Larry groaned, raising a middle finger in Dawn's direction. She slapped him on the back.

'You'll be all right, our kid, as soon as you've got the hair of the dog down you.' Dawn offered Larry a greasy sandwich. So packed were they with bacon, eggs and ketchup that she had to open her mouth wide to take a bite of her own. 'I feel your pain,' she said, swallowing her mouthful. 'My bedroom was a terrifying spiny place when I woke up this morning. Thank goodness for Ralph,' she said, her smile cheerfully wide. 'My very clever chef of a hubby is great at getting rid of the goblins that creep in during the night and decide that my head will make the perfect addition to their percussion band.'

Larry's head still felt woolly, but at least the pounding headache was starting to ease and he didn't feel half as nauseous as before. He looked up to see Dylan was already ploughing through the work Larry should have completed in his absence.

'Er, sorry about the paperwork, boss. I don't know how on earth you manage to keep up with it all. The last few days have been really busy, haven't they?' He looked towards Dawn for support.

'Hey, I might bring you the perfect hangover remedy, but I'm not so soft in t'head that I'll be your alibi.'

Dylan raised his head. He wrinkled his nose and his voice was gruff. 'Tell me, Larry, have you been home yet?'

'Please don't,' Larry said, clutching one hand to his head. 'Not so loud. I went clubbing and I met Gwen. She's an old flame. How could I say no?'

'You mean Gwen, the hippy shoplifter you bailed last week?' asked Dawn. 'I saw her drop you off in her rusty pink tin can.'

Dylan shook his head.

Larry stood up and attemped to balance himself as the world took another sickening spin, placing his hand on Dawn's shoulder. 'I've got clean clothes in my locker. I'll go have a shower and I'll see you at the briefing. Nothing happening is there?'

Dylan shook his head again.

'You do realise, one of these days he's going to end up dead?' said Dawn when Larry had gone.

'Won't we all?'

Dawn laughed. 'Touché!' She paused. 'But seriously, have you met Gwen's husband? He's a bare-knuckle fighter.'

Dylan had his head down, reading. 'I'm not his mother,' he said.

'Last week he was bragging about being chased by an irate husband wielding a weapon!'

Dylan looked up. 'Have we had a complaint?'

Dawn pulled a face. 'Not that I know of.'

Dylan nodded and continued reading.

'He's always on the take, though, and that makes him vulnerable.'

'Spreading rumours and a bit of bragging is what Larry does. The rest, well, it's best I don't know. If I do know DS Banks though, he'll smarten himself up ready for the briefing. He might play hard, but he works pretty hard too.'

Larry Banks slowly made his way to the gym. In the changing-rooms he discarded his clothes on the floor of the cubicle and lay naked on the warm glass of the sunbed. As soon as his body felt the heat from the bulbs, he closed his eyes against the bright lights and fell into a deep sleep.

One hour later, he opened his sore eyes to the sound of the buzzer. It was dark and, although his body was hot, he felt a chill from the fan. A distinct smell of body odour wafted under his nose; his throat felt as dry as dust. Clutching at the sunbed, he lay very still and tried to gather his bearings as he recalled the vision of a roll of smoke and a bang louder than fireworks, which had resulted in the panic still tight in his chest. The images hadn't been quite like a dream, but definitely weren't reality; they had felt vivid, but also distant. The long, winding ribbon of undeveloped upland trodden by the Pennine Way he knew so well had stretched out before him and in his wake was Dylan, chasing after him relentlessly until his legs were weak and wobbly. Larry's lungs had felt a tightness he'd never known before and he'd struggled to breathe. He'd known that if he'd stopped running, even for a second, Dylan would catch up with him. At the top, around a hairpin bend, the road had vanished – he was heading nowhere at all. Larry's legs had cramped and he'd fallen, the palms of his hands landing on wet turf. Tentatively, he'd glanced behind him to see Dylan standing there and Kay's face looming over her husband's shoulder. 'Dylan must never know,' she'd breathed down the back of her husband's neck.

Just remembering it made shivers run down his spine and his skin turn cold.

Larry headed for the showers, stopping at the sink to splash cold water on his face. She was right; Dylan must never, ever know about them. The cool water trickling down his warm skin was a refreshing sensation. He put his face up to the shower head and rubbed his eyes to clear the tiredness. Leaning against the tiles, he let out a quiet groan. It was going to take more than coffee, greasy sandwiches, a sunbed session and a shower to completely shift this hangover.

'You fit?' Dylan said to Larry twenty minutes later when he walked past him, chatting and laughing with two of the typists, on his way to the briefing room.

'You bet,' he said, downing the coffee he'd snatched from Lisa's desk. The pretty young girl from admin giggled at his grimace. 'No milk or sugar? You need to get a life.' Larry leaned on her desk and whispered into her ear, 'Stick with me and I'll show you the world,' giving her a wink as he left.

Dylan didn't need to turn around to know it was Larry that was hurrying down the corridor behind him moments later, because the strength of his aftershave gave him away. Approaching the briefing room, he slowed down to allow Larry to catch up. 'When are you going to grow up?' he asked as they reached the door.

Larry grinned. 'Never, I hope,' he said, putting his hand on the door handle. 'But I am going to cut down on my drinking, if that's what you mean.'

'Of course you are,' scoffed Dylan as he squeezed past him. 'Or do you really mean it?'

Larry nodded emphatically.

Heading a morning briefing when all the shifts collided and the whole office was working at the same time always felt like the start of a new adventure to Detective Inspector Dylan, especially with Detective Sergeants Larry Banks and Dawn Farren at his side, and this day was no different. The number of people in attendance meant that not all the team could sit around the table; some staff had to perch around the periphery of the room.

Dawn sat at the front of the room, two empty seats alongside her awaiting their arrival. From her buff-coloured file she produced the information Dylan and the team needed to be briefed about. All eyes were on her until Lisa brought in plates of warm toast and butter, and hot drinks were placed on the table before them. Much better in Dylan's view that the team were fed and watered and ready to listen, rather than fidgeting in their seats willing the meeting to be over.

Larry adjusted his cuffs for the second time in two minutes. He looked very smart in his designer suit and shiny shoes, a total transformation from earlier. If he'd meant what he said, there were going to be fraught nerves and many other withdrawal symptoms, Dylan was more than aware, but he would support his friend and colleague as much as he could, rather than see him become an addict.

There had been a couple of brace and bit burglaries overnight but, apart from that, it had been relatively quiet. When Larry gave his update on the issues that had occurred in Dylan's absence he tapped the table with his pen. The light caught his shiny cufflinks. *The dandy detective*. Dylan smiled. He was pleased to see Larry back on form.

'The burglar is linking the crimes nicely for us. So, once he is identified, traced and arrested,' said Larry, 'he'll have a hell of a job disproving his involvement, just so long as we recover the brace and bit used in his possession.'

Detective Constable Ned Granger leaned back and crossed his arms across his chest, just above his beer belly. 'Why do we need to recover the brace and bit in his possession?' he asked, tapping his foot.

'Because,' Larry snapped, his eyes locking on to Ned's, 'the drill holes from this make of drill will all be the same size and will match the bit, so we need to find it in his possession to show it's his, you numpty!'

Ned held Larry's stare and lifted his hand to scratch an already stubbly chin while he pondered Larry's answer. Dylan could see the mischief in him, as he tried to come up with something else to say that he knew would rub the detective sergeant up the wrong way.

'If uniform got their heads out of their arses, they might catch them on the job, and then we could deal with serious stuff,' was the best Ned could muster. This time his jibe was addressed to Vicky Hardacre, the younger, blonde PC who was with the team on secondment, and who sat next to him.

Dylan could hear a couple of the others rustling their paperwork and he watched Larry's facial muscles contract and his mouth tighten as if he was about to yell something abusive.

'Any MISPERS we should be aware of?' started Dylan.

'Yes, sir, there have been two separate reports of two girls going missing from home, not connected, as far as we are aware and – as far as we know – they don't know each other. The only thing they have in common appears to be that they are both fourteen years of age.'

'So, both vulnerable.'

'Yes, boss.'

'And what are the circumstances?'

'The first is a Tiffany Shaw, who is described as a good, clean-living girl and from a respectable family. Her mother is reported to have been the last to see her yesterday when she left after breakfast, purporting to be off to spend the day with "friends". Her parents have checked with all her known associates but have had no luck tracing who she was supposed to be meeting, or where,' said Dawn.

Dylan frowned. 'I gather she didn't turn up at school this morning either.'

'No, sir.'

'And she's never gone missing previously?'

Dawn shook her head.

Police Constable Vicky Hardacre cleared her throat. 'Her friends have hinted to me this morning, sir, that she might be seeing an older boy.' She paused.

Dylan's eyebrows rose in anticipation.

'But they are unaware of who he is. Or that's what they're telling me.'

'And, you don't believe them?'

Vicky shrugged her shoulders. 'Her parents refute the accusation as "absolute nonsense" and tell me she has no interest in boys whatsoever.'

Ned turned his head in Vicky's direction and muttered, 'She'll be the first fourteen-year-old girl who hasn't an interest in boys that I know of.' He sniggered.

'What's that DC Granger?' Dylan asked. Ned Granger excused himself to answer the phone he extracted from his jacket pocket. Vicky looked puzzled: she hadn't heard his phone ring. Ned perched on the edge of the desk next to the door and listened intently, as it seemed.

'So, we follow the usual procedures, liaise with uniform to see what priority enquiries are already in motion and ask them whether any searches are taking place. I want us to support them when and where we can.'

'The second missing girl is a regular, boss. Tanya King: well known to the welfare authorities and to us. According to the night report, uniform have liaised with the children's home where she lives and asked them to let us know when she turns up.'

Larry leaned forward and poured himself another strong coffee. 'I don't think we need to be concerned about Tanya going AWOL. Everyone who has dealt with her knows she's streetwise. Only yesterday I had to eject her from an off-licence. She had been drinking and was causing bother, as usual.' Larry took a sip of his drink. 'She told me she was on her way to see her boyfriend, Tariq, and we all know what that means. She'll no doubt turn up sooner rather than later.'

Dylan stood up and started pacing around the room, as he often did in briefings when he was thinking. 'Okay, to start with, whatever your views about them, they are both young girls and both vulnerable. We need to trace them ASAP. So, especially while there isn't much happening elsewhere, I want you to assist uniform as best you can and, while you're at it, let's rattle some cages at the children's home, and find out exactly what's going on with Tanya.'

Dylan was standing by the door, seeming to all intents and purposes ready to close the meeting, when he put his hand out, took the phone from Ned and pressed the loudspeaker button. The dial tone rang out loud and clear. He raised an eyebrow at Ned. 'You're such a tosser, Ned Granger. My office now and, on the way, make yourself useful and put the kettle on.'

Ned, red-faced, nipped through the door to the sound of the others' laughter.

Chapter Eleven

Numerous enquiries were made throughout the day but by five o'clock neither of the girls had been traced or had turned up at their home addresses. The search was widening under Dylan's instruction but, with no new leads to work from or with, he decided to return home to see how Isla was faring, planning to return to review the MISPER situation in a few hours. He was growing more and more concerned for the girls as the passing hours quickly turned into a day. Sometimes when children went missing it was blatantly obvious they had been snatched, at other times not so; but all missing children or vulnerable adults required a professional approach in their investigation and that would be exactly what would happen in Dylan's safe pair of hands.

When Dylan arrived home, to his surprise, Kay was dressed up to the nines, make-up on and all ready to go out.

'Going somewhere?' he asked, trying his best to appear nonchalant.

'Have you forgotten?' she said, head turned away, as she fiddled with an earring with the aid of the mirror over the mantlepiece. She felt sick to her stomach seeing the confused look on Dylan's face reflected in the mirror, clearly caused by her actions, and hearing the pained tone of his voice.

'It's that blasted reunion,' she said, trying to relieve his angst. 'I told you about it ages ago, don't you remember?' Kay turned to him, a half-hearted smile pasted on her face. 'I'm sorry. I won't be that long, not more than a couple of hours at the most. I really wish I didn't have to go, but I promised to pick some of the gang up,' she said, standing on her tiptoes to kiss Dylan on the cheek.

Dylan remained perfectly still, his face devoid of all emotion.

Kay rubbed her forehead, the way he knew she always did when she was thinking. Then she busied herself collecting her things together and shrugged her arms into her best jacket. When had she become such a proficient liar?

'I'll need to take the car,' she said.

'Okay,' said Dylan, his voice flat. 'But when you get home, I'll need to go back to the station. We have two vulnerable young teenage girls missing.'

Kay looked shocked and briefly felt a sense of guilt, but the moment passed quickly.

'Where's Isla?' Dylan asked.

Kay lowered her voice, her eyes darting up towards the ceiling. 'Up in her room where she's been most of the day.'

'How's she been?' Dylan's voice was full of concern.

'How do you expect an addict to be when they've gone cold turkey?' Kay snapped as she raised her eyebrows at him.

Dylan tutted. 'When did you become so insensitive?'

Kay picked up her handbag and held out her hand. 'Keys!' she demanded.

Dylan gripped the car keys tightly in his jacket pocket. 'Did you manage to phone the doctor?'

Kay checked her watch. She seemed flustered.

'Well, did you?'

'Yes, yes, of course I did. But they can't offer her an appointment until a week on Wednesday.' She rolled her eyes. 'And a fat lot of good that is!'

'Did you explain the situation?'

Kay scowled and drew back from her husband. 'What do you take me for, a complete imbecile? There's a pizza in the freezer for your tea. Like I said, I'll be a couple of hours max.'

Dylan watched her turn and walk through the hallway, slamming the front door shut behind her without a backward glance.

He walked back to the foot of the stairs, put his hand on the bannister and listened. All was quiet and still above. Next to the telephone, there was a framed photo of him and Kay that had been taken by Isla on Christmas Day. He picked it up and, staring at it, carried it into the kitchen. He was thoughtful. Happy times. His smile quickly fell from his lips. Who was he kidding? He placed the photograph face down on the table as he started to prepare a brew. He stood for a moment, recalling that Christmas day ... Now he thought about it, it was very unlike Isla to have chosen to wear a baggy jumper and tracksuit bottoms over the new clothes she'd just been bought. 'Keeping them for best,' she'd said, and he'd bought the lie. Consumed as he was in work, it had been easier not to think about it. In the same way, he'd known deep down back then that something was not quite right between him and Kay.

'Pizza again!' Isla's words startled him. 'And it's a crap one!'

Dylan gave her a lopsided smile, put his arms around her shoulders and placing a kiss on the side of her head, he squeezed her tight. 'Hey, we've eaten worse,' he said, and sighed.

'What's with Mum wearing stockings anyway?' Isla's dark-rimmed eyes were suddenly dancing, teasing.

'Was she?' Dylan said, surprised. His stomach churned. 'How'd you know?'

'I watched her getting ready. She didn't know I was watching her. She looked nice, don't you think?'

Dylan nodded as he bent to put the pizza in the oven; he couldn't look at her, fearful she might notice the sadness on his face.

Twenty minutes later, Isla sat at the table, a slice of pizza hanging from her fingers. She picked the photograph up firmly in her other hand. She smiled, there were tears in her eyes. 'Aw ... That's a lovely picture of you and Mum,' she said. 'What would I do without you?'

Dylan reached out and softly stroked her arm. 'The feeling is mutual,' he said. 'I hear you can't see a doctor until next week?'

'Yeah, the receptionist was really great, though. She sent a message through to the doctor and said he'd more than likely ring me sooner. I also stopped off at the chemist and the pharmacist there was great, too. He gave me lots of information to read and advised tablets for stomach cramps – in fact, I think they've helped already.'

'Your mother never said she'd been to the doctors?'

'She hadn't. I went on the bus.'

Dylan's brain was in turmoil. Had Kay really left their weak and damaged daughter to make her own way to the doctor? His logical side urged him to deal with the situation as quickly as he could. It also reminded him that to act in haste was to repent at leisure. The emotional side of his brain wanted to believe that Kay was not lying to him and he felt guilty for questioning her. But why, then, was she acting so strangely?

'I've read up on what to expect, Dad. I know I'll get withdrawal symptoms, mood swings and suchlike, and I also know they will be hard to cope with, but the reading material they've given me says that they'll subside. Besides,' she said, picking up her plate and planting a kiss on the top of Dylan's head on her way to the bin, where she deposited the uneaten pizza, 'I also know while you and Mum are here to help me, I can conquer anything.' She scowled and patted her stomach. 'I just wish the cramps would hurry up and go.' Isla went to the doorway and leaned against the frame.

'You'll tell me if you are worried about anything, won't you? I don't want you trying to do this all on your own,' said Dylan.

''Course I will,' she said with a little laugh before she turned away to leave him alone with his thoughts.

Kay pulled into the lay-by. She looked solemnly at herself in the driver's mirror and wondered for the millionth time if she was doing the right thing. She knew that, whatever she decided, in the end her life was never going to be the same as it had been before Kenny Fisher.

Fisher's car pulled up behind her. He had been waiting for her for a while, parked up in another lay-by further up the road so that he could watch her arrival. She saw the look of utter satisfaction on his face when he saw her step out of her car and get into his.

It was too late for Kay to back out now, but that wasn't the reason for her wanting to go out with him tonight. She wondered briefly how Dylan would react if he found out, but the conclusion she arrived at was not one she wanted to think about right now. If she played her cards right tonight, he would never need to find out about them. She rubbed her forehead as if trying to remove her husband from her thoughts. Dylan would be hurt, that much she knew for sure. But why should she care about that? It was his continual neglect of her feelings that had driven her to be here in the first place.

The Miller's restaurant in Redchester had been impressively

restored, embracing the building's history. Housed in what had been an old bakery, the oak-beamed bar showcased a working mill wheel. The staff seemed to know Kenny Fisher well, or perhaps it was merely his appeal that made it seem so; everyone instantly warmed to his friendliness and charm.

Sitting at the beautifully dressed dining table, overlooking the most amazing views of the moorland, Kenny placed his hand possessively over hers. She took three long, deep breaths, holding back tears; though whether they were tears of fear or sadness she did not know.

'I'm sorry, Kenny, but I can only stop for a couple of hours. Dylan's got to go back to work and I need to get back to Isla.'

'Let's eat first, then talk, shall we?' Kenny clicked his fingers and summoned the waiter. 'Champagne! The best you've got for my girl!'

Kenny was in a curiously joyous, if not jubilant mood. Kay tried to stay calm. Gulping down the wine in the crystal champagne flute, she prayed that it would give her the strength she needed to stand firm; furthermore, she conceded that after the second glass she would need it just to give her enough strength to get her behind off the chair.

His talk centred around her leaving Dylan; hers around the fact that it was simply not possible. Her words appeared to fall on deaf ears: deaf, sober ears, as Kenny didn't drink and drive.

Kay ate her food quickly. If the conversation didn't give her indigestion, then gulping her food down surely would. She didn't want another argument with Dylan about being late and she was mindful that she and Kenny still needed to have the conversation she'd planned in her head earlier.

To those looking on, Kenny played the perfect attentive partner. His lips formed the perfect lover's smile offering sweet nothings in her ear, but what he actually said was far less palatable. 'Don't mess with me, Kay,' he whispered, menacingly. Looking into her eyes, he was met by her troubled stare. 'You turned up just like I asked. You've even gone to the trouble of dressing up for me.' He winked at her, and his smile widened. 'Don't think I haven't noticed the stockings and suspenders.' His warm hand stroked her leg, promising more. 'You're a tease, Kay, that's all, just a big tease. *I* know what you really want and, if you're honest with yourself, you know exactly what you want too. And that's me. You know it is only me who can ever make you completely happy.'

Kay's expression was pained as she began to realise just how serious he was. 'You don't understand, Kenny. I can't leave, not now, not with Isla being so ill.'

Kenny sat up, leaned across the table and put a finger under her chin. Their eyes locked, but it wasn't a lovers' stare. 'You can. And you will,' he whispered. 'Do you understand?'

Kay's eyes closed slowly and she nodded her head. Her voice wobbled. 'Yes,' she replied.

The sex they indulged in before they left for home was not what she had become accustomed to. Kenny was the patient lover no more; this time he was extremely rough.

Shocked, and a little frightened, Kay ran from his car to hers and locked the doors. This was not fun. Unusually, he drove off before her and a blanket of darkness fell all around her the moment he was gone. She replenished her make-up. Her mouth felt sore; her body bruised. Had the aggression been intentional? She was torn: a big part of her wanted to end the relationship but – if she was honest – as Kenny had said, there was a part of her which didn't.

She put her head back on the headrest and closed her eyes. She recalled the first time: the smell of him on top of her, the heaviness of his powerful body, the passion in his voice as he'd asked if she was sure. She'd wallowed in the attention he gave her, the excitement of their clandestine meetings and the idyllic fortnight they had just spent living as man and wife while Dylan had been away. For the third time that night she rubbed her forehead to break her reverie. *How could their affair have turned out the way it had?* Then she remembered how the real argument had started, the words still fresh in her mind: *When are you going to leave?*

Kay had wondered at first whether she had understood him correctly. Even to her ears, her response had sounded lame. '*When* am I going to leave …?'

'Leave Dylan and come to live with me?'

The words bounced off every bone in her body. Leave him? Leave … *Leave Dylan?* No, she wasn't ready for it, nor had she ever truly thought she would leave him.

Kay banged her fist down hard on the steering wheel. Why had Kenny gone and spoiled it all? What she wanted, what she *needed*, was for their secret affair to remain forever just that: a secret.

Chapter Twelve

Taking several deep breaths, Kay smoothed out the creases of her clothing, double-checked her make-up in the driver's mirror and ran her fingers through her hair. She checked her phone. It had been over three hours since she had left, but she knew the lightheartedness she must portray to her husband would only be required for a few minutes, because as soon as she walked through the door, Dylan would be on his way out.

'Good do, was it?' Dylan called from the lounge when he heard the key in the lock and the gentle click of the door shutting behind her.

Kay came to stand by the door. 'No, not really,' she said.

Her hair was dishevelled and, Dylan thought, there was something about her: her eyes were bright, sparkling … perhaps she had never looked lovelier. And then she was gone.

'I'll just run up and grab a shower and get my comfies on and I'll be straight back down, Isla,' she called to their daughter as she ran up the stairs, adding as an afterthought, 'The car keys are on the hallway table, Jack!'

Dylan rose to his feet, bent down to gave Isla a habitual brief kiss on the forehead and asked, 'Will you be okay?'

The build-up of sleepless nights was now clearly visible on Isla's face. 'Stop asking me if I'm okay, will you?' Her voice was raised. 'Actually, it makes me feel much worse. How many times do I have to tell you I'm fine? And for your information I don't need babysitting.'

Dylan fastened the top button of his shirt and tightened the knot in his tie. 'It's only because I care,' he murmured softly. He walked into the hallway and looked up towards the sound of the running shower. He felt a faint stirring within him and sighed, wanting nothing more in that moment than to go to his wife, talk to her, hold her and make love to her like he used to. Instead, he stepped forward to pick up the car keys and as he did so there was a tug at his sleeve; it was Isla come after him.

She wrapped her arms around his neck. 'I know you do, Dad ...' she said. Her eyes looked redder in the hallway's bright light: tired, swollen and stressed. 'It's the withdrawal: makes me feel irritable all the time ... I'm so proud of you. I hope you find those missing girls soon, so that you can come back home to us.'

'I'll do my damnedest,' he said, with a half-hearted smile. As he held her, he looked up the stairs. The shower had stopped but there was no sign of Kay.

Isla pulled away. 'If you're waiting for Mum to come down, you'll still be standing here in the morning. If I know her, she'll be straight to her bed, no matter what she said before.'

Catching sight of his face in the hallway mirror, Dylan saw himself frown. Perhaps it was time to grow a backbone and simply face up to the fact that Kay might be indulging in an affair. After watching Isla go back into the lounge, he gathered up his coat, grabbed the car keys and shut the door behind him. 'For better or for worse,' he announced to the night air. Now, as then, he meant every word he said.

The cold afternoon, accompanied by a light breeze, had turned into a blustery evening and the wind blew his thoughts away. He pulled his coat edges closer together when a gust caught him off balance. As he drove towards the police station, his thoughts turned to the missing girls and his concern grew. Time was of the essence when someone was vulnerable; the course at Hendon had reinforced his awareness that precious minutes saved lives.

He had learned that predators could groom their prey for weeks, even years, watching and waiting for an opportunity to pounce, and a child could sometimes disappear in the blink of an eye. But with two incidents occurring in one day, and knowing the different circumstances, it didn't strike him that this was what had happened here. However, the words of his mentor, Peter Reginald Stonestreet came back to him: 'Never assume, son,' he'd said. 'Never assume anything.' Dylan guessed that applied to his home life as well.

Kay gave a deep sigh of relief as she sat down at her dressing table in the darkened room, a towel draped around her body. She had waited at the window to see Dylan reverse the car down the driveway. He'd stopped and looked up at their window, and she'd immediately drawn back. Still thinking of Kenny, she put on her pyjamas and headed for her bed.

Hearing the pull-cord in the bathroom a few minutes later, Kay suspected that her daughter was heading for a relaxing bath before bed – just what the doctor would have ordered. She smiled and nuzzled down further, breathing in the lavender pillow spray Kenny had bought her.

Half an hour later, still tossing and turning, she could not get to sleep. She felt bad. Kenny's mood earlier, she conceded after some consideration, was just a reflection of his disappointment and frustration. Who wouldn't be angry and upset, considering how she was treating him?

For the fourth time in less than fifteen minutes she picked up the phone. He was a good man, a kind man. He made her feel special, he made her feel loved and she didn't want to lose him. But neither could she face thinking about leaving Jack (and particularly Isla) at the moment. What she wanted was his patience. What she needed was to hear his voice – but what could she say to a person who she loved, but who she was hurting so deeply?

For over an hour she stared at the phone, making excuses for her actions, practising exactly what she would say to him, ever so sure she would have a response that would satisfy him, since he loved her. However, as she sat in silence on the edge of the bed listening over and over to the ringing tone, she became less sure.

'Hello?' said Kenny eventually. His voice sounded groggy as if he had been fast asleep. She clasped the phone tighter, a little annoyed that he was able to sleep when she couldn't. If he loved her as much as he said he did, how could he manage to sleep so soundly after their row?

'Meet me tomorrow. We need to talk,' was all she said before putting down the phone.

Kenny smiled to himself. He looked at the clock. Almost midnight. *And she acts like she doesn't care? Bullshit!*

Dylan looked at the clock. It was midnight when the knock came at his office door. Detective Constable Benjamin entered. Yawning widely, Dylan rubbed his eyes. 'Now then, John,' he said, 'what can I do for you?'

'Can I sit down?' John asked.

'Of course,' Dylan said, feeling encouraged. He guessed the news was good by the big, black gentle giant's toothy smile.

'Tanya King's been found,' he said.

Dylan blew a long breath out from pursed lips, leaned back in his chair, stretched his arms upwards and linked his fingers together behind his head.

'But ...'

Dylan had always found John to be loyal and calm when the job called for it, but with a temper that he could unleash at any time. He was a father to two children and a keen rugby player. Dylan rated him highly; he'd get the next boards, Dylan was in no doubt. He'd be proud to have Benjamin as a detective sergeant on his team.

'She's at the hospital. I've been informed that all units responded to several calls about an hour ago. A young lad and lass, both semi-conscious, were found laid on a grass verge leading to the dual carriageway into town. At first those attending thought the youngsters might just be drunk or had both overdosed. However, when they got them to the hospital they soon realised that both had been badly assaulted. According to the medical staff they have several other injuries, which they suggest are consistent with both recent and historic violent sexual abuse.'

Dylan grimaced. 'Do we know where the lad lives?'

'They're both from Field Colt Children's Home, sir. As you're aware, Dawn is covering for the DI over at CPU this week and she's been called out.' Benjamin made a move to stand. 'I'll go and put the kettle on, shall I? She'll be calling in here prior to going to the hospital. In fact,' he said, looking at his watch, 'she should be here any minute.'

'Teenagers, they think they're streetwise ...'

John nodded in agreement.

'But sadly, there will always be those who take advantage.'

'On a positive note, though, have you heard that the other missing girl, Tiffany Shaw, is back home? Tail between her legs, apparently. Uniform are round at the house now hoping to find out where she's been,' John raised his eyebrows, 'and who she's been with.'

'No, no I hadn't heard, but then I'm not officially here ... working that is.'

'I find it hard when I'm off duty to put the job out of my head too, especially when it's an ongoing incident ...' John said as he turned to walk out of the office.

'Yes, but you must, John. Otherwise you'll end up living for the work ... And, as a wise man once told me, I must work to live. It's just a job at the end of the day ...' Dylan said, to himself as much as to the DC.

Before John could leave, Dawn arrived at the office.

'Well, all I can say is, if you do have to get out of your bed, Dylan's office is at least decently furnished, with a good carpet and comfortable chairs, unlike mine in the CPU.'

Her straight face and her wicked sense of humour could warm even the coldest of nights. The men rose to greet her.

'It's like walking into the land of the bloody giants with you two. For goodness' sake, just sit yourselves down, can't you?'

'What's the news, then, Dawn?' Dylan said, sitting back down.

'News is that Nick Towler and Tanya are just the latest kids to be hired out by Field Colt Children's Home as "entertainment" for parties given by the rich. These are usually large, private house parties. Maybe we'll learn more about what has happened to them if we can gain their confidence and get them to open up and talk to us,' said Dawn.

John looked from Dylan to Dawn.

'We've come to be made aware of these sorts of "parties" more and more recently, but it appears that, up until now, those connected to them have been too frightened of possible reprisals to speak to us. And without their statements there's nothing we can do,' said Dawn. She'd somehow managed to drop her biscuit into her coffee while dunking it and was now busy chasing it around with a spoon. 'I've been told that if the kids speak out or say anything negative about the home, then they are moved on to another one. It's hard enough for these kids to form any kind of relationship with each other, let alone the people who are supposed to care for them. Being constantly moved around leaves them feeling even more isolated, so apparently, according to my little friend who's a cleaner at Field Colt, they put up and shut up!' With a look of great satisfaction, she popped the retrieved soggy biscuit into her mouth.

'The protectors are turning out to be the abusers, then. They're probably only drawn to the job because they're sick individuals who get their kicks out of abusing kids,' said Dylan. His tired face was puffy and grey.

John appeared thoughtful. 'Or might it be possible that someone is getting paid handsomely to farm these kids out?'

Dylan sighed and shook his head resignedly. 'And no doubt the heads of the children's homes involved all know each other and won't waste any time in calling them troublemakers in order to justify their continual movement.'

Dawn looked at Dylan. 'It's a vicious circle.' Her brow furrowed. 'Do you remember Larry mentioning Tanya at the briefing, saying that he'd ejected her from an off-licence last night? He said she'd told him she was going out with a lad called Tariq? What do we know about Tariq?'

Dylan looked at John. He shrugged his shoulders.

Dawn scribbled a note in her book.

'Ask her,' said Dylan to Dawn.

'I've just made a note. Trouble is these kids are allowed out and about unsupervised and they mix with undesirables who end up grooming them.'

'I guess the kids think it's a case of better the devil they know? At least that way their destination is in their own hands – or so they like to think,' said John.

'The suggestion is, at least according to my friend the cleaner who often overhears the kids talking, that the kids at Field Colt are regularly invited to these parties. Basically, it sounds like they're supplied on demand, just like you and I would ring up and order a takeaway.'

Dylan picked up his pen, his right hand twitched and he tapped it on the desk. 'This suggests to me we might be hitting on a network that's been around for a while, and right under our very noses.' The others agreed. 'If the offenders have a direct contact inside the home – and it must be someone in authority so as not to arouse any suspicion – we need to find out precisely who that person is.' Dylan wrote on a piece of paper which he'd extracted from his printer.

'Number one, I want you to collate as much evidence as possible, as quickly as possible. Number two, we need to speak to all residents and staff; and number three, log all the incidents we've been made aware of in the past in relation to Field Colt, even if they have come to nothing. Get your coat, Dawn. I'm coming with you to the hospital. I want to hear what Tanya and Nick have to say first-hand.'

Dawn looked at Dylan, noticing the huge dark rings that had formed around his eyes. 'Why not go home, eh? Get some rest. I'll take it from here and I'll speak to you tomorrow morning. You look all in.'

Dylan appeared not to hear her, or simply chose not to. 'We've got someone experienced talking to Tiffany, haven't we?'

'Yes, Kelly Armstrong. She's good. We can rely on her to get to the bottom of whatever's been going on.'

Dylan rose from his chair, but the sheer effort it took generated a groan from deep inside him. He opened his drawer and took out a packet of paracetamol and a can of Coca-Cola, popping two pills from their plastic covering. The Coke fizzed as he opened it and he swallowed the pills down in two huge gulps.

'Right, what are we waiting for?' he said to Dawn.

Chapter Thirteen

The accident and emergency department was the latest part of the old Harrowfield General Hospital building to have been relocated, redesigned and thoroughly modernised. Dylan stepped through the automatic sliding doors into the bright and airy, well-planned triage area and remembered the shabby old canteen which had once stood on that very spot.

The detectives waited for over an hour, before they finally heard that Nick Towler had been seen by a doctor and had had all the necessary scans.

'He needs emergency surgery,' announced a nurse, before fleeing to an alarm raised by a colleague. 'Excuse me,' she said, squeezing past Dawn and quickly disappearing behind one of the cubicle's dark green curtains, which opened slightly to reveal the bare soles of two soiled feet.

The ward where the detectives waited had been broken up into twenty separate cubicles. The curtain behind which Nick Towler was being treated was parted slightly. They glimpsed the doctor through the gap, looking somewhat flustered. A sudden cry came from within, followed by the doctor's raised voice. 'I'm trying to save your life, man! Listen to me!' Towler was refusing to have a tube inserted into his body while he was still awake. The doctor rushed to restrain his patient with outstretched hands, one palm steadying the rising teenager, the other attempting to hold him down.

A member of staff sitting at the doctor's station lifted his head from the computer where he was studying the scan results. He was dressed in dark blue scrubs; a stethoscope hung around his neck. He looked drained. 'He's got several internal injuries which are causing us some concern,' he said.

'Has he said anything yet?' queried Dylan.

The medic nodded his head, and stood up, a host of printouts clutched in his hands. 'Yes, he told me he was picked up by taxi with Tanya King, and they were both taken to a party at a large house. They were given drugs and drink. Apparently, he was then subjected to a sexual assault by at least eight men ...' He sighed. 'And then instead of being returned to the home, as promised, they were dumped at the roadside – no longer of any use I guess, in the state they were in ...'

One of the two medics seeing to Towler could be heard trying to calm things down from behind the curtain, her voice resonating over the multitudinous sounds in the bustling department. Her voice rose even louder.

'Let's get this off now, shall we, Nick?'

'Gerroff! Fuck, that hurts!' Towler yelled, followed by a piercing scream and a tussle.

Dawn raised her eyebrows at Dylan. There was silence, followed by a sharp intake of breath.

'How long has it been like this?' the doctor asked.

A pause followed. 'I don't know ...' Towler's voice wobbled. 'Can you make it better?' he asked, this time sounding as timid as a little boy.

Dylan and Dawn heard a few more noises from the patient that made them wince, and expressions of astonishment and disbelief from the attending medics.

'We'll get you into theatre as soon as we can, I promise. Try not to worry … it's going to be okay.' The voice of the doctor was calmer and much more sympathetic now.

The curtain swished back and two women swiftly passed through the opening, one in front of the other, carrying in their arms bowls covered with paper towels. Beneath the covering could clearly be seen a plethora of blooded gauzes, soiled tubes and discarded needles. A single tear rolled down the cheek of the younger of the two women and she dipped her head as she passed the detectives.

'Is it?' said Dylan to the passing doctor.

'Is it what?'

'Is it going to be okay?'

She rolled her eyes at him. 'What do you think?' she said. 'It's never going to be okay. Not till the bastards who did this to him are removed from the streets.'

The medics had left the curtain slightly open so that Towler could stay under close observation from the doctor's station.

Alone at last, Nick Towler lifted his head slightly and looked down at the plaster covering the cannula that had been inserted into the back of his hand. His head dropped to the pillow almost immediately, the exertion too much for him. He felt drowsy and warm, comfortable now that he felt safe. He turned his head slowly to face the grey, plastic chair at the side of the bed where his soiled clothing now lay in shreds. In his drug-induced state his lip turned up at one corner of his mouth. There was no danger of him running away. His eyes found the ceiling, but just that slight movement of his body was agony. 'Fuck! Fuck! Fuck!' Hot tears ran down the side of his face onto the starched white pillow. He squeezed his eyes tightly. 'Please make it stop hurting,' he sobbed.

Tanya King had been heavily sedated, and they were told they would have to wait to speak to her, so the detectives headed back to the station.

They walked down the main corridor in the older part of the hospital to the exit. Although the walkway connected the wards that held all the staff and hundreds of patients and was bright with natural light in the day, in the middle of the night it felt like a different world. Claustrophobic and airless, it was occupied only by those who had no choice but to be there: the cleaners, the clinicians and the undertakers. Despite the harsh fluorescent lights it seemed a deep, murky world and, although doctors could prolong lives, the atmosphere here suggested the inevitability of decay and death. They walked in silence, each with their own thoughts, the measured pace of their footsteps echoing on the solid floor.

The path of the new line of enquiry was like a wall of darkness pressing against him. Dylan's thoughts turned to the mechanics of the investigation. How he could help support Dawn, new to the CPU role, and temporary cover at that. First, he could offer the staff he had working in CID, to assist her where necessary – there was little else he could do for the two victims, at least tonight.

'We haven't got enough detail to locate the house in question,' said Dawn as they drove through the dark town of Harrowfield back to the police station. 'And by the time we do have any leads, it's highly likely that it will have been cleaned up.'

Dylan turned to her. 'In the past I've known someone to have changed the furniture altogether to try to make the property look nothing like what a victim might have described to us.'

Dawn looked at Dylan as he steered the car into the backyard which was empty bar a police van and a Traffic car. 'Really?'

'Really. It totally threw us until we found paintings and furniture described by the victim up in the attic and, on closer scrutiny, marks on the walls and indents in the carpet where the old furniture had been.'

'Just to suggest that the victim was describing somewhere else? How devious!'

'Exactly. That's why this type of investigation can often be quite lengthy.'

The CID office looked just the same as it always did at night when the lights were dimmed and there was no one at the twelve desks lining both sides of the room. The wooden desks, a few with typewriters, were stacked with paperwork and piles of files of various colours, and strewn with an A4 black binder or two. There was one landline. Mostly the detectives still used paper; the latest computer technology was available for checking databases, but it wasn't used for much else.

Dylan was exhausted from lack of sleep, but his mind still felt sharp and replayed every word of the conversation that he, Dawn and the medics had had that night, searching for a way forward. Pushing open the door marked 'Detective Inspector', he turned on the light. The fluorescent bulbs juddered into action. He stood for a moment, fingers on the metal filing cabinet that stood directly inside to steady himself, squeezing his eyes tightly shut. He needed time to adjust to the brightness.

Dawn had continued to the kitchenette. 'Do you want a coffee?' he heard her call, but he didn't answer. He should go home, but before he did so he glanced at his desk to make sure that nothing important had been placed on it since he'd left for the hospital.

On the way out, he sought Dawn. The corridor leading to the stairs and the upper floors of the police station also served as a passageway to the toilets and the Gold Command Room where ongoing major incidents were centred: those defined as kidnap, terrorism, firearms incidents and the odd chase or two. It was locked.

Around the small table in the kitchenette were four chairs. An old fridge stood next to the door and there was room for little else in there apart from a waste bin. The fridge was open. It held various sizes of Tupperware with names marked on them and the words KEEP OFF written in big, bold, black lettering on the milk containers, a pointless exercise because no one adhered to the instruction.

A microwave stood on the worktop above the fridge, which also held a kettle, and he found Dawn reaching into the cupboard full of mismatched crockery that sat alongside shelves stuffed with coffee, tea, sugar and a variety of food the officers had brought in for personal emergency consumption.

'I'll be going now,' he said, just as his pager vibrated in his pocket.

Dawn and Dylan's eyes met. 'It's John Benjamin,' Dylan said. 'He's on his way back into the nick and wants to discuss some information he's been given from an informer regarding Field Colt.'

Dylan had discovered from DC Benjamin that plans were in hand to close the children's home because of a lack of funding so he was keen to see the man in charge of Field Colt early next morning. Peter Donaldson had overall responsibility for the children in his care at the residential home, though he failed miserably to live up to it in the detective inspector's eyes.

On his arrival, Dylan was told by the receptionist that her boss was in a case-conference meeting and wouldn't be available for the rest of the day.

'That's okay, I'll wait,' said Dylan, much to her surprise. 'It's of the utmost importance that I speak to him.'

'What's it about?' she asked, giving a dry, smoker's cough.

'I'd rather not say,' said Dylan, 'but if Mr Donaldson does not manage to find time to see me, then I will have no choice but to have a team of police officers search the premises.'

Dylan watched as, looking flustered, the woman tottered down the corridor on her high-heeled shoes without offering him a seat, or any refreshments.

While he waited, he took note of his surroundings. The wide staircase had a threadbare carpet; the gold-leafed bannister was faded; the dark, oak panelling was heavily scratched; the ceiling plaster was stained and flaking and the red and gold flocked paper on the walls peeled at the corners. Taken together they gave him the impression of a crumbling slum rather than a place where children found refuge. Funding was clearly one of the children's home's issues. The foyer was scattered with chairs of various shapes and sizes; all the upholstery, whether it be cloth, velvet or leather, was worn and thin and looked ill-treated.

But there was something else missing from a place where children lived. There was no scampering around, no hollering, shouting or abandoned laughter. This place had an empty, unconnected feeling, as if the sadness here had taken on a life of its own.

A door could be heard opening and, quickly after, softly closing.

Dylan heard a brief distant murmur, the kind which only a bar full of contented drinkers could usually produce. But it also brought about with it an inviting smell of freshly cooked food.

Five foot six, approximately sixty years old, overweight and balding, Peter Donaldson crept up on Dylan silently from between two huge stone pillars. The rolls of fat around his middle bounced up and down as he approached offering a podgy, white, liver-spotted hand.

'Hello, Inspector Dylan,' he gushed, with a highly perfected shibboleth grip which Dylan was aware all Freemasons used when seeking protection by a brother of the craft. 'Why don't you come into my office, and we can have a little chat?' Cake crumbs had lodged at the corners of his mouth and his sickly smile was wide, showing the remains of chocolate fondant stuck between his teeth.

Dylan's feet sank into deep-pile carpet as he entered Donaldson's office. Donaldson went to sit behind his oak desk and waved the detective inspector into the high-backed leather chair opposite him. Behind Donaldson was a flamboyant marble fireplace over which hung a large oil painting of a Knight Templar.

'I'm not a member,' Dylan said flatly, the minute he sat down. With fingers entwined on his lap, he waited.

Donaldson blushed and lowered his face, but he recovered quickly, fixing his pig-like eyes on Dylan and rubbing his hands together. 'My colleague tells me that you needed to see me urgently? I must advise you that I'm due to attend a case conference shortly. Will this take very long?'

'That depends,' said Dylan.

'Depends on what?' His eyes looked up towards the ceiling. 'Don't tell me, some of the residents have been causing havoc again? If so, I apologise in advance. It's very difficult for my staff to watch over them twenty-four seven. Some – most – of them suffer from extreme behavioural or severe psychological problems, as you are probably aware … I know that is no excuse …' His voice petered out at the sight of Dylan's shaking head. But he wasn't finished. 'There's never a dull moment here, that I can tell you.'

Dylan tried to keep his tone neutral so that Donaldson could not interpret it. 'I've come here to inform you that my officers are currently investigating two serious and extremely violent sexual assaults that have occurred within the last twenty-four hours, on two children who are residents here. They were found dumped at the roadside by members of the public, injured and requiring urgent medical treatment.'

Donaldson's hand went up to his mouth and, with his elbow on the desk, his stubby fat fingers remained hovering over his pale lips. His eyes were downcast and suddenly hooded. 'How awful! Tell me, have you caught those responsible?'

Dylan shook his head.

'Is there any suggestion that this took place here at Field Colt?'

Dylan's lips curled up at the corners. 'No. If that were the case, my officers would be crawling all over this place right now securing evidence. It took place elsewhere, or so I am told. But we also have intelligence that this home has been complicit in providing children for parties for wealthy paedophiles.'

Donaldson gave a little gasp and jumped back in his seat. 'Goodness me,' he cried, incredulous. 'Well, we must quash that little rumour straight away, mustn't we?' He had turned as pale as an oyster. 'I can assure you that is most definitely not true. I've been here for six years now, and I … Well, I can't believe that even those two would make up such spurious allegations.'

Donaldson didn't appear to realise he had slipped up. Dylan cocked his head and frowned. So, Donaldson did know more than he was letting on. What Dylan had yet to find out was how much. 'Those two?' he asked.

Donaldson took one look at Dylan, hunched over and tried to hide any further reaction.

Dylan leaned forward. 'All investigations are about ascertaining the truth, so if anyone is lying or assisting the offenders then we will find out soon enough, don't worry. I need you to assure me that you and your team will give us your full co-operation. In the first instance, I will need a list of all staff together with details of their duties and any other information you feel obliged to share with us. We will need to examine records of all telephone calls made and received at Field Colt by both staff and residents.' Dylan's expression became even more serious. 'I also need to know which taxi firms you are in the habit of using.'

Donaldson shifted uncomfortably in his chair and, with shaking hands, filled a glass of water from a jug on his desk. He took a huge gulp.

Dylan could see beads of sweat beginning to appear at his hairline. He nodded towards the damp stains slowly spreading underneath Donaldson's armpits. 'You okay?' he asked, frowning.

'What you've told me is very upsetting and I find all this questioning extremely intrusive, not to mention unnecessarily disruptive: I've got lots of guests out there, all wondering where I am, no doubt. I haven't got time for this. Look,' he said, physically shaking, 'complaints are made almost daily in a place like this, about all sorts of things. It goes with the territory, so to speak. Very few of those made, after investigation, have been discovered to have any foundation whatsoever. The staff here work very hard, solely for the benefit of the youngsters and the wider community. Who are the two that are involved?'

Dylan's eyes narrowed. 'Well, I thought you might be able to tell me who was missing this morning, Mr Donaldson!'

Donaldson looked embarrassed. 'It goes without saying you can be assured of my full co-operation and that of my staff,' he said.

'Tanya King and Nick Towler are the names of those being treated in hospital.'

Donaldson threw his arms up in the air. 'Pfff, well,' he said with a half-smile on his face. 'And, guess what, surprise, surprise, those two have both been severely reprimanded for their recent bad behaviour: failing to comply with house rules, drinking, smoking, running away ... You name a rule, they've broken it.'

Dylan's lips were set in a tight straight line. 'I understand that they might be difficult, but one thing they can't do is physically injure themselves, at least, not in the way which they have been ... Let me tell you, the injuries inflicted on them are so severe they require surgery.'

Donaldson was immediately on the defensive. 'I'm not saying for one moment, Inspector, that they have caused the injuries themselves, but I've been told that, outside the home, they both have a habit of mixing with some very undesirable people. Of course, what has happened to them is unfortunate, but I can assure you it is nothing at all to do with anything at Field Colt.'

Dylan got up to leave. 'I am sure you will agree, Mr Donaldson, that every complaint must be investigated diligently for the benefit of everyone concerned. Transparency and co-operation are all I ask.' Dylan turned to go.

'And may I reiterate,' replied Donaldson, 'that all my staff members are professionals who are forever under the microscope, by all different kinds of authorities, to ensure that our duty of care is constantly of the highest possible standard. They have it hard enough, without the addition of police investigations. So, may I ask you to kindly bear that in mind when you are dealing with your enquiries?'

Donaldson led DI Dylan back into the reception hall. Dylan held out his hand.

'I'll be in touch,' he said. 'I can promise you there will be a full and rigorous investigation on our part. This home,' he said, taking in all the disrepair around him, 'should be a place of safety.'

There was a certain desperation in Donaldson's voice when he called after him, 'I'm sure if you speak to your boss, Hugo-Watkins, Walter will assure you of my dedication and commitment to all the youngsters here.'

When Dylan didn't respond, he added, 'He's a very good friend of mine.'

Chapter Fourteen

Jennifer Jones stood rooted to the spot outside the Chief Superintendent's office, trying desperately hard to block out the words she'd just overheard her new boss say about her to Walter Hugo-Watkins. His office door was slightly ajar and Avril Summerfield-Preston was standing half in, half out. Her long, pointed fingernails gripping the metal handle were as bright red as freshly spilled blood. She leaned inward, her face unseen, but Jen could sense that she wanted to impress him. Her perfume was strong and heady; in fact, it was so overpowering that while Jen waited patiently in the corridor to hand over some papers for him to sign, she had to stifle a cough. Avril either didn't know, or didn't care, that her cutting remarks could be overheard.

'She's a hairdresser, no less. Comes from the Isle of Wight, where …' here Avril's voice lowered a little, 'I've heard there's a lot of inbreeding. I fear she's the archetypal dumb blonde.'

Jen continued to listen, hearing a man's snooty voice ask, 'Not a graduate, then?'

'I don't think they actually have a university on the Isle of Wight,' Avril sneered and giggled. 'But then, for the pay on offer, what sort of people do HQ expect to attract?'

Jen's eyes began to fill up, and she swiped angrily at the single stinging tear that slipped down her cheek as the woman continued her character assassination.

'You should see what she's wearing today, too. Talk about mumsy!'

Jen looked down pensively at the wraparound navy-blue and white polka dot dress with its asymmetric hem, frilled short sleeves and attached patent leather belt. It had seemed highly suitable for working in an office when she'd purchased it. But now, as she began to scrutinise the material in the unflattering corridor lights, she conceded that it might be a bit frumpy, just as Avril had implied. In her defence, when choosing what to wear she had made a conscious effort not to fuel Martin's jealousy. In the process, perhaps she had managed to lose a vital part of herself: her femininity and pride in her appearance.

Taking a deep breath, she straightened her back and turned away, anxious that Avril should not catch sight of her tears, and walked straight into the arms of Rita.

'Loitering with intent?' Rita whispered jokingly. At the sight of Jen's crumpling face, Rita's jaw dropped. 'Whatever's the matter?' she asked, concerned, pulling a tissue from her pocket and steering Jen along the corridor to the steps that led to the outside yard and the property store. Looking over her shoulder, Rita saw Avril Summerfield-Preston step out of the office, with her nose in the air, and totter off in the opposite direction.

Jen and Rita sat huddled together in the property store. There was so much that Jen needed to learn about the job she would ultimately cover, but for now Rita was more interested in what had happened to upset her young colleague so much. Of even more concern to Rita was what had caused the massive bruise on Jen's neck.

Simply listening to Rita's soothing voice had a positive effect on Jen, so she confided in her precisely what had happened when Rita had dropped her off at home on the night of the retirement party – omitting some of the most horrid details – and on what course she feared things were ultimately heading. She sighed, long and deep, her head bowed down.

'Everything is pointing in the same direction. It seems that I'd best go back home to the island.' She looked up momentarily into her friend's kindly face with doleful eyes. 'Maybe I'm just not destined for a life on the North Island.'

'The North Island?'

Jen gave Rita a brief smile. 'It's what the islanders call the mainland.'

Rita reached out for her hand. 'Well, I think you're like a breath of fresh air around here: keen to learn, always helpful and willing and never without that lovely smile. As far as we're concerned, Personnel couldn't have chosen anyone more suitable to complete our little admin team.'

Jen remained unconvinced. 'Look at me though, Rita. My life's a complete mess. I don't want to cause problems for you, especially since I won't be around for long either way.'

'Why ever not? Don't you like it here?'

Jen's eyes flew open. 'Like it? I love it. It's just ...'

'Just what?'

'I heard Ms Summerfield-Preston telling the chief superintendent that, well, basically, she didn't think that I was ... let's say the right person for the job. I doubt she'll sign off my probation at the end of the month.'

Rita scowled. 'I don't see how she can't. I typed up your report from the chief inspector in Personnel and it's excellent!' Rita's eyes softened. 'Welcome aboard the train, Jen. I've a feeling you're going to be here for as long as you want to be.' Rita squeezed her hand. 'You'll get to know all about Avril Summerfield-Preston and Hugo-Watkins. And don't beat yourself up about your failing relationship with Martin either. The most important thing is that if you want to, we can get you out of that, and very quickly. I'll help you all I can. In fact,' Rita paused, a twinkle in her eye, 'I happen to know about a two-bedroomed terraced cottage that's coming up for rent in Brelland. I could put a word in for you, if you think it would suit you and Max.'

Jen found herself feeling suddenly optimistic. 'Really?' she asked.

Rita put her arm about Jen's shoulders and hugged her tight. 'I reckon after all these years in the job I'm not a bad judge of character, and I reckon you are one of the good guys who's just having a shitty time. We've all been there at one time or another. Believe it or not, I was bullied because of my ginger hair and freckles – and for being six feet tall – by my first boss. He was four feet ten in his stockinged feet.'

The smile spreading across Jen's face made her look younger and even prettier. It was the first time she had seen Rita let her guard down and she warmed to her even more.

'Now then,' said Rita, slapping the palm of her hands on her thighs and standing up. 'If you're going to get any work done, and I'm going to see about that property, we'd better both get our skates on. Catch you later, eh?' she said with a reassuring wink.

Whatever Jen had once seen in Martin, or felt about him, certainly didn't exist any more. She had wondered why the sickly feeling rising in her stomach at the end of the working day had begun the minute she'd started her new job at the police station. On Fridays, when everyone else in the office was excited about their plans for the coming weekend, she would hope against hope that she'd be asked to work some overtime. After all, she said to Martin, the police station opened twenty-four seven and there was always something to do. But she knew that the lies couldn't continue for ever.

When Dylan had left Field Colt, he had intended to drive straight back to the police station. He realised that he'd have rattled a few cages and once Donaldson got in touch with his Freemason friends there would be some sort of fallout heading his way. He sat in his car and switched on the engine, wondering exactly what that would turn out to be.

He noticed among the cars in the car park a private registration plate which he knew belonged to Marcus Thornton MP. He frowned and muttered to himself, 'That was fast. I wonder what he's doing here?' His eyes scoured the building, checking out each of the windows one at a time. 'If I find out you're involved, I'll have great pleasure in feeling your collar, Mr Thornton,' he said to himself.

His mobile phone rang, making him jump, his heart rate quickening when he saw the caller was Isla.

'Dad?' she said. 'I've been offered a place at a residential home in North Yorkshire to undergo therapy and observation. There are workshops there that the doctor thinks might help me.'

'And have you accepted?' Dylan asked eagerly. He waited with bated breath for her reply, knowing this would be a voluntary admission.

'Yes, Dad, I have. The doctor says that the place comes highly recommended and that I am really fortunate to have been given this opportunity at such short notice.'

'Good. How do you feel about it?'

'I feel lucky, but also a bit sad, because I know that the person in the queue before me, who had been waiting for the chance, didn't make it. So, I guess I'll have to make it count for them too, eh?'

Dylan swallowed the lump that rose in his throat. 'Yes, I guess so,' he said, softly.

There was an eagerness in Isla's voice. 'When are you coming home? I could do with a hug.'

'Tell you what. I'll drop by on my way back to the nick and have a sandwich with you, shall I?'

'That'd be nice. I've got lots of paraphernalia to work my way through, if I'm to be prepared for next week.'

When Dylan arrived back home, there was a letter waiting for him. He opened it, read the contents and put it back in the envelope, leaving it lying on the kitchen worktop.

'Looks like we're both going to be away next week,' he said to Isla, who was busy chopping tomatoes.

'Huh?'

'I've been invited to go on a two-day conference in South Yorkshire, including a buffet reception, no less, the night before.'

'Mm … Well, I hope the menu is better than mine. I've got to gain weight, the doctor says, and at the clinic all the meals are monitored so that I get the right number of calories.' She quoted rough extracts from the brochure and scowled as she continued reading the material the doctor had given her.

'HUGS, NOT DRUGS; ONE DAY AT A TIME; YOU ARE BEAUTIFUL; EATING DISORDERS THRIVE IN THE DARK BUT DIE IN THE LIGHT,' she read.

'What are you thinking?' he asked.

'I'm trying extremely hard to rein in my sarcasm and negativity, if I'm honest. This positive-attitude, recovery-speak propaganda is utter bullshit, if you ask me.'

When she looked up, she saw what looked like disappointment in his eyes. 'But anything is worth a try, isn't it, Dad?' she said, giving Dylan a forced smile.

'Where's your mother?' he enquired.

'Oh, I don't know. I think she said something about being called in to work when I saw her dashing out the front door earlier.'

When Jen arrived at Martin's house that night, she had only one thought in her head: she was moving out and taking Max with her. Unusually, there was a smell that reminded her of her mother's Sunday roast coming from the kitchen. Max pushed himself through the gap in the open front door and bounded towards her.

Martin was down on his hands and knees in the small cupboard space under the stairs. Years of rubbish, it seemed, was piled high around him in the hallway. Noticing the puzzled expression on Jen's face, he said, 'My mother used to make me hide in here, when I was little. I didn't understand why at the time, but from the peephole I made in the door I could see everything, and now I understand that she was just trying to protect me. The vegetables won't be long.'

'Protect you from what?' Jen said, putting her work bag down on the floor. She removed her shoes and bent down to fuss Max, closing the door behind her.

'My philandering father,' Martin replied, fingering a tiny hole in the dark wood panel of the door. 'I never knew she was aware that I'd made this, until one day when he came home from work and I was under the stairs, just playing. She shut the door; I had a bolt on the inside to keep me safe. I heard her saying to my father that she knew he was going to leave us. He got very angry – I'd never heard my father so angry, he'd always been quite kind and loving and reassuring towards my mother until then – I couldn't hear exactly what was happening, but suddenly my mother was wielding the kitchen knife at him, the one I'd seen her use to peel the vegetables earlier. There was a struggle and I saw my mother fall to the ground. As she bled on the carpet, her life leaving her, she caught my eye and smiled and I knew she was at peace at last.'

Martin held out the knife as he stood, a photograph of Jen and her ex-fiancé Shaun in his other hand. Suddenly, the meal didn't smell so good.

Jen's screams had been heard outside and a neighbour had reacted to them. When uniformed police officers spread out across the garden, Max barked incessantly, thus unintentionally shrouding the noise. Jen had tried to comfort Max and her sense of relief at seeing a uniformed officer at the kitchen window was overwhelming. How would Martin react, though, once he knew the police had arrived? She knew she should try to distract him until they were ready to intervene. However, frozen to the spot, with the sharp-bladed knife fixed in the stud wall next to her head, all she could manage to do was stare into his eyes, pleading with him to let her go.

She could feel his warm breath on her face: it didn't smell of alcohol. He pulled the knife out of the wall with ease and, although he held it to her throat, she didn't feel at all threatened by his actions even when he gently traced the outline of her face with its tip. Maybe it was his words that calmed her.

'We *will* be together,' he whispered in her ear.

Surely he wasn't planning to kill them both?

Taking her shaking hand, he brought it up to his lips and kissed it tenderly, before closing his eyes and looking down at the photograph in his hand.

'No!' He spat the word out and ripped the photo clean in half, removing Shaun from it, then he kissed the other half and tenderly placed it in his top pocket. From another pocket he produced a book of matches. With pure hatred glinting in his eyes, he lit a single match and, when the flame became strong, slowly slid Shaun's picture into it. Flames shot up the sides and Shaun's face began to distort and melt. Martin smiled at the sight, but didn't let go, even when the flames licked his finger and thumb. Little pieces of ash drifted down to settle near their feet and for a brief moment Martin looked perplexed. Then he ground the ash into nothingness beneath his shoe and proceeded to take Jen's half of the picture out of his pocket, sucking in his breath.

'I know one thing for sure,' he said, staring at Jen with wide, vacant eyes. 'If I can't have you, then no one else will either.'

She was by no means out of danger yet.

The sudden banging at the door startled him. He put a finger to his lips. 'Sh ...' The knife's blade stroked her cheek. Martin's eyes darted from Jen to Max and back again. He didn't move. 'Quiet,' he whispered. 'They'll go away.'

The banging persisted, accompanied by the shout, 'It's the police. Can you come to the door, please?'

'They'd better go away, because if they don't, there's only one thing left for me to do. I'll stab you and I mean it. I'm serious, Jen. It'll be them who'll have blood on their hands, not me.'

Without any warning the front door suddenly flew open, crashing noisily against the wall. When Jen opened her eyes she could see one, two, three, four police officers standing at the entrance to the kitchen.

'Step away,' the police officer with stripes on his epaulettes shouted at Martin. When Martin didn't move, he shouted again. 'That's an order! Not a request!'

Martin took two small steps backwards. Jen found herself holding her breath. She didn't know what she had expected when she'd arrived home, perhaps another argument, but certainly not this. Martin held the knife tightly in his right hand, waving it in Jen's direction. Confusion showed on his face, as if he was trying to process what was happening.

The sergeant took a step forward and spoke to him calmly. 'Put the knife down now, there's a good lad. Now! Before someone gets hurt.'

Martin was not yet ready to relinquish the weapon. 'Don't tell me what to fucking do, in my own fucking house,' he screeched. 'If you know what's good for your friend here, get out, or she's going to get seriously hurt. Do you understand?'

Jen's eyes silently pleaded with the officer to stay.

The four stood their ground.

An ongoing stand-off situation meant that, behind the scenes, the request had already been made for the on-call negotiator to attend. The officers' remit was to continue an open dialogue with Martin, although his attention remained focused on Jen.

'Is one of them your boyfriend?' he screamed at her.

'Martin, stop. Please, just stop,' Jen begged, as tears rolled down her cheeks. Trembling now, but with every piece of courage she could muster, she spoke calmly. 'The photograph you just burned was one of my ex-fiancé Shaun. He was the reason I left the island, remember? He's got someone else, he isn't a threat to you.'

Martin turned angrily on the officers, his eyes bulging and foul expletives pouring out of his gaping mouth. Jen could no longer recognise him as the man she had once fallen in love with.

'Get out of here now,' he screamed. The knife was once again pressed against her throat. 'Unless you want to see your friend here start losing blood.'

If his intentions hadn't been obvious to the officers before, then the swift stroke across his own throat with his free hand couldn't have made things any clearer.

Sensing the threat, Max emitted a low growl and started snarling as he crawled on his belly, inch by inch, towards Martin and Jen.

'Do you fucking want some as well?' shouted Martin, wielding the knife threateningly at the golden retriever. But Max, too, stood his ground, his lips curled back to display a set of sharp white teeth. His snarls grew more persistent, louder than anything Jen had ever heard from him before.

While Martin was glowering at Max he had briefly turned his back on the officers and, although it was only for a split second, seeing the knife suddenly safely away from Jen's neck, the quick-thinking sergeant took his chance, rushed forward and flattened Martin to the ground.

In the blink of an eye all four officers fell upon Martin, who continued to struggle wildly, spitting at one of the police officers. The spittle landed on the gloved hand he'd put up to shield himself. Instantly, he returned the unwanted gift by wiping it roughly across Martin's face. Blood seeped from Martin's nose as, kicking and shouting, he was led away towards the marked police car.

Sergeant Wheelwright stood above Jen, who, with arms wrapped comfortingly around Max's neck, was sobbing uncontrollably. 'Good boy,' she said encouragingly. 'You're a very good boy.'

She wiped the tears from her eyes with the back of her hand. 'Thank you,' she said, looking up at the uniformed officer who held out a hand towards her. She stood up painfully.

'He can't hurt you now.'

'How did you know he was …?'

'One of your neighbours rang three nines when she heard your screams.'

'What'll happen now?' asked Jen.

'Well, he's been arrested for making threats to kill. But, tell me, how did a nice girl like you end up with a nutter like him?'

Jen found herself smiling weakly. 'I don't know. I guess I fell under his spell. Miles away from home, alone, new job … he was nice to me. He wasn't like that when I first met him, believe me.' Jen blushed. 'I feel so embarrassed … I've only just recently started work for the police, in admin. I'll never live this down, will I?'

The kind eyes of the officer crinkled. 'It'll be news for a day. Believe me, I know others who have been involved in a lot worse.' His face turned serious. 'Have you got somewhere else to go? It could be that he'll get bail once he's calmed down.'

Jen looked anxious.

'We'll go for a remand in custody but there's no guarantee that's what will happen. My advice is to pack up your things and move while we've got him locked up.'

'Don't worry, even if we need to stay in a B&B we'll be out of here tonight.'

The sergeant's radio sounded. 'Negotiator, stand down.'

Jen looked at the sergeant quizzically.

'The negotiator. He's been told he's no longer required to attend,' he said, with a smile. 'You gather some things together and I'll come back shortly once we've dumped mi'laddo in a cell. I'll need a statement from you, but I guess I know where to find you?'

Jen nodded her head. 'Don't worry, whatever happens I will be in work tomorrow. Will it wait until then? I can't risk giving Avril any ammunition with which to fire me!'

'Avril Summerfield-Preston? Beaky's your boss?' he said.

Jen nodded.

'If you want some of the lowdown on that vicious cow, I'm the one to come to. Any time. Just say the word.'

Jen smiled gratefully. Perhaps the day hadn't turned out that badly after all.

Chapter Fifteen

DI Jack Dylan sat in the Traffic car next to Traffic Police Officer Cane who had just turned off the blues and twos when, two miles away from the address provided, they'd been stood down. However, the adrenalin had already kicked in and, not now needed, made him feel slightly drunk, his eyes out of focus. He became aware of the beads of sweat that had formed on his brow.

The brief of the domestic had been sketchy, with updates given from the operator at Force Control en-route. The challenge of a life-and-death situation had taken his mind away from his own problems and given him a feeling of purpose. It had been bizarrely exciting and now, pulled up at the kerb and feeling calmer, he felt somewhat disappointed he hadn't made it to the scene, as well as sorry for the unknown victim's situation.

There was no reason to fear the speed at which Chris Cane had driven – he was well accustomed to getting to an emergency in the quickest possible time – but Dylan was always anxious when not in control of the vehicle. With their ever-increasing speed, adrenalin had pumped through Dylan's veins, pedestrians had leapt out of the way, cars had slowed and pulled over and, where necessary, Chris had steered the car across to the opposite side of the road to pass vehicles, avoiding any delay.

It was Chris who finally broke the silence. 'Back to base, boss, is it?' he asked, glancing in Dylan's direction as he drove away. 'No fun travelling at speed when you're not in control, is it?'

'I was just thinking the same,' Dylan said, wiping his forehead.

'Not that bad a driver, am I?' the Traffic officer laughed heartily.

Dylan smiled. 'No. No misjudged corners, or unnecessary risks. I was impressed.'

'You're an advanced driver yourself, sir?'

Dylan nodded. 'Last time I was in a Traffic car I was driving down the motorway at a hundred and thirty miles an hour.'

Chris pursed his lips and sucked in his breath. 'You don't blink at that speed, do you, sir?'

'You certainly don't.'

Dylan stood in the doorway of the CID's kitchenette. Dawn was eating a sandwich. The kettle was on the boil. Tiredness showed on her face.

'Any update from the hospital?' he said.

She shook her head. 'Nothing yet. I'll be on my way shortly.' She took a sip of coffee. 'What's the update on the incident? I heard the shout go out,' she said.

'Nothing much, other than it was a domestic between a male and female. Male, threatening female with a kitchen knife, was disarmed by uniformed officers after a violent struggle and subsequently arrested for threats to kill.' Dylan took the steaming mug of coffee from her. 'I guess that's all the information I needed to know.'

'A regular?'

Dylan shook his head. 'No names given yet, but I'm sure it will all come out in the wash, as they say.'

Jennifer Jones stood for a moment surveying the mess in the hallway, looked one more time at Max's doleful expression and set off up the stairs two at a time. Max bounded into action, following her. At the bedroom door she was shocked to see her clothes and possessions scattered everywhere. Some she recognised from boxes she hadn't even opened since leaving the island. She dropped to her knees and retrieved two suitcases from under the bed. Very quickly she assessed what was important to her, what had not been broken or ripped to shreds and, in what felt like a wild panic, grabbed what she could and threw it in. She worked systematically through her drawers and the wardrobe, all the while choking out sobs.

When her suitcases were full, she grabbed a plastic bag and sought out her toiletries, throwing them on the top. She closed the first suitcase with a groan, shifted some things to the other, sat on it and struggled with the zip. After a few attempts and sweating like mad, the deed was done. She pushed the top of the second suitcase down by pressing on it with her knees and, after a few tries, she managed to secure that zip too. Looking around the room she double-checked that she had everything she was able to carry, pulled the handles out of the suitcases and stood them on their wheels. One step at a time she clumsily manoeuvred the cases down the stairs to the front door where she grabbed her bag from the floor, put on her shoes, slung her coat over her shoulder and opened the door. Max scuttled out behind her as the door closed with a thud.

There was no awkward moment when Rita came to collect her, just a hug of assurance from a friend, and Jen immediately felt safe. Rita opened her car boot and together they threw in her cases. More sobs rose up from her throat as she sat down in the passenger seat. She slammed the door.

'Ready?'

'Go,' Jen barked. 'I don't care where to, just go!'

The house Rita had secured as Jen's refuge was furnished. 'Do you want me to stay the night?' she asked when they'd settled Jen in.

Jen shook her head. 'No, you've done more than enough. How can I ever repay you?'

'You don't have to. Just say you'll stay here for a while before you decide whether to go back to the island or not. Contrary to what you may believe right now, Yorkshire folk are about the friendliest you'll ever meet.'

'Well, that would certainly make a change. You could live next to someone on the island all your life and still not know your neighbour.'

Rita hadn't been gone long when there was a knock at the front door. Max barked, and Jen jumped in surprise. Who could that be? Because as far as she was aware, no one knew she was there, except Rita and her new landlord.

When the Dylans arrived at the Rehabilitation Centre at the end of the week it was raining. But Dylan was pleasantly surprised to see it wasn't anything like he'd imagined and its pleasantness managed to push the rain into the background.

Stauer's Hall Mansion had been built in 1788 according to the shiny gold plaque in the entrance hall. A private residence in the countryside for the mill-owning Ainsworth family, the place was surrounded by acres of parkland and contained many ancient trees. It had been converted into an asylum in 1904, been renamed The Mansion Hospital and had run independently as a hospital ever since; most recently being upgraded at huge cost to become a residential retreat for people suffering from addictions of one kind or another.

'Apparently it's haunted, you know,' Isla reached up and whispered in Dylan's ear, as they waited for someone to greet them. She reached for his hand; she was shaking.

'Really?' said Kay with a sigh. 'How old are you?' She looked at her watch, drew in a sharp breath and, finding a bell on the reception desk, hit it with the palm of her hand.

Dylan looked slightly surprised at her harsh tone and even more so at her impatience.

'Yes, it's actually haunted by the ghosts of the former hospital patients who, for one reason or another, never checked out.' Isla giggled. She seemed in a carefree mood but Dylan sensed a wavering, a vulnerability on her face, a tightening of her jaw and a fear behind her smile.

Isla seemed eager to please the young, good-looking guy, whose full lips promised a hint of a smile and who advised her parents that it would be okay for them to leave. On the surface, Isla appeared keen to get started on the programme, and although the young man made it clear that it wasn't going to be easy, he promised he'd be there for her whenever she needed him. As Dylan and Kay got ready to leave, Isla shrugged her shoulders and, with a forced smile, sat down on the bed in the small Room 8, that would be hers for the foreseeable future.

'I guess I'll see you in a few days then,' she said. 'When I've been assessed and they've decided what to do with me?'

Dylan affirmed. 'Yes, I'll be back from the conference by then. We're both going to be behind the eight ball in the next few days, aren't we?'

'Yes, Dad, I guess so. Love you.'

'I love you more,' Dylan said as he bent down to kiss her cheek before following Kay out into the main corridor.

Strange faces and voices surrounded Isla, pressing in on her from all sides, searching, probing, but she could make no sense out of the reassuring words or the kindly smiles of the strangers around her.

Kay began to feel slightly panicky. She felt as if she was imprisoned with Dylan as she sat at the bar of the Armitage Arms, and yet they were only having a spot of lunch together before he left. What if she was pushed against him by the other diners, forced to feel the warmth of his body, sense the close familiarity of his skin?

The couple next to them snuggled even closer, very obviously madly in love. It took her back to the early days, when she and Dylan hadn't been able to take their hands off one another. Then normal life had taken over. Her daughter Isla had grown up, but their own children had never come along. Dylan had moved up in the police force and Kay had become more restless as he spent longer and longer hours at work and she felt obliged to spend the same number of hours at home alone. Eventually, they'd started to drift apart.

'If you don't want me to go, I can still cancel,' Dylan said, sensing her uneasiness. 'I appreciate that I've only just returned from Hendon. But it's an honour to be asked. Not everyone gets invited to attend these events, especially someone of my rank.'

Her heart was beating quickly as she looked at the clock above the bar. If she didn't go soon, Kenny would think she wasn't coming.

'For God's sake, Jack, it's only two nights. You're literally an hour away. If I need anything, which I won't, I'll call you. I can cope. I always do. Just go.' Her hands pushed him way. Her angst was growing by the minute, but Dylan didn't give up.

'But, with Isla being away ... I know you must be worried.'

'Look,' Dylan could see beads of sweat shining on her top lip.

'Fingers crossed, this rehab will identify a way forward and Isla will be back home with us, and everything will be back to normal before we know it. I'm not worried, so you shouldn't be either. She's an adult. She's made her choices. We can only do so much.'

Kay moved as quickly as she could towards the door, frantic to get away from Dylan. She needed to meet up with Kenny to tell him that this time it was well and truly over. She'd been agonising over it since their last meeting and he wouldn't like it, she knew. But she couldn't continue with the deceit any longer; her nerves simply couldn't take any more. It had been fun while it had lasted but it had to end. Only then could they all try to get back to normal.

She was unable to get past the group of walkers putting on their muddy boots on the pub steps. Dylan was also held up by them, impatient as they were to get back on the moors. For a moment, Dylan and Kay were trapped together in the narrow passageway. She prayed that he wouldn't ask her to drop him off at the train station. That would mean waiting with him at the station for his train to leave.

Finally, she reached the bottom of the steps. As she headed for the car, the cool air hit her and it was with great relief that she heard her husband's footsteps fade away as he headed for the canal bank that she knew would take him, by foot, back to the police station. From there he'd be able to get a lift to the train station.

As she put her key in the car door, she heard someone calling her name. She turned to see Dylan running towards her. Her heart sank. 'Haven't we forgotten something?' he asked. Kay automatically turned her cheek to accept a kiss, which never came. She felt slightly disappointed as he lifted the car boot and took out his overnight bag. As he walked away, she called his name. He turned.

'Tell you what, if you let me know what time you finish in Sheffield I'll drive over and pick you up. That way we can go and visit Isla together on the way back.'

Dylan smiled and waved. 'Bye!' he shouted.

Chapter Sixteen

A full briefing had just taken place in the CID office and Detective Sergeant Larry Banks, preparing to take charge while Dylan was away, had retreated to the DI's office. He sat in his chair, finger pointing to a telephone number in his little black book and picked up the phone. He was about to put his feet up on the desk when Dawn entered the room.

'Tut tut!' she said. 'You know what happened the last time Dylan caught you with your feet up on his desk. You nearly wound up two inches shorter.' Dawn put the file she was carrying on the corner of Dylan's desk, breaking eye contact with Larry.

'You won't tell?' Larry said laughing.

'You're right. I'm not a snitch. But don't you think you owe it to Dylan to be a bit more respectful?'

Larry stared at her, finding it difficult to come up with an answer.

'Those puppy dog eyes only work on bimbos, Larry. Don't bother wasting them on me ...'

Larry's shoulders slumped. 'I'm putting my feet up on a piece of wood, not shagging his wife,' he called after her retreating figure.

Minutes later Larry heard Dylan approaching and quickly whipped his feet off the desk. After speaking to Dawn, Dylan put his head round his office door to see Larry with one hand to his forehead, his pen hovering over a batch of papers. He looked up sharply.

'I'm expecting a delivery, Larry. Allegedly, it's a bullet-proof jacket. Hopefully, I'll never have to test it. It's part of the negotiator's kit and it's supposed to be here this morning, but it hasn't arrived yet. Will you sign for it and keep it safe if it turns up?'

Larry nodded emphatically. 'Of course, I'll drop it off with Kay. I'd hate to think it was stuck here in the office if you needed it.'

His eyes returned to the papers requiring his immediate attention. Dylan remained with his hand on the door handle. 'And Larry,' he added, 'make sure that paperwork is done by the time I get back.'

Larry groaned. 'I think I might have a stab at this promotion lark myself. Courses, dinners, beer trips, new clothes … How you getting to Sheffield?'

'Taking the train.'

Larry looked surprised. 'You haven't heard?'

'Heard what?'

'There's a strike started, I heard it on the news this morning.' Larry tossed his head back in the direction of the yard. 'Better take the fleet vehicle. I can use my own, if the others need the CID car.'

Dylan knew better of Larry Banks. He had no intention of going for promotion. He was a detective sergeant, the best job in the police force in his eyes. Always someone above him to shoulder the responsibility and getting paid for his overtime, something the rank of inspector and above didn't qualify for. In addition, it meant that he had others of a lower rank than him to call upon to do the dirty work.

Larry could see that Dylan was engaged in deep conversation with Dawn; there was no chance of him getting out of the office anytime soon.

Dawn's plan, she explained to Dylan, was to get Tanya King and Nick Towler to take part in a video interview, now they were both on the mend. But, although their physical injuries were healing, it was highly possible that their emotional scars would never leave them.

A dark shadow crossed Dylan's face. 'Do you think they will dare to risk the wrath of Peter Donaldson?' he asked.

'I would definitely have said no if Field Colt was going to remain open, but it does seem it's going to close down.'

A glimmer of hope filled his eyes. 'So, let me get this right. What you're saying is they might just go along with it. After all, what've they got to lose?'

'That's exactly what I'm saying! I hear you went over to Field Colt to have a chat with Donaldson.' The sparkle in her eyes suddenly vanished. 'Please be careful. I hear he's quite well connected.'

'How long have you known me?' Dylan said. 'Have you ever seen me back away from anything, even if it's to my detriment?' Instinctively, his fingers touched the scar at his temple and the one on his nose.

'Touché! It's him and his colleagues who should be worried.'

Dylan focused on Dawn's face as he leaned forward. 'Look, I don't care if he is a good mate of Hugo-Watkins like he said, or of the Chief Constable; or even the bloody Commissioner. The bastards who are involved in this crime need to be put behind bars, and the sooner the better.' He prodded the desk. 'I want no stone unturned in this case. If the evidence is there, we'll put them before the courts as soon as physically possible.'

'Well, as you're aware, rumours have been rife about Field Colt for as long as I care to remember. We have lots of paper reports and several allegations that go back years, all carefully stored in the archives. The more recent ones are on the electronic databases, I've checked. Most have been written off as No Further Action. Because, let's face it ...' Dawn paused, sighing heavily, '... in the end, without the victims' co-operation, we're stuffed. And the bloody abusers know it.' Dawn's large brown eyes looked sorrowful. 'I sort of get it in a way. Remember, these kids in the home have nothing but tales from their elders to go by. Who the hell can they trust? If they test the water – and most of them do stand up for themselves at one time or another – they're simply branded as troublemakers, even if they do then bow down and refuse to co-operate with the police. I've found out recently that the "problem child" is often moved on repeatedly – away from their friends, sometimes at very short notice – and the others aren't told where they've gone and aren't allowed any communication with them from then on. How frightening must that be for the child who's been moved? But also, what does it say to those left behind?'

'So, the kids think it's better to put up and shut up,' said Dylan, his eyes taking on a glazed look. 'And who knows what horrors the next home will bring them?'

Instead of using the conference facilities at the police training school, which was world-renowned for its excellence and had its own bedrooms on site, Dylan's latest course had been scheduled at a very expensive offsite location in a beautiful-looking country hotel. As Dylan had driven up towards the entrance, he'd been stopped by a tall, serious-faced young man wearing a uniform, who'd insisted on parking the car for him.

Dylan had taken his bag from the passenger side and got out, handing the young man the keys. He'd then been greeted by an older gent in a top hat who'd extended a firm handshake and a hearty greeting, taken the bag from his hand and led him into the foyer where he'd waited patiently with Dylan until he could be booked in. The old man had looked somewhat relieved when the policeman had declined his offer to show him up to his room on the top floor.

Once there, he'd unpacked the few pieces of clothing he had brought with him, made himself a drink and sat on the chair by the window which overlooked a glorious garden. It was quiet, it was peaceful and he'd felt quite serene. Then he'd reminded himself that the tax payer was paying for this. What the hell was he doing here?

Twenty minutes later Dylan was being handed his name tag. Not an ordinary paper sticker, or even one with his name handwritten on it with a marker pen; no, this had been a custom-made tag with his name and title engraved on a thick plastic plaque with a pin attached to the back.

But the plush exterior hadn't reflected the reality. His room had been damp, despite the antiquated heating system which had kept him awake throughout the first night, pumping water around the creaking radiators. By morning it had given up the ghost, resulting in the need to wear coats throughout the day. The food provided had been a cold buffet, hardly enough to satisfy the average Yorkshireman's appetite, and it did nothing to help maintain body heat.

The first speaker had been arrogant and patronising, devoid of any sense of humour; the second, vain and supercilious, mocking the first speaker's pompous tone. Dylan's companions were sullen and silent, hardly speaking at all save to make an occasional sardonic remark about the worthlessness of the event.

With the promise of much of the same to come, Dylan had decided he would leave early the next morning. Why bother staying? Most attendees would no doubt be sleeping off the heavy drinking session from the night before. The morning plan allowed for further socialising, sexed up by naming it 'Networking', before they all returned to their native forces, and largely to allow time for the alcohol absorbed the previous evening to leave their bloodstreams – another working day lost.

During the break for lunch, Dylan's phone beeped a message and he picked it up, hoping it may be Kay, or Isla with an update. It was Larry. His 'suit of armour' had arrived.

Unbeknownst to Dylan, the jacket had caused some amusement in the CID office. To all intents and purposes, the body armour looked like a normal, caramel-coloured anorak, which was obviously the idea behind the design. However, it was also patently obvious when it was placed before the officers on the office floor that it had zero flexibility. In fact, when Larry tried to lift it he found it took both hands and an extreme amount of effort. Wearing the garment would hardly make someone discreet, he thought, as he walked across the office in it, looking like the Tin Man from *The Wizard of Oz*.

A little later, Larry pulled up outside the Dylans' house. Their car was parked on the driveway, which he hoped meant that Kay was at home. As he approached the house, he could hear raised voices. He recognised Kay Dylan's. The other had the deeper pitched tones of a man. He was surprised. He listened for a moment but, try as he might, he couldn't make out a single word of what was being said.

He knocked on the door. Instantly, the shouting ceased. He knocked again, louder this time, and waited. After a few moments the door flew open and Kay stood before him, looking a little flustered. He offered her the parcel.

'Jack's bullet-proof jacket,' he said. 'Its heavy! You'll never carry it. Aren't you going to invite me in for a coffee?' he asked, looking over her shoulder.

There was nothing he didn't like about Kay Dylan. Everything was exactly to his taste – her long, dark hair; her soft, bronzed skin; the full lips; her sexy, hazel, come-to-bed eyes, high cheekbones and long, lean face. But, just like lightening, the flash had passed almost before the thought could form.

Kay coloured deeply, staring at him in an embarrassed silence. Now he thought about it her hair was dishevelled, her silk blouse in disarray, her cardigan half on and half off. 'Is everything all right?' he said.

'It's nothing you need concern yourself about, Larry.' She attempted a smile, but it did not quite reach her eyes.

Larry scowled. 'Tell me you're not seeing someone else behind Dylan's back?'

Kay's sheepish look was semi-apologetic. 'It's over now. I promise. That's the reason for all the shouting you heard. He's not happy, but I've made my decision.'

'Are you sure everything's okay? I can come in and see him on his way if you like.'

Kay shook her head. 'No need, Larry. He's not violent, just upset.'

'As long as you're sure you're not in any danger. You're lucky it was me calling and not Dylan bringing it home himself now that there's a train strike.'

Kay's eyes flew open wide, she scoured the street outside her door.

Larry smirked. 'Don't worry, he's taken the fleet car instead.'

Larry turned to leave. Kay put her hand out to him. 'Don't you dare say anything to Dylan! It's ended. What he doesn't know can't hurt him, can it?'

'You're playing a very dangerous game, Kay, bringing your lover to your house.'

Kay stared into his eyes. 'Like I said, it's over, okay?'

Larry raised an eyebrow in a knowing way.

'I mean it, Larry. You tell Dylan about this and I'll just have to tell him about us, and that would stir up shit that neither of us could handle.'

Larry raised his hand as he walked down the pathway. 'Okay, okay. Message received and understood. Bye!'

Kay dragged the heavy coat inside and shut the door. It stood in the corner like a bodyguard. She watched Larry drive away before going into the lounge where she knew Kenny would be waiting impatiently. She flopped down in the nearest chair.

'That was lucky, it was Dylan's sergeant. I told you we can't talk here; anyone could turn up, like I've said a hundred times before. Now do you believe me?'

Kenny appeared sombre. 'It's a shame it wasn't the big man himself. It's about time he knew.'

Kay was edgy. 'Let's go out for a while, shall we? I need a drink.'

Dylan stood at the window of his hotel room, looking out into the darkness and wondering what he should do. Being away again had given him space to think. He was in no doubt that if he carried on down this path, he would lose his wife, his home and maybe his daughter. He wondered what Kay was doing now? She was his safety net; he liked having a home to go back to, even if he had rarely seen it of late. And he loved Isla as if she were his own flesh and blood.

'So, what happens now?' he whispered. Making his mind up eased his tension. He took his phone from his pocket and dialled.

'Can I come home?' he said to their answering machine.

Chapter Seventeen

Open wounds always aroused questions but Detective Inspector Jack Dylan's bruised heart couldn't be seen by others and would be less easy to heal than any physical injury. Kay still hadn't returned his call.

Though there had been total silence from Kay, Stauer's Hall had at least confirmed to him that Isla had settled in nicely and was responding well both to her counsellors and the other residents.

Tired of listening for a call he'd accepted was never going to come, Dylan switched off his mobile phone. He had finally come to accept that his marriage was over. Contrary to Kay's belief, he was neither ignorant of her indiscretions, nor as stupid as she liked to think. Not being a quitter, he'd always said that what he didn't know or look for, couldn't hurt him.

That may once have seemed true, but he'd come to realise that what it could do was cause deep mistrust and an uncertainty about the future that he wasn't prepared to ignore any longer. One thing Terry Spence and his family had taught him in the brief time he had spent with them at the retirement party was that life was for living, but it was only worth living with those who reciprocated love and loyalty wholeheartedly.

Dylan took his time on the journey home. He had lots to think about. As he neared Harrowfield he was drawn towards a childhood haunt named Castle Hill, a heritage site that had been a settlement for almost four thousand years. With an icy wind biting round his ears, he stood and stared thoughtfully at the ancient monument overlooking the town. His back to the ancient stones, he prayed for a sign that everything was going to be okay and as he did so he watched his breath slowly drift away through the cold air. The pale winter sun shone on his face as it broke through a cloud and he began to reflect gravely on his life. Wasn't it true what his hero and teacher, the great man Harry Wallis, had said: 'When winter comes, and darkness falls, man is able to look into himself and read his own heart ...'

What came next?

'... But, with the coming again of the summer, and of light, their eyes are blinded. Yet even so, though deep is the abyss, men's hearts look forward after the long Northern winters to a spring of joy, to the smell of green leaves and dry leaves, and hay in the barn when we can trace the rainbow in the rain ...'

Tears ran down his cheeks as he turned to leave, ready at last – he thought sadly – ready now to face whatever lay ahead.

When he got back to the car, he switched on his mobile phone and was startled to see the number of early morning calls from Larry Banks. He rang him back and waited, anticipating that if he'd been out all night on a job he may have returned home to sleep. To his surprise, the call was answered quickly.

Larry's choked voice, and his uncertainty about who was on the other end of the phone, brought a smile to Dylan's face.

''Course it's me, who the hell do you think?' he said. 'Have you been drinking?'

Larry was unable to speak for a second or two, overcome by emotion as he was. 'Boss, is that really you?'

'Who the fuck do you think it is? If you've slept in my office all night and it smells like a brewery when I get back, I'll bloody kill you!'

Larry's voice sounded strange to Dylan: hollow, and disorientated.

'No, of course I haven't.' Although just then he wished with every fibre of his being that he could drink something alcoholic, anything that would help to make his next task easier.

The detective sergeant's voice sounded quite untypical of him. For once, Dylan could hardly hear him. 'It seems I've got a really poor signal. What did you say, Larry?'

'Can I meet you at your house? There's something personal we need to discuss urgently, away from the office. And I've got some news. We have a partial fingerprint for our brace and bit man, good enough for a search.'

A surge of anger and frustration came over Dylan.

'I can't leave you for one minute, can I? What the hell have you done this time? Some irate husband chasing you again? Don't tell me you've been caught in the act? There is only so much I can do you know.'

'No, no, it's nothing like that.'

Dylan's voice softened. 'You're not seriously ill, are you?'

'No, I just need to have a private chat. I'll explain when I see you. I don't want to do it over the phone.'

'That sounds ominous. I'll be home within the hour.'

'Okay.'

'Oh, and Larry,' he said, 'I can't get hold of Kay, so if you get there before me ask her to put some bacon under the grill, will you? I didn't bother stopping for breakfast. I just wanted to get home.'

Larry's voice remained sombre. 'I haven't been home yet either, you know me, but it's not like you to miss the full English. Anyway,

I'll see you back at yours.' He hung up. He was immeasurably relieved that it wasn't Dylan who was in the intensive care unit fighting for his life. Now, though, he had to tell him that his wife had died in a car accident, in their car, which was being driven by an unknown man.

'Shit! Shit! Shit!' Larry kicked the waste bin, opened his drawer, fumbled around in the back and was much relieved to see that the bottle of whisky he'd secreted there wasn't empty. With trembling fingers, he unscrewed the cap. Then he heard the door. About to let go of the glass bottle he saw the door slowly opening and Dawn standing before him, dishevelled, her red-rimmed eyes bloodshot, still wearing the clothes that she had worn the day before. It was obvious that she hadn't been to bed either.

Larry looked from her grey face back to the bottle. His eyes wide he told her, 'It's not Dylan.'

Dawn staggered towards him, her hand clamped tightly over her mouth. She started to cry with relief. Reaching out, she took the bottle from him and took a huge swig. She screwed up her face.

'Nasty enough,' said Larry, his quivering lip curled at one corner.

She nodded her head. 'For you?' she said.

'No, not really. For Dylan. It's almost time for the shitty part; I need to break the news to him about Kay.'

Larry pulled up outside the Dylans' house. He wanted to make sure that he arrived before his colleague. Outside, the early morning mist had turned into a solid wall of fog, the earlier pale disc of the promising sun now totally obliterated. Turning off the car engine, he rested his head back and considered how to break such devastating news. There was no easy way. It was best simply to relate the facts, the way his boss always did. There was no point in trying to soften the blow, to ease the pain. Not that it would sink in for a while.

He wondered how Dylan would take the news; just what exactly would his reaction be? Although they had worked together, he didn't know a lot about Dylan the private man, only Dylan the boss. Jack Dylan was a nice man who had got Larry through some tight scrapes. What had he ever done to deserve this avalanche of shit landing on his doorstep?

The fog muffled the sound of the fleet vehicle Dylan was driving as it pulled up outside.

Seven fifteen, Larry noted on the clock in his car; most people were still in bed.

There were no lights on in the house and the curtains were drawn back, Dylan noted, but his attention quickly shifted when his colleague greeted him.

'Good God, Larry, you look like total shit! You can't keep burning the candle at both ends, mate; you're going to end up killing yourself!'

Larry stared down at the floor, his stance unusually shifty. He couldn't look Dylan in the eye.

'Yeah, it was another late one. I guess it goes with the territory.'

Dylan flicked open the boot, taking out his overnight bag.

'So, is it somebody's husband after you again? He walked ahead to the front door and put his key in the lock. Larry followed him. He turned. 'Kay's probably still in bed,' he said. 'Better be quiet.'

Larry shrugged. 'I've only just got here so I haven't even knocked.' He couldn't tell him the truth, not on the doorstep shrouded in fog.

'It was beautiful when I left Sheffield this morning,' Dylan said as he opened the door and put his case in the hallway. There was post behind the door and he picked it up and put it on the hallway table.

As he turned to close the door, he saw the anorak standing upright at the bottom of the stairs and attempted to move it.

'Bloody hell,' he laughed. 'It's supposed to stop a bullet, not give you a bloody hernia. I'd better start coming to the gym with you.' Dylan looked up the stairs, saying nothing. He took off his coat and slung it over the bannister, before heading for the kitchen.

'I did warn you,' said Larry. 'Are you putting the kettle on?'

'Why?' asked Dylan, turning to face his detective sergeant. 'Am I going to need a strong coffee?'

'Better make it a strong, sweet tea,' he replied.

Larry sat down at the kitchen table facing Dylan.

'Do you want to tell me about it before Kay comes down?' Dylan asked, his eyes on the kitchen door.

'Please, Jack. Don't make this any harder than it is.' Larry paused, leaned forward and looked at the wooden floor between his legs.

Dylan's mouth had gone dry. 'Come on, just spit it out for God's sake. Has something happened to Isla?'

Larry looked up, seeing pure fear in Dylan's eyes for the first time ever.

'No, Jack, it's Kay. She was killed in a road accident last night.'

Chapter Eighteen

A sledgehammer slammed into Dylan's stomach. Every function of his body went numb for what seemed like an eternity. Dylan recognised the mask of the detective that had settled on Larry's face. Seeing tears begin to gather in the detective sergeant's eyes, a tingling sensation began to spread through his veins. He slowly shook his head.

'Larry, that's not funny,' he said, coming round the table, grabbing his colleague by the throat and pulling him to his feet with a power that could only be explained by an adrenalin rush. The two men stood nose-to-nose. Dylan tried to control his breathing as his heart began to pound in his chest and a vein on his forehead throbbed.

'She's not dead! There's no way she's dead. I'd know if my wife was dead!' he yelled. After a moment Dylan released Larry unceremoniously, dropping him like a lead weight back onto the chair before dashing to the stairs and leaping up them two at a time.

Dylan's breath came in short bursts. His legs felt like rubber as he stood at the foot of their bed; it hadn't been slept in. Kay's discarded nightclothes lay strewn, as always, over the pine rocking chair at her side of the bed, where she had nursed Isla as a baby.

When Dylan re-joined Larry in the kitchen a few minutes later, he found him making tea. Tears had begun to trickle down Dylan's cheeks; he knew very well his colleague wouldn't joke about something as serious as this.

He slumped in a chair at the kitchen table, his eyes glued to the face of the man who came to lay a gentle, reassuring hand on his shoulders. Dylan's first reaction was to push him away, but Larry held on tight. The release of built-up tension was like the bursting of a dam. Dylan's entire body shook in spasms so violent and overpowering that he didn't notice the tears also rolling down Larry's cheeks. After a few moments Larry sat down opposite him. Dylan calmed himself and took a sip of his hot drink.

'Tell me ...' said Dylan. 'I want to know everything.'

'Your car was being driven over the tops from Redchester on the A62 when it left the road. Kay was pronounced dead at the scene.'

Dylan looked confused. 'Why am I only getting to know this now?'

Larry chose his words carefully: Dylan knew all the professional jargon and its underlying technical meaning. 'When the car left the road, it ended up on its roof in a deep ravine. It wasn't the easiest place to retrieve it from, as you can imagine. Eventually, the Traffic police from Redchester identified who the vehicle belonged to through the registration number. They contacted us because you, the owner, were identified on the system as living on another force's patch, hence our lads then contacted me. The Redchester police had no idea you were a police officer, but obviously our guys did. After they'd got in touch with me, I tried getting hold of you, hoping that you were alive and still at the conference.'

Dylan put his head in his hands, his fingertips rubbing his forehead. 'Did she suffer at all?' he asked, his hooded eyes looking up and searching Larry's face.

Larry shook his head. 'I am reliably informed that Kay's injuries were such that she would have died instantly. No, she wouldn't have suffered.'

There was a long silence between them. Larry had literally taken his breath away, and Dylan was finding it hard to form structured sentences, his brain full of unanswered questions caught up in a tangled web, each fighting for supremacy.

'Was she driving too fast, or perhaps there was ice on the road? Did she swerve to miss an animal?' He paused, a sudden memory producing a fleeting smile. 'I've seen her slam on the brakes for a damn crow on the road tucking into roadkill; terrified both me and Isla – and the driver behind us, no doubt.' Dylan paused. He looked puzzled. 'What the hell was she doing over there in the first place? She'd not mentioned going out, let alone out of the county. I don't understand.' Dylan stared into the teacup on the table before him, the cold brown liquid only half drunk. Larry never had been good at making a brew. He rubbed his finger around the rim. 'There was definitely nothing wrong with the car. It was serviced by Luke, you know Luke Henderson, the police mechanic?' Dylan stared at Larry, searching his face for more.

'Another reason,' Larry paused, struggling to force the words out, 'another reason for the delay in contacting you was because she wasn't the driver of the car.'

Dylan looked wary.

'Kay was the passenger in your car and the driver survived, but he is on a life-support machine.'

'What?'

'Everyone assumed that the male driver was you. When I heard about the accident and I checked with the hotel porter, he confirmed that you'd left the conference, but he couldn't tell me exactly what time.'

'Reception was closed, so I just chucked my keys in the express drop-off.'

'Exactly, but not as early as I initially feared. For all I knew you could have come home after the event had finished the night before and gone out with Kay.'

'So, this person who's lying in hospital. I guess he can't be identified?'

Larry shook his head. 'And now you know why I was so shocked when you rang me.'

Dylan's face was solemn. Larry could see he was working through the information he had been given and trying to put all the pieces of the jigsaw into place. 'Okay,' he eventually said, 'let me get this straight. What we do know is that Kay was the passenger, but we don't yet know who the driver is?'

'That's right.'

'Had she been kidnapped, do you think?'

'The driver is badly injured; his face and hands so badly burned that they are completely covered in bandages, besides which he's been put into an induced coma. There is nothing to suggest Kay was kidnapped.'

Dylan sat in silence, tears trickling unchecked down his face.

'If she wasn't kidnapped ...' He stared at Larry.

Larry swallowed hard. 'When I dropped the anorak off, she was dressed ready to go out. There was someone else there—'

'Are you telling me Kay was seeing someone?'

Larry nodded. 'Looks that way.'

It was Dylan's turn to shake his head. 'Who the fuck?' he spat through gritted teeth. 'I'll fucking kill him.'

'I don't know. I didn't see him, I only heard his voice.'

Dylan gave him a deadpan look. 'You mean you don't know, or you won't tell me?'

When no answer was forthcoming Dylan rose from his chair and walked into the lounge to find the answering machine flashing.

Larry appeared in the doorway, a questioning expression on his face.

'I left a message last night. She never heard it …' Dylan lifted his face to the window and looked out onto the empty driveway.

'Honestly, no one has any idea who the driver is yet. The main thing is, it isn't you.'

Dylan turned. 'I need to see her. And *him*.'

'I told you, the driver is covered in bandages so there's no point going to the hospital. You won't be able to see anything.'

'But he's fucking alive, Larry! Kay's dead. Where's the fucking justice in that? Perhaps it'd have been better if they'd both died.' Dylan walked into the hallway and picked up his coat. 'Let's get to the mortuary. I need to see Kay and then I want to go to the hospital. I need to see him …'

'But …'

Dylan raised his arm. 'I know what you're going to say. It may sound stupid to you, but I've got to see him and I also want to see my car. The Traffic department might know more than me about cars, but they're not trained investigators. I need to satisfy myself that everything that can be done, is being done. Only then will I accept the outcome.'

Larry fumbled in his jacket pocket for his mobile phone. 'I'll just make a call and let the divisional commander know that you're safe – and arrange for the coroner's officer to be there at the mortuary for the viewing. You'll need to formally identify Kay.'

'I doubt Hugo-Watkins will care whether I'm dead or alive. He's probably already got one of his yes men lined up as a replacement.'

The closer they got to the mortuary, the more agitated Dylan became. He glanced over at Larry.

'Thanks,' he said.

'Thanks for what?'

'It can't have been easy, telling me ...'

Larry smiled. 'Hey, I'm just thankful you're still here. Who else is gonna save me from myself?'

Neither man said a word as they walked down the corridor to the viewing room at the mortuary, somewhere they'd walked together a hundred times before; but this time it was different. Larry glanced over at Dylan. The police force must have replaced his blood with ice water – the mask of the detective was locked in place. Their footsteps reverberated, adding to the tension of the moment.

Dylan's mind was focused. His marriage might have been over in his head before all this, but it was his heart now taking supremacy. Had his wife lived, and it had been proven that she had been having an affair, she would have been dead to him – there were no grey areas in infidelity as far as he was now concerned.

Dylan knew the coroner's officer, former police officer Derek Booth, quite well. He was waiting for them through the swinging doors. Derek was a tall, grey-haired man, with a stubbly grey beard. He was a sensitive soul, with a firm handshake which Dylan noticed hadn't weakened at all over the years.

'Hang in there, boss,' said Sir Derek, as he was affectionately known by both his colleagues and the local community where he had served as community constable until his retirement. He put an arm around Dylan's shoulders; there were tears in his eyes.

'There's some jewellery in an envelope and clothing in there,' the mortuary assistant advised, pushing a brown paper bag towards

Dylan. The lump inside Dylan's throat became a rock. Swallowing was all but impossible. His heart wanted to stop, too, as he stared at the bag. Larry took it for him.

Derek looked towards the viewing room. 'When you're ready,' Derek said. 'Take as long as you like. I'll go and put the kettle on and when you're finished maybe we can have a brew together, eh?'

Dylan nodded, glad it was Derek on duty and not a stranger. He took a step towards the door. His knees almost failed him and he stumbled slightly. He felt Derek's hand squeeze his arm. It gave him some comfort and encouraged him to go on. The metal door handle which he had turned many, many times for victims about to view the bodies of their loved ones, today felt very different in his sweaty palm. The door opened slowly to reveal the familiar dimly lit room. Sympathetic music played low in the background and the sweet smell of potpourri hung in the air.

The strawberry birthmark on Kay's left forearm was easily identifiable even amidst all the cuts and bruises and burnt flesh. It told him instantly, if he had been in any doubt at all before, that it was his wife's body laid out before him. Her eyes were closed on her swollen and distorted face, but it was definitely her.

The injuries from the fire and being thrown through the car windscreen made her battered body appear mannequin-like. Dylan's throat tightened; he was more than slightly aware of the wounds that the crisp white sheet covering her must conceal. His chest shuddered and his tears were uncontrollable. She looked unbelievably peaceful, like an angel; yet the sight of her was also grotesque.

'Why, Kay?' he asked. A sob caught in his throat. 'What the hell were you thinking? Was I such a bad husband?'

He looked up at the ceiling. 'How the hell do I break this news to

Isla?' His eyes were drawn to the gaping wound on Kay's face, stretching from her forehead right down to her chin. A second one extended from her nose to her ear. He knew it was true that her death would have been instant. He was glad she had not suffered.

He couldn't bring himself to touch her, let alone to kiss her. He felt totally betrayed. His sadness mingled with anger and he breathed in deeply. 'Even though I know you were seeing someone else, I still wouldn't wish you in here. If you weren't happy, you should have said. I loved you enough to let you go.'

Part of him wanted to pick her up and shake her; part of him didn't want to leave her alone. He knew that her soul had gone from her body. He also knew that once he had left, her carcass would be lifted on the tray beneath and slid back into the fridge to lie on a shelf alone, but surrounded by strangers. She'd undergone a post-mortem examination and he knew exactly what that would have entailed. The mere thought of it turned his stomach. She was now nothing more than a statistic. The shell he would leave in the room wasn't Kay.

He managed somehow to stop himself from collapsing, allowing himself the comfort of anger as his primary emotion. He remembered their lunch together a few days before. Why hadn't he confronted her then? Why had he left things to drift? Then his thoughts went back to a few days before that. She had gone out in stockings, Isla had said. Presumably she had been going to meet *him*. Even when Isla so desperately needed her mum? Had he ever really known his wife?

The only way he would get through this was by keeping the mask of the detective in place. In his eyes, Kay was now a stranger, no longer the person he'd thought she was. She'd chosen to go off with someone else. Their relationship was in the past and that's where it would remain, in his past. Shivers ran down his spine. Dylan was not distressed by the chill, he knew full well that the room was kept cool in order to slow the decomposition of the body on the table. He looked down at the corpse before him. That's all it was to him now, just a shell.

Composed, he turned and walked from the room. He had seen what he needed to see.

Derek Booth lifted his head when he walked out of the door. His eyes asked the burning question.

'Yes,' Dylan said. 'It's Kay Dylan. My wife.'

In the kitchen Derek pulled out a chair and handed Dylan a mug of coffee, pushing a plate of Rich Tea biscuits in his direction. 'Just how you like it, sir,' he said. 'And I've taken the liberty of writing out your statement identifying her, for you to sign. Now, sit down, read and sign thereon. You know the routine better than most.'

Dylan sat down next to Larry. Derek patted him gently on the back as he watched him sign his signature. He felt for him, but he also knew, just as Dylan did, that if you got too deeply involved with other people's sadness you wouldn't be able to do your job.

'Thanks, Derek,' said Dylan, offering him the document across the table.

'You're more than welcome, sir, more than welcome.' The coroner's officer looked across at Larry. 'Your colleague has updated me, so we don't need anything else from you at this moment. We can speak later,' he said kindly.

'I don't know about you, but I need a drink,' said Larry, as they crossed the car park.

Dylan walked ahead of him; a man on a mission. 'Not until I've seen the bastard who put her in there,' he said.

'When they say it's an accident, then it is an accident,' said Larry. 'You've just got to accept it and move on.'

Dylan stopped and turned. His eyes were the colour of steel. 'Until I've reviewed all the facts for myself, just as usual, I won't be assuming anything. And you won't either. Do I make myself clear Detective Sergeant Banks?'

Chapter Nineteen

Bill Jones, Jen's new landlord, had gone way beyond his remit to ensure her safety by calling in to fit deadlocks on the doors at the little cottage. Her new home had a lovely little garden out back for her to hang out in and plenty of room for Max to play. Out at the front she marvelled at the magnificent views of the valley below and the spectacular surrounding hillsides.

'Rita wanted to make sure you felt safe,' Bill had said. 'Now, I don't need to know what's gone on, but I can't have a junkie living in my property, no matter who vouches for your character. Do you understand?' The balding, pot-bellied man in overalls peered sternly at her over his glasses.

Jen suppressed a giggle. 'I can promise you, Mr Jones, I don't do drugs of any kind. Never have.'

He raised an eyebrow. 'What, never?'

'No, never. And I never will. I'm just an old-fashioned girl.'

'Well, that's quite a revelation by today's standards. Even I smoked a bit of pot at college.'

His confession made Jen chuckle, which brought laughter lines to his eyes and to the corners of his mouth.

'There's some lovely walks around here for you and the dog. You'll love it!' he said.

When Bill Jones had gone, and with her security assured, Jen had still found herself checking from time to time that the doors were locked and no one could enter, such was her fear that Martin might find where she was living.

'You'll be all right now,' Rita had assured her a few days later as they sat eating fish and chips straight out of the paper and drinking the white wine Rita had brought out of cheap and cheerful glass tumblers.

'I guess he doesn't want to encourage drinking either,' Jen said.

Rita frowned. 'What do you mean?'

'Oh, nothing,' she said, feeding Max the leftover scraps. 'How'd you get to know Bill anyway?'

Rita smiled widely as she took a sip of wine. 'Because his nosy neighbours – he calls them Mr and Mrs Can't-Mind-Their-Own-Business – don't know the difference between a cannabis factory and a darkroom.'

Jen screwed up her nose. 'Eh?'

'We ruined three days of his work when we barged in and turned the lights on while he was developing some film and I ended up with the property seized in the store.'

'Really?' Jen's eyes were wide.

'Really. There's one thing that's true, life is never dull working at a police station.'

Suddenly, Jen looked serious. 'You don't think Martin will come looking for me, do you?'

Rita shook her head. 'I doubt it. He'll be warned off trying to contact you and, besides, he's a wimp. He knows he's lost you, and no doubt that's what he's always been afraid of. But he was the author of his own disgrace; he certainly didn't need a third party's help.'

Jen slid down onto the floor and put her arms tightly around Max who, lying comfortably on his side, put his head on her knee and looked up at her with his big brown eyes. 'Maybe I should just resign myself to the fact that I'll never meet anyone who'll love me the way Max does,' she said, ruffling his ears. Moaning contentedly, Max nuzzled his face in her lap.

'Well, he obviously likes the idea, but I don't think someone like you is destined to remain a spinster for ever,' Rita said. 'Mr Right will appear one day when you least expect it, and only then will you realise that the others really meant nothing.'

Jen sighed heavily. 'I wish I had your faith, but right now I am more than happy with a roof over my head and a job I love that gives me enough to pay the bills. And I like it just being me and Max here. Although, if I'm honest, another person's contribution towards the rent would be a great help. But I can manage, just, and that's all that matters right now.' A huge smile lit up her face. 'I've never had an en-suite bathroom before.'

'There's always a positive in everything. Sometimes it takes some bloody finding, but I've always found that as one door closes another one usually opens.'

Martin Schofield entered the pub and headed straight for the bar. After being released from the police station on bail he'd got a taxi home, where he'd discovered all Jen's personal belongings had gone and found a brief note telling him it was over between them. He ordered a beer and a shot, then another and another. In no time at all Martin was very drunk – and very loud.

'Good riddance is what I say!' he said to the landlord before sarcastically raising his glass to make a toast. 'Here's to the exes and the goody-goody police officers who kiss ass,' he said. 'Nothing but trouble, you women.'

'Aye, you can't live without 'em and you can't live with 'em,' said the landlord, taking Martin's empty glass and refilling it for the umpteenth time.

Arriving at the intensive care unit, Dylan flashed his warrant card to the woman manning the nursing station.

'We need to see the injured driver, please,' said Larry, with a close-lipped smile.

Unquestioning, the nurse led them down the corridor.

'Could you update me on his condition?' asked Dylan. His voice sounded strange to his ears.

'No change,' she said.

'And we still don't know who he is?'

She shook her head in reply as she walked ahead, briefly peering into each room as she passed. Each door had the patient's name on. When she came to the door without one, she put her hand on the handle, knocked gently and pushed it open to show the officers the patient lying prone on the bed, connected to intravenous tubes and wearing an oxygen mask. The bandages wrapped around his head were thicker on the right-hand side, giving him a grossly misshapen look. His hands were also wrapped in bandages, which formed thick white mittens.

There was a nurse at the foot of the bed, filling in an observation chart. She nodded to the detectives and whispered something to her colleague, then they left together.

Dylan took a step closer to the bed, his fist forming a tight ball. He swallowed hard and felt his stomach clench. Larry, sensing his distress, gripped hold of his arm, feeling the raw hatred pouring out of every pore of Dylan's body.

The man in the bed lay still as death, breathing with the aid of the mask, but showing no signs of consciousness at all.

'What if he never wakes up?' said Larry in a whisper.

Dylan opened his mouth and then shut it. He gave a slow shake of his head. 'It's not an option. He has to,' he said matter-of-factly.

For a few minutes the two stood in silence, Dylan motionless, scanning the patient with his trained eye, searching desperately for something about him that would tell him who he was. But he could find no clues.

'It'll take time, but you'll find out soon enough,' Larry said, as if reading his thoughts. 'Why don't you go now and leave this to me? You must break the news to Isla, before she hears it from elsewhere.' He tugged at Dylan's arm. 'Come now. There's nothing we can do here.'

Dylan didn't move. Larry tried again. 'Let's go and grab a coffee, eh, and maybe something to eat? We can talk about how you're going to tell Isla?'

At last Dylan spoke, but his eyes didn't leave the patient.

'Don't worry. When I hit him I want him to be conscious – and to know it's me.' Dylan screwed up his face. 'Who the fuck is he anyway?' he said with venom.

Dylan held Isla's hand while he broke the news of her mum's death to her, awaiting some sort of reaction, but there was none.

'That's sad,' she said eventually, wiping away a lone tear. 'Can I see her?'

'Of course,' said Dylan. 'We'll go straight away.' He looked across at the nurse standing beside them. 'I need to make sure it's okay with the staff first,' he said. The nurse nodded her consent.

Isla wanted her father to comfort her; she didn't like seeing him looking so tense and powerless. It wasn't like Dylan to be so reserved, as if he was detached from reality. His reality, to all intents and purposes, was also her world – one that had just been blown apart. She tried desperately hard not to show him, or anyone else, how upset and frightened she was really feeling, in order to help ease his burden.

While Isla went to get her things, Dylan spoke to the nurse. It concerned him deeply that after hearing such devastating news Isla had yet to show any kind of emotional reaction.

'Don't worry, Mr Dylan. It'll be the medication she's taking; it's helping to keep her calm.'

Perhaps when he took her to see Kay's body she would be different. He would be prepared for her reaction and, of course, would be there for her for as long as it took.

Why was it Mum who died? Isla asked herself repeatedly as she stared out of the car window. *Maybe if I hadn't been away from home, she'd still be alive.* Her questioning lasted the entire journey, until they pulled up outside the mortuary.

When he stopped the car, Dylan laid a hand on hers. 'There was nothing you could have done,' he reassured her. 'Your mum's death was out of our control. I want you to remember that.'

But she couldn't take in Dylan's words. She felt numb. *If only he hadn't gone to that stupid conference*, she thought to herself. *You were her husband.* You *should have been with her.* But she couldn't speak those words out aloud to him, as she became increasingly confused about what she should say or do. The mind-numbing medication didn't help.

In his own state of shock, Dylan assumed that her calmness was a sign that she was coping, little realising just how much she needed him to console her.

It was the first time she had ever seen a dead person, let alone the cold, dead face of someone she loved. Isla could never in a million years have prepared herself for what she saw, or for her reaction to the waxwork-like mask that had taken the place of her mother's beautiful face, which was purposefully laid on one-side for the viewing. Although the mortician had done his best with the make-up, the body lying in front of her was unrecognisable as the person who'd cared for her and nurtured her from birth.

A stifling sensation crept through Isla's brain, her pulse began to race and there was an intolerable struggle inside her. Strange lights flashed before her eyes and an unearthly singing rang in her ears. For the first time in her life Isla fainted.

Once again, Derek Booth was there and when he heard Isla's breathing getting shallower and saw her swaying, his eyes met Dylan's over Isla's head and he reached out ready to catch her.

'You okay, Isla?' she heard her father's voice, as he dabbed at her forehead with a cold cloth. She was lying down on a sofa and Dylan was putting a cold glass of water to her lips, encouraging her to take small sips. 'When you're ready,' he said gently. 'I'll take you back.'

'Will she be cremated or buried?' Isla asked, struggling to sit upright. Her head felt fuzzy. Dylan put a hand on her shoulder and gently pushed her back towards the cushion that acted as a pillow.

He couldn't believe her calmness and was somewhat shocked that she should already want to know about her mother's funeral arrangements.

'What do you think your mum would have wanted?' he said.

She seemed to be contemplating his question. He squeezed her hand. 'It's okay to cry, you know,' he said softly.

Isla looked confused. 'Don't fuss. I'm fine. I've seen her now and I know she's not coming back. We've got to move on. I think she would have wanted to be cremated and, to be honest, I don't like the idea of putting her in the ground for the insects to eat her up.' Isla got up. 'Shall we go now? I don't want to miss tea.'

'She's not grieving,' Dylan told one of the rehabilitation staff.

'Give her time,' the nurse replied.

At the police station the news of Kay's death had spread as quickly as an outbreak of flu. Detective Inspector Jack Dylan's wife had been killed and the sour gossip was spreading throughout the building like wildfire. Who had been driving Dylan's car? Was the man really her lover? Malicious tongues were extrapolating further: she'd been going to leave Dylan for another man.

Dylan could not deny any of it. But they were all surprised at him turning up at work. As far as he was concerned, he had a job to do and he needed to focus on that to get him through, with the help of the many friends and colleagues who truly cared about him and chose to ignore all the gossip.

'Boss, what are you doing here?' asked Larry.

'I can't be at home.' Dylan reached for the paperwork in his in-tray. Surprisingly, most of it had already been done. Dylan raised his eyebrows at Larry. He looked at his friend knowingly. 'So, you can do it if you put your mind to it.'

Larry smiled. 'How's Isla? Or is that a daft question?'

'She looks and acts like a zombie. But the staff at rehab tell me that the medication she is on is helping her to cope with the situation.'

'It must be good stuff.'

'Or bad, depending on how you look at it. But she did say she was looking forward to her tea, so if she's managing to eat now, at least that's a positive.'

'Talking of food, have you eaten anything since this morning?'

Dylan's eyes were on his computer screen as it pinged into action. He didn't reply.

'Didn't think so. So, how about we get out of here and go across to the Armitage Arms and get ourselves a couple of pints of anaesthetic and a sizzling hot beef sandwich? The others are setting up in readiness to pick up James Vincent Maloney Junior, the brace and bit burglar, tomorrow morning. I'll tell them not to bother us unless it's urgent.'

'Obviously learned everything he knows from his dad. I've locked Vincent up a few times.' Dylan looked thoughtful. 'How come it's always the wrong 'uns that seem to live till a ripe old age?'

Larry shrugged his shoulders.

'Tell me,' Dylan said as they stood at the bar. 'Why do you think people cheat on each other?'

Larry picked up his pint and eagerly put the golden nectar to his lips. The cold liquid felt good to his parched throat. 'Excitement, the thrill of the chase? Who knows?'

'You've been in some close scrapes with the husbands of your "acquaintances", so what's it all about for you?'

Larry tipped his head back and finished his pint. He nodded at Dylan's full glass. 'Drink up,' he said, handing his empty glass to the bartender.

Dylan looked at him questioningly.

'Sex! I don't know what else you want me to say! Sex without any strings attached. If the ladies need my services, then I'm available. And luckily I'm a fast runner.' He laughed, trying to make light of the situation as he accepted the second pint and paid the bartender.

'Do you never think about the husband?'

'No,' he said, pulling back. 'Why should I? When all's said and done, I'm not the one who's doing the cheating.'

Dylan managed to produce a brief smile. 'Aye, and it's me that's left to deal with all the shit when they make threats against your life!'

Chapter Twenty

Surely Kay couldn't have known how her philandering would pan out and the hurt it would consequently cause her husband and her daughter. She couldn't have been that selfish, could she? As Dylan lay on the sofa in the darkened living room, an intense welling up of pity for Isla and loathing for his wife churned together like a whirlpool in his stomach. He let his chin fall to rest on his chest and was grateful for this moment of solitude to think things over.

No matter what he'd done to cause her to take a lover, there was no reason for her to have neglected her own daughter to pursue her own self-gratification; but she'd paid the ultimate price – and her lover was still alive. Dylan squeezed his eyes shut and let the alcohol numb the pain, but it sent his mind reeling with unwanted thoughts.

What twists and turns their lives had been dealt. They'd been happy once, simply out of their love for one another. But was it love he had felt? He questioned himself now. Had it merely been a fierce need to protect the lovely young woman and the little girl who'd been parted from her father after a fatal freak accident at work? All that seemed a lifetime ago now: a lifetime since he'd been the young CID aide called upon to comfort a victim's wife. However, all that was inconsequential now, in light of the recent tragedy that had befallen them.

What he was currently going through didn't compare with Kay's loss at that time, or with Isla's now. Kay had lost the person with whom she had chosen to spend the rest of her life, the father of her baby; Isla had lost both her birth father and, now, her beloved mother.

When Dylan had married Kay, his promises to her had been set in stone. He had fully intended them to last a lifetime. *To have and to hold from this day forward ... until death do us part.* Now, hurtful as it was, he was forced to accept that for her the words she had spoken in front of the registrar back then had meant nothing. Just the thought of it gave him pain, and moisture began to fill his eyes. Was it shameful of him to be angry with a dead woman? Hastily, he brushed the tears away with the back of his hand. He sat up and shook his head. *Get a grip!* What good were tears anyway? The past was gone. A past that apparently had never really mattered to anyone but him. That was the stark truth.

He poured himself another glass of whisky. The alcohol was working, soaking up his thoughts and pushing away worry, and he solemnly waved his glass in the air.

'Here's to the future, whatever that may be ...' His voice wavered. He was successful, he had a career, he still had a life. His head bowed. The sad thing was that, according to Larry, Kay's death was even more of a senseless waste because to her lover she had been just a conquest, whereas to Dylan she had been the whole world. What else could he have done to please her? He had done everything she had asked of him: worked hard and earned enough money to give her the comfortable lifestyle she craved – which, until now, he'd believed she'd enjoyed. But he was forced to admit that it hadn't been enough, maybe nothing he could have done would ever have been enough; he wasn't Richard, Isla's dad. How foolish had he been to try to make himself believe that he could ever be enough for the lovely, vivacious Kay?

All this time she might just have considered him as a provider: the one who gave her the material things in life. Today he had been faced with a harsh reality and he couldn't even ask her why. She was gone from him. The real truth could be that she had never really been his.

He couldn't remember a time in his life when he had felt as helpless as he did now, and he wasn't quite certain what enraged him more: Kay's clever attempts at hiding her indiscretions, or the fact that he had failed to act on his instincts sooner. But then he hadn't really wanted to think her capable of such deceit. How could he ever trust anyone again?

He turned his face into the cushion and let the tears flow. It was time to let go. He gulped his drink down and reached for the bottle, aware that if he drank any more he would become entirely numb and end up not feeling anything. He poured himself another whisky.

The next two days passed by in a blur. Then he remembered there was a funeral to plan.

It appeared that Kay had pushed Kenny Fisher closer to insanity every day. When news of her death was broken to him by doctors, he seemed to smile with satisfaction, rather than show any signs of being upset. *No one else would ever be able to have her now.* His lack of control over his facial muscles was put down by the doctors to him being taken off the medication to allow him to wake up from the induced coma. Besides, the staff monitoring him were more than aware that everyone reacted differently to news of a death.

Medical staff continued to perform tests on him, those that had had to wait until the patient was awake. Previously undetected brain injuries, usually a result of a lack of oxygen, but occasionally from a stroke, had been known to occur while patients were in a drug-induced coma in the past, and this was a consideration in his case owing to his strange reactions since being woken.

Kenny had no such injuries. He was patiently biding his time until he felt strong enough to leave the hospital, knowing full well that the doctors wouldn't allow the detectives anywhere near him until he was deemed fit to be interviewed.

The police in charge of the enquiry had been told that the unnamed man involved in the fatal accident was off the danger list – his visible wounds were healing quickly and quite well, and he was both eating and sleeping – but his mental health was causing the doctors concern. Also of deep concern, to the police and hospital staff alike, was that no one had reported a man of his description missing.

It was all part of Kenny Fisher's clever planning. He had no family, or none that would miss a short absence, and his work force were never shocked by him 'upping and off' when he pleased. For some time, he had done the bulk of his work by telephone or using the latest computer technology.

Days passed and his identity was still unknown. In his mute state he appeared gracious and grateful to the staff who nursed him. His wounds were still such that the authorities would not show them to the media – they were simply too shocking.

When he did finally speak, he expressed a wish to leave hospital as soon as possible.

Two rest days at home and Dylan was back in the office, early as usual. He wanted an update on the accident, intending to use his experience as an investigator to understand what had happened to his wife. He was ready to go to the scene to see for himself the stretch of road where the accident had taken place. Photographic evidence and witness statements were all well and good, but he was more than aware that nothing beat being at an actual crime scene to get the feeling for both the time and the place.

His thoughts were interrupted by the sight of Dawn in conversation with the uniformed inspector. 'Everything okay?' he asked when she tapped at his door and entered his office a few minutes later. She sat down opposite him.

'An update regarding Tiffany Shaw. Remember? The schoolgirl who went missing the same day as Tanya King.'

His look was wry. ''Course I remember. I might have a lot on my plate right now, but I'm not senile yet.'

'Touché,' she said, with a bob of her head. 'Tiffany has confessed to spending the night with an older man – her teacher – but she is adamant that he didn't force himself on her, and that intercourse was by consent.'

Dylan nodded. 'But she can't legally give her consent because she's only fourteen years of age.'

'Exactly. Well, I didn't want to disturb you last night, but it appears that the fact that her dad is a builder and built like the proverbial brick shit-house – and has a put a price on the teacher's head – has dampened her lover's ardour a bit. He's come out of hiding and into the station with his solicitor. He's admitted everything and been arrested for rape. He's up for remand this morning.'

'Well, he couldn't very well argue that he didn't know her age, could he, since he taught her?'

'No, he's only twenty-three himself, and has ruined a very promising career by all accounts.'

Dawn saw Dylan bite his bottom lip. He sighed. 'Another one who's fucked it up for everyone then, just because he can't keep his dick in his pants.'

Dylan parked up on the A62 near the remnants of police tape dangling from a bare branch of a leafless tree and flapping in the wind. More tape still divided the area where the car had left the road from the rest of the world. Tempted as he was to get out and tear it down, he resisted: it reminded him that it was here Kay had died, with her as yet unnamed lover beside her.

He remained seated inside the car for some time. Radio Leeds had been playing in the background all the while, but his attention was suddenly drawn to the lyrics of the current song, and he reached out to turn up the volume. It was 'I'd Do Anything for Love'. Transfixed by the tune, he continued to listen as the words built up the suspense, portraying a romance-consumed lover who pledged to do anything in the name of love except 'that', a mysterious thing that he won't specify. The revving of the motorcycle, the police chase ... the song went on and on, and he with it, until the conclusion where the woman predicts what he will eventually do and the singer denies that he will ever leave her and start screwing around.

Dylan stared out across the bleak wilderness, beautiful, challenging and unforgiving, his whole being consumed with grief. Would he not have done that?

After a while he stepped out of his car and headed towards the guardrail that protected tired drivers from the almighty drop into the wilderness beyond. He passed a waist-high concrete bollard that had obviously been hit at speed for it to have crumbled as it had. At its base lay a bunch of freshly picked wild flowers; his eyes searched for a note – there was none. Before he could ponder on this, the wind picked up and hurried him along towards the grass verge where there remained clear evidence of the path the car had travelled before going over the edge.

It was as if he was there as it had happened. He could hear the sound of a car hitting a bollard, so real it seemed that he quickly looked over his shoulder towards the road. He heard the terrifying screeching of brakes and put his hands over his ears, screwing up his face and tightly closing his eyes in an effort to block out the nightmare images dancing through his mind. When he opened them again he was surrounded by a low, white cloud that spread towards the ravine, abruptly halting at its edge. The cloud tops were as smooth now as the surface of the road. Then a thunderous smash made him jump. Seconds later it was followed by a booming sound, as the ghost car came to an abrupt halt below. The apparition had him rooted him to the spot and he heard his own voice crying out into the ether, pleading, 'No! NO!'

He stepped forward and, tentatively looking down into the ravine's belly, spied two red lights, the width of a car, staring back up at him from the abyss. Then there was nothing but an eerie silence.

Dylan stared into the ravine, surveying the expanse of plants and trees, blending together every possible shade of green. The clouds parted and the sun came shining through. A brilliant white light shone down towards the earth and met the dispersing cloud, forming a 'stairway to heaven' – or was it hell, given the circumstances?

Walking back to the road, he felt strangely empowered. He had a desperate need to see the car that had been involved in the fatal accident, but he knew it was still on the ramps in the police garage, waiting to be examined by the vehicle investigation branch, so that was impossible. He had promised himself he would not interfere with the official investigation into Kay's death, but that wouldn't stop him doing his own. Only then could he accept the outcome, which he hoped would result in a substantial jail term for the driver.

Back at the station he searched the computer database for the latest information and his heartbeat quickened on seeing that the driver had been identified as one Kevin Fisher. He was taken aback: the only Kevin Fisher he knew was Kay's boss, Kenny.

The Road Traffic sergeant dealing with the accident was Barry Thewlis. Dylan wanted to get to Fisher, he wanted to get to Fisher so badly, but he knew he had to bide his time, so he went to speak to Thewlis.

Dylan found Thewlis in his office, doing paperwork. It was dark outside and he looked to be concentrating, head down. As he came up behind him, Dylan put his hand on the sergeant's back and gently patted it so as not to startle him.

'How's it going?' asked Dylan.

Thewlis looked over his shoulder. 'I think it's me who should be asking you that,' he replied.

Dylan sat in the chair next to him as Thewlis opened a file drawer in his desk. He selected several papers and spread them out in front of him. 'I'm guessing you want the lowdown?' His eye caught Dylan's.

He nodded. 'Please. Whatever you can tell me.'

Thewlis tapped his pen against the desktop thoughtfully, then put it down and cracked his knuckles. 'Your vehicle is still being examined but rest assured it's being treated as priority. They want to be absolutely sure there weren't any mechanical defects that might have contributed to the accident.'

'I read Frank Bland's witness statement, the one he gave about the vehicle prior to the accident. Is it possible to have a copy of that faxed over to my office so I can study what he said? If he got the impression the erratic driving was deliberate, then maybe this wasn't quite the accident we've been led to believe it was.'

Thewlis nodded. 'The driver of the car was stone cold sober at time of the accident, whereas your wife was three times over the legal limit. Which might explain why she was in the passenger seat. It's most unfortunate that her airbag didn't deploy.'

'But the driver's did?'

'Yes.' Thewlis paused. 'I know it won't give you much comfort, but your wife died instantly.'

Dylan's face was impassive, but he carried on as if he had his own agenda. 'I see that it's been confirmed that the driver was a Kevin Fisher?'

Thewlis blinked. 'Yes, we were contacted by the hospital when Fisher confirmed his details to them. Does the name mean anything to you?' Thewlis sat back in his chair and chewed the top of his pen.

Dylan's mouth twisted. He paused and looked down at his hands. 'Yes, it does,' he answered. 'Kevin, known as Kenny, Fisher is – or rather was – Kay's boss.'

The corner of Thewlis's mouth turned down. 'Oh, I see,' he said. 'I am sorry.'

Dylan didn't acknowledge his sympathy, afraid that if he did he would lapse into speaking as the victim and not the investigator. 'Do we know why her airbag didn't deploy?' he asked.

Thewlis straightened up. 'No, not yet. That question will form part of the examiner's findings.'

'And Fisher hasn't been interviewed yet, I understand?'

Thewlis hesitated. 'We're waiting for the hospital staff to give us the green light, but as soon as he is fit for interview, we will be speaking to him.'

Dylan sat forward. 'And you'll let me know what he says?'

Thewlis smiled slightly. 'Of course. I can guarantee that.'

Chapter Twenty-One

This can't be happening, thought Jen, when she saw Detective Inspector Jack Dylan put his head around the admin door and motion to her. Her face flushed as she rose from her chair to walk towards him. At six foot, Dylan was tall. If that didn't separate him from the rest of his colleagues, his chestnut brown hair, blue eyes and handsomely chiselled features, which were normally devoid of any emotion except for the rare moments when he was mildly amused, would have captured anyone's attention.

The soulful eyes which had greeted him when they were first introduced at the retirement party now appeared like large blue saucers, lost as they were in the depths of her now gaunt face. She appeared to have lost weight since he had last seen her. Her A-line skirt hung loosely about her hips and the elegant blouse she wore hung off the shoulders of her delicate frame. A walking coat-hanger was the description a few of her colleagues had started to use.

Jen wasn't sure what the correct words of condolence were when speaking to an officer of Dylan's rank or, indeed, whether she should mention his private life at all. After all, she barely knew him. Yet she felt a strange connection to his world, having registered the details of his wife's death in the Accident Register, marking the booklet with the ghastly red pen which was kept aside specifically for use on such dire occasions. It had been her first fatality in the job.

Dylan forced his mind back to the reason for him being there.

Jen tried to speak, but the words stuck in her throat. She coughed and tore her eyes away from his.

His voice was even and polite, 'I am told that you're the one to speak to regarding the Accident Register?' he said, in order to break the silence.

Jen nodded.

'I'll be in sitting in the kitchen along the corridor. Would you mind joining me?'

Jen shook her head and he was gone. She watched him walk down the corridor.

Rita's desk was next to the shelves where the Accident Register was kept. She raised her eyes to meet Jen's as she lifted it down, her expression full of empathy.

Dylan prowled the kitchen. He turned when he heard the door open and immediately sat down at the table.

'I'm so sorry to hear the sad news about your wife,' Jen said, doing her utmost to avoid direct eye contact. Dylan held his hand out for the book. The tension between them was palpable. There was some awkward fumbling owing to the register's large size; as it left Jen's hands, her fingers touched his and a shock wave like a mild electric pulse passed between them. Her eyes met his, but didn't find the look she'd expected; instead there was a childlike vulnerability in his gaze, which made her want to reach out and give him a hug.

She moved over to the kitchen worktops and, needing to do something with her hands, filled up the kettle and plugged it in. She could hear him turning the pages, then he stopped. Jen held her breath for a moment, then pulled two cups out of the cupboard and fiddled with the screw cap on the coffee jar, busying herself until she got up the nerve to turn around.

Dylan scanned the entry, hoping and praying that he would find some answers, but there was nothing other than the facts he already knew. When Jen turned, he was slamming the register shut. She carried the cups to the table, her hands shaking. 'I'm sorry,' she said.

Dylan gave a weak smile as she put a cup down in front of him. 'For what?' he asked.

'For not being able to help.'

Dylan shook his head. 'I don't really know what I was expecting.'

'Answers?' she suggested, taking a sip of coffee.

'I guess so.' He sighed heavily.

'And all the register will give you is the bare facts: day, date, time, location *et cetera*. I could have told you that if you'd asked,' she said softly.

'I had to see it for myself, for my own peace of mind.' He smiled briefly. 'It's the investigator in me, it's a curse; I can't leave anything to chance.' He put one hand on the table and stood with the cup in the other before emptying it. 'Thank you for humouring me,' he said sincerely.

Jen sat for a while after he'd left. *Why do terrible things happen to nice people?*

Returning to his own office, Dylan was surprised to see Larry, clutching a brown envelope in his hand.

'Where've you been, Jack? I've been trying to get hold of you for ages.'

Dylan took out his phone and checked it, seeing three missed calls from Larry. His pager also showed that he had been bleeped several times.

'What's so important?' Dylan asked, sliding behind his desk.

'Kenny Fisher is on the mend. They're hoping to speak to him soon.'

'I know,' Dylan said, pressing the button to start up his computer.

'You know already? How come?'

Dylan nodded. 'I spoke to Thewlis.'

'Did you know that the blood tests showed Kay was well over the limit?'

Again, Dylan nodded. 'I did.'

'Don't you think that's odd? She was practically teetotal!'

Dylan narrowed his eyes. 'I didn't know you took so much interest in my wife's drinking habits?'

Larry cleared his throat, suddenly looking hot under the collar. 'She never accepted a drink from me ...'

Dylan smirked. 'And that makes you an expert?'

When Larry didn't respond, Dylan felt guilty. After all, he was only trying to help. 'Mind you, I lived with her, and it turns out I didn't know her any better than you. She was shagging her boss right under my nose, for God's sake!' Dylan absentmindedly shuffled papers around his desk. 'And come to think of it, I think she might have been drinking more lately.' He suddenly recalled the image of Kay the night he had gone to the retirement party, standing in the living room with a large glass of wine in her hand. He'd known something was odd, but with his other suspicions swirling round his mind hadn't worked out what was wrong with the picture.

'I know it might sound trivial at the moment,' Larry went on, 'but would Fisher have been insured to drive your car? Bearing in mind it's a write-off.'

'I think having car insurance is probably the least of his worries right now, don't you?'

'I'm just trying to be practical.'

Dylan stared at him thoughtfully. 'I'm sorry, I know. I guess I can't get away with using the firm's car for ever.'

Larry frowned. 'Don't you want to go and see him?'

Dylan looked at him askance.

'Fisher! Don't you want to have it out with him?'

Dylan sat back in his chair. He looked deflated. 'You know I do,' he said. 'Trouble is, I don't trust myself.' He paused. 'I know I've got to be patient. Thewlis is dealing with the enquiry and I've got to trust him to inform me of any developments, especially in regard to Fisher.' Dylan's voice was even and calm. He paused again. 'However, I'm going to have a drive over to the police garage and see the damage to the vehicle for myself. If there is any evidence to be found, I'll be damned sure not to miss it!'

Larry grinned. 'That's more like it!' Then he gave Dylan a grave look. 'I've been thinking. Do you suppose it could've been Fisher that put you in hospital the other week?'

Dylan frowned, watching closely as Larry took a stack of photographs out of the brown paper envelope.

Larry paused, eyebrows raised in question. 'Or did he pay someone to get rid of the competition?'

Photographs of men recently released from prison flashed in front of him as Larry dealt them out in front of Dylan like a pack of playing cards. On the eighth turn of the card, Dylan stopped him and took the picture from Larry's hand. He looked at Larry, then at the picture and back at Larry again. 'Patrick Todd! It was him who I saw on the train. How bizarre is it for his name to suddenly come to me now?'

'Guess that's what they call a lightbulb moment,' said Larry, grinning from ear to ear.

'What worries me is how come he's out of prison?' said Dylan. 'I put him away for armed robbery. Surely he's not out yet?'

Larry collected all the photographs together, bar the one of Todd. 'I'll do some checks,' he said, waving the picture in the air.

Dylan followed him through the doorway and into the CID office. It was relatively quiet, with most of the officers out on enquiries and the majority of the admin staff either typing, filing or discussing cases. They kept their voices down, respectful of colleagues whose jobs required concentration.

'Come to think of it, he did threaten me in court when he got sent down,' said Dylan pensively as they approached Larry's desk, one of the few placed near the door. The desktop was messy, but not half as bad as some of the others, with a semblance of organisation in the separate piles of paper.

The chair was turned to the door and Larry dropped into it, spinning around to face Dylan, his expression philosophical. 'Don't they all?'

'True,' said Dylan, perching beside Larry. 'But that's Patrick Todd without a shadow of a doubt. That's definitely him, the chap I saw on the train, one hundred per cent. I remember smiling at him, obviously unaware of his identity. And he recognised me as well, I'm sure of that.'

Larry fired up his computer. 'He's changed quite a bit,' he said, scrutinising the mug shot. 'More muscular than I recall.'

'Well, he would be, wouldn't he, having spent the last eight years in prison?'

Dylan's eyebrows knitted together. He was distracted; something was bugging him. 'Is hitting someone over the head really his style?'

'Who knows? What I do know is that if it was that violent twat who hit you, you're lucky to be alive.'

Dylan swallowed hard. *Could it have been Todd's intention to murder him?*

Larry scrolled through screen after screen of intelligence on the computer system. 'Let's see what we can find out about his release,' he said. He turned to look at Dylan. 'If we've housed the bastard, then we'll know where he is and we can go feel his collar.'

Dylan nodded.

Larry pointed at the screen. 'Remember when we picked him up for that spate of street robberies? The witnesses were petrified and no one dared pick him out on the ID parade. We were about to release him and then you told him you were sick of being messed about and that the people he had robbed had seen him, and he just rolled over!'

'There's a first for everything. I think it was about the only time we didn't have a fight bringing him in either, because although we didn't have any evidence, he thought we had, which is always helpful.'

'He didn't fall for that again, did he? Sadly, he's broken a few officer's noses since,' Larry snarled. 'Nasty bastard!'

There was a holler from the outside corridor, a shaft of light as the CID office door opened and Detective Constable Ned Granger barged in larger than life, chuntering to himself. His eyes swiftly explored the room and, on seeing Dylan, immediately lit up.

'Just the person!' he said. He aimed a thumb over his shoulder. 'Divisional commander wants to see you urgently, sir.'

'Did he give a clue as to what it's about?'

'Nah. I told him you were out, but then he started shouting, telling me to get you back in now. He's a pillock.'

Dylan stood up and stretched. 'Well, I suppose I'd better see what he wants. I'll be back in five. Put the kettle on, Ned, will you? I have a feeling I'm going to need a caffeine boost.'

As he walked down the corridor, Marcus Thornton MP passed Dylan, heading in the opposite direction towards the exit. The limp biscuit had a grin on his face and Dylan had a wild desire to wipe it off.

Chief Superintendent Hugo-Watkins's secretary nodded and smiled at Dylan, ushering him into his office with her eyes as she continued to type some recorded dictation.

Dylan knocked lightly on the door and walked in. A wave of heat and a nauseous smell of tuna and tomato sauce sandwiches hit him. Hugo-Watkins waved him towards a chair and took a sip of tea from his bone-china cup. Dylan watched him eat. When he'd finished, he got up, went to his en-suite and washed his hands before settling once again behind his desk. He took another sip of his tea and dabbed his mouth with a napkin. A large custard tart on a plate beside him awaited his attention and his greedy eyes were focused on it. A loud burp preceded his tight-lipped smile, followed by a hollow apology.

'I've had a complaint about you,' he said, finally.

Dylan nodded. 'Yes?'

Hugo-Watkins's brow furrowed. 'I've been extremely annoyed lately by reports of your unprofessional – cavalier even – behaviour whilst dealing with the, I have to say spurious, allegations against our local children's home. I have had complaints from some stalwart members of the community.' He threw his hands in the air. 'And now the local MP's on my back! I've been forced to assure everyone that this attitude will stop immediately. I've no idea what the hell's got into you! But, since you ... well, let's say, since you are grieving, I'll make allowances for your errors of judgement just this once. Now go, before I change my mind,' he waved a hand in dismissal, his eyes returning to the custard tart. He picked it up and took a bite.

But Dylan was not for leaving. There was not a flicker of emotion as he edged forward in his chair and leaned towards the little man, forcing him to make eye contact.

In a menacing voice, he began, 'If you think Marcus Thornton is a stalwart member of the community, you'd better think again. Don't you know he's currently under investigation for falsely claiming expenses? If I didn't know better, I'd think that you were trying to protect a fellow Lodge member.'

Hugo-Watkins turned so red that Dylan feared he might burst. 'How dare you?' he spluttered, the unswallowed mouthful of custard tart spraying wet crumbs all over his desk.

'If you think that I have been unprofessional in any way throughout this investigation of the serious sexual assault of two young children, then go ahead! Be my bloody guest! You might be annoyed. I'm fucking *raging*!' Dylan stood and put his palms flat on Hugo-Watkins's desk.

'There's a group of wealthy people in this community having sex parties with under-age kids. They ring up for them to be delivered, just like a fucking takeaway. I think Peter Donaldson – who says he's a friend of yours and that you can vouch for him, by the way – knows all about it. I've told him I intend to investigate what's been happening fully and, by God I'm warning you now, I won't give up until everyone, and I mean *everyone*, involved in that particular paedophile ring, no matter how high a profile they have within the community, is brought to court and summarily dealt with.'

The room was quiet, so quiet that Dylan could hear the tap, tap, tapping of Janet's keyboard outside.

When he finally took his hand away from his mouth, Hugo-Watkins's voice was notably quieter, almost a whisper. 'Yes, well, that said, your approach does seem to have been a little heavy-handed to me.'

Dylan's eyes widened in amazement. 'Heavy-handed?' he shouted. '*Heavy-handed?*' Once again, he bent over the commander's desk and this time, as he slowly shook his head, he too spoke almost in a whisper. '*Nobody* is above the law, so I suggest you get your head out of your arse and realise what's going on around you. The only reason they've got away with it so far is because they're all mates together, feeding from the same trough. But, a word of warning, the lid is about to come off.'

'You can't talk to me like that! I will not allow you to do ...'

Dylan raised an eyebrow as he spat through his teeth. 'Won't allow me to do what? Investigate the crime? Just you watch me.'

The ring tone of Dylan's phone broke the ensuing silence, seeming to bounce off the walls. He took the call while holding up one hand like a traffic signal to prevent his commander from speaking. When he ended the call, his face was grave.

'There's a life-and-death situation. I've got to go.' He turned and headed for the door. With his hand on the handle, he turned.

'I'm sure you meant to say "sorry for your loss",' he said.

The door slammed behind him and the stud wall shook. As he ran down the corridor, the adrenalin pumped through his veins. He took the steps out of there two at a time.

Time, he was well aware, was of the essence.

Chapter Twenty-Two

The single-crewed Traffic car, blue lights whirring, was waiting for Dylan directly outside the front doors of the police station. He jumped into the passenger seat to see Chris Cane behind the steering wheel. The traffic officer gave him a candid smile and put the vehicle into a rear wheel skid before Dylan had even secured his seatbelt. As they swung out into the main road the two-tone sirens sounded the alert to anything obstructing their free passage. Dylan was thrown from side to side as the car bounced along at speed. The radio communication was full of static and pauses, forcing the two to listen intently and repeatedly ask for clarification.

Harrowfield town was busy and it seemed to Dylan that some drivers took for ever to pull over to allow the police car to pass. Defiantly, Cane kept his foot down. He approached the red traffic lights on the ring road at high speed, on the wrong side of the road, overtaking the queuing stationary vehicles at the roundabout. As the police car approached oncoming cars, some drivers moved up onto the central reservation, having nowhere else to go in order to evade the emergency vehicle ruthlessly bearing down on them, refusing to give them any leeway. At last they were in sight of their target destination. As they rounded a corner, Dylan could see a marked police car parked broadside across the entry to the bridge. It had its blue lights on, blocking access to all traffic.

'They're going to have to put a diversion in place up on Burdock Way, otherwise the town's going to be gridlocked in no time,' said Cane. 'Bet when the Victorians built the bridge they didn't consider it attracting people intent on ending their lives,' he said, weaving in and out of the cars that were at a standstill. 'How many would-be jumpers have we already had so far this year, boss? I'm aware of at least five.'

As soon as they'd stopped, Dylan opened the car door and quickly pulled himself out of the vehicle, thankful for the fresh air. Already planning his next steps, he shut the door and continued towards the police car on foot.

Meanwhile, Cane turned the car round. 'Good luck!' he said, from the open car window as he passed Dylan. 'I don't know how you've got the patience. Life's too precious to throw it away in my book.'

Dylan tossed his head in the jumper's direction. 'They can't be thinking straight,' Dylan said. 'There but for the grace of God ...'

'Give us a call if you need collecting, boss,' Cane called, before heading back to town.

As Dylan stood thinking, contemplating the best approach to take, he looked up towards the dark skies. Night would be falling soon, and so would the rain he saw brewing overhead. Before him, the nearly one hundred metre span of North Bridge's carriageways was unusually empty. Empty, that is, except for a hooded figure perched high up above on the ironwork.

Some of the motorists delayed by the incident had no sympathy for the individual on the bridge and weren't shy in voicing their displeasure, calling the attention-seeking stranger a damn nuisance.

The anger and frustration behind him was palpable, but Dylan couldn't afford to be sidetracked.

At the south-west turret of the bridge, next to a drinking fountain, was a burly young man in a police uniform. He was deep in conversation with an irate man and two women. At the sight of Dylan, the police officer excused himself and walked towards him, leaving the three arguing between themselves.

'Any update?' Dylan asked, his eyes fixed on the lone figure, still standing solid for the moment at least.

PC Mohammed shook his head. 'No, they've not moved. But according to a witness there's no cords tied to the feet, nor any sign of a 'chute strapped to their back. Not even a can of Red Bull in sight. I think it's safe to say it's not someone seeking a thrill, rather than oblivion.'

'Do we know whether it's a male or female?'

Again, the police officer shook his head. 'No, and it doesn't help us that both sexes all dress the same these days. My orders are just to stop traffic at this end and my colleague's doing the same at t'other side.'

'Okay. Keep within earshot, will you, just in case I need something urgently? But keep at a distance so they can't hear your radio.'

PC Mohammed observed the look of steely determination on Dylan's face.

'And have we got an ambulance waiting down below?'

The young officer shrugged his shoulders. 'I was just told to stop traffic …'

Seeing PC Mohammed's hesitant expression, Dylan continued with his instructions. 'Tell Control to get an ambulance down there as a matter of urgency.'

Dylan concentrated hard on putting one foot in front of the other as he began the 'long walk', aware that this was his first real test as a negotiator and that all eyes would be on him. Nothing other than the cool breeze on his cheeks and his own purposeful heavy footsteps were noticeable to him, such was his focus. His eyes were fixed on the lone, dark figure on top of the central pier, twenty-three metres above the main road. It was a good sign, he knew, that the jumper was still on the bridge.

As he edged forwards he felt the wind pick up, his footsteps now merely a whisper as his thoughts turned to wondering what might be holding the person back: fear of the unknown, guilt? Whatever it was, it was Dylan's job to find out. He felt completely alone and with that loneliness came a rhythm to his footsteps, a kind of music that Dylan had never heard before. The music changed rapidly as he crossed the bridge and looked down at the River Hebble below, listening to the sound of rushing water. The blue lights of the ambulance reflecting off the river's surface alerted him to its welcome arrival.

He was nearing the hooded figure and his heart quickened. *Would the sight of him send them over the edge?* Suddenly, a poignant thought came to him: he was possibly the only thing standing between this person living or ending their life.

As each step took him a little closer, he was pleased that, so far, his movements hadn't brought about any untoward responses from the jumper. As he got nearer, his pace slowed. The dark figure, facing away from Dylan, didn't budge. He was now within shouting distance, but he assumed wouldn't be heard over the wind.

He could see that the person was clinging on to one of the parapet's ornate decorations. Clothed in a dark hoodie and jeans, the figure's facial features were concealed and Dylan couldn't make out whether the person was male or female. Not that it mattered. He crept a little nearer and began negotiations slowly, exactly as he'd been taught.

'I'm here to help you. Whatever has happened, we can sort it. Just come down from there and let's talk, eh?' He spoke loudly, without actually shouting, so as not to startle the jumper and cause an accidental fall.

Without turning around, the figure confidently released one hand from its grip on the Maltese cross and flicked two fingers at him.

The fact that whoever it was had decided to engage in discourse, however abusive, was at least an acknowledgement of his presence. Dylan was pleased. He tightened his overcoat lapels around his neck and pulled up his collar.

'You may not want me here, but I can assure you I'm not going anywhere. Whatever the problem is, we can sort it. There is no need to do this.'

All the while as he talked, Dylan took small steps forward – a slight shuffle now and again – and he soon found himself just a metre away from the skinny individual, the trainer-clad feet now at the same height as his shoulder. Allowing him to come so close was a good sign, but he wouldn't test his luck any further, for now.

The ledge on which the jumper was perched above him was dangerously high. Dylan felt a few cold splashes of rain on his face. Suddenly, he felt the urge to move negotiations forward at a quicker pace.

'Whatever the problem is, I can help. Talk to me.'

There was no answer. Dylan shivered.

'Aren't you cold up there? Do you need a hot drink or anything? I know I do. Come down and talk to me.'

The lonely figure didn't flinch when a fierce gust of wind threatened to catch them both off balance. It was the kind of wind that forewarned Dylan that a storm was about to unleash its pent-up fury.

Instead of being afraid, the jumper looked up towards the heavens, seeming to relish the sting of the droplets of water.

'If you fall, the likelihood is that you won't die, but you will be seriously injured and in a hell of a lot of pain,' Dylan said. 'That's why there's an ambulance down there.'

He shuffled just a fraction nearer as he spoke. The move was unchallenged. He was just about an arm's reach from the person who hadn't yet said or done anything other than flash the 'V' sign at him and look up at the sky. *A true player would have stepped over into the end of time before now – wouldn't they?*

Just because the jumper wasn't responding didn't mean Dylan would stop talking. Perhaps him talking was what was taking attention away from the idea of going over the edge. He was in no doubt that the outcome of a jump would in fact be instantaneous death, but he preferred to frighten the figure with the thought of a grim survival. If jumpers thought they were going to experience a great deal of pain, he had been taught, it might possibly make them think twice about making the final move.

As he stood there, chilled to the bone, Dylan was acutely aware that the hooded figure was going to become colder, hungry and weaker and could slip, faint or go over accidentally at any time, especially as the wind speed was increasing at such a fast rate.

'Why not come back to this side of the bridge and have a fag or a coffee? Just while you think about things. I know you can't see a way through whatever problems you have right now, but there will be one. Let me help you find it.'

Dylan moved from one foot to the other as he craned forward, desperate to make eye contact, but the hood totally shielded the solitary soul's face from his view. He could feel a frustration growing within him, becoming as strong as the fear of the wind that threatened to take the jumper with it.

Please don't rain, he thought, just as a blanket of rain began to drape the horizon. Within minutes it was pelting down in unrelenting torrents. The bare bits of his skin grew cold and his clothes became soaked through. He could see the dark figure above him wobbling from side to side and he feared the movement was unintentional.

'If you go over,' he shouted, taking a different tack, 'I'm going to get such a rollicking because I've failed.'

Half an hour had passed and though the rain began to abate at last both were now shivering and shaking uncontrollably.

'I lost my wife recently, my daughter is ill, and my whole world as I knew it has fallen apart,' he said, in a quieter, softer tone. 'I've probably reached the lowest I ever could … Everything I loved has been taken away in the blink of an eye.' He paused. 'Turns out I've been living a lie; nobody ever really knows what another person is thinking or feeling. But things will change; they *will* get better. Let me help you. Let me help you sort out whatever the problem is.'

He paused again, coughed and shivered. 'I'm here getting piss wet through like you because I want to help you, not judge you. So, why not come down? Let's both go get a hot drink and have a chat and sort things out, eh?'

The person on the bridge was clearly now soaked through and it was obvious to Dylan that it would be a few degrees colder up on the ledge than where he was standing. He coughed again and suddenly the figure turned towards him, the movement causing a heart-stopping unsteadiness. He recognised the wobble. And the face.

'Dad? Please help me. I'm frightened,' whispered Isla.

Chapter Twenty-Three

'Isla?' Dylan's voice cracked with shock.

Isla was leaning out over the ledge, looking down and holding on to the cross with only one hand. The other hung loosely by her side. Dylan watched as she slowly shut her eyes.

His heart was palpitating so hard and fast that he thought it would burst. Light as she was, her weight might still take him hurtling over the edge with her if he reached out, but he had to try to save her. Dylan moved forwards as swiftly as a striking snake, rulebook forgotten, grasping her cold, wet, slippery hand in his before gravity took over.

A short command burst from his lips, laced with such power and energy it made the hairs on his own arms stand on end. The eyes that turned to meet his in response were wide and unfocused. Isla blinked and was suddenly possessed by an aura of unnatural calm. With a tug on the bottom of her hoodie, Dylan spun her towards him and his foot slipped on the wet pavement.

Too surprised to scream, Isla saw Dylan's face distort as he flung her to the ground. The force had knocked him backwards. He was winded from the impact of the fall, but leapt up to ensure that she was safe, sprawled out yards from him. He had brought his daughter back from the brink of certain death.

Dylan crawled across to her and knelt down by her side, totally drained. An emergency siren blared in the distance. When Isla didn't respond to his touch, he scrambled to pick her up. Shivering uncontrollably, she pulled her knees up to her chest and huddled up into a ball. Grief rumbled through her like a bulldozer without brakes rolling down a hill. Her entire body shook, as she sobbed to flush the pain away. He placed his strong arms around her and pulled her to her feet. Her knees buckled and he held her tightly, soothing her with encouraging words.

'It's all over, Isla. You're safe. You're safe now, I promise,' he muttered, staggering to the barrier with her, where they would be afforded a little shelter. Sitting with their backs against an iron girder, Isla clung to him as if he were the only person in the world that could save her from herself.

'I'm sorry, Dad. I'm so sorry ...' she sobbed, burying her head in his shoulder.

'It's okay, you cry. Let it all out. It'll help.'

He pulled her closer to him and placed a hand on her head, gently stroking her hair. 'I thought you were at the clinic. You're the last person I expected to be up here.'

'They gave me pills ... I heard voices. They told me I needed to die ... it's my fault Mum's dead. I couldn't bear it. She's always there, whether I'm awake or asleep ... calling me to go to her.' Isla looked up at him. 'Then I heard your voice, Dad. It was stronger than hers. You said you could help me ... that you weren't going to leave me. I don't want to die, Dad. I don't want to die.'

Dylan looked away, tears welling up in his eyes and snaking down his face, despite his attempts to hide them from her. 'Shush ... shush ...' he soothed. 'It's okay, it's okay.'

Isla gazed up at him through blurry eyes and blinked. He brushed away her tears. His hands were incredibly gentle. She had never seen him cry before and it frightened her.

The bridge was still closed. Dylan became aware that nothing would move until he gave the command. Isla shivered and sneezed. Dylan spoke softly. 'I think we need to think about moving, don't you, before we get hypothermia?' There was a moment of silence. 'You okay with that?' he asked.

Isla hiccupped and moved away from the security of his arms. She gave him the fleeting ghost of a smile and gently nodded. Only as she released her grip on his hand did he feel a stickiness on his skin and realise how hard her nails had been digging into him, enough to produce blood.

As they stood up, she kept hold of his arm tightly so as not to fall and he held her upright. 'I'm here with you, don't worry,' he reassured her.

His eyes were sympathetic yet showed no pity, thank God. She didn't need pity.

Glancing over her head, Dylan could see a semi-circle of pedestrians at the mouth of the bridge, waiting. He also saw the unmistakable flashing light of the ambulance as it wove in and out of the stationary cars to get onto the bridge and closer to them. Finally, the ambulance pulled to a stop, the doors swung open and the paramedics jumped out.

Dylan stood at the open door as the medics helped Isla into the back. Her eyes were sunken and her skin grey, and a sliver of blood was running down her face from a cut to her forehead that he hadn't noticed before. The youngest paramedic on the scene, who couldn't have been much older than his daughter, looked at Dylan in a questioning way and he gave her a nod to let her know he was okay.

'Nothing else required at this time,' Isla heard Dylan tell PC Mohammed via his radio. 'I will be accompanying the young female to the hospital and I'll update the control room later.' He had no intentions of telling them anything else while Isla was still in earshot.

While Dylan was sitting in the rear of the ambulance however, next to the paramedic who had draped a foil blanket over Isla, he explained who he was and that the patient on the stretcher was his daughter. He reached out for Isla's hand, but instead of taking it in hers as he'd hoped she would, she turned away.

The paramedic gently placed a hand on Isla's shoulder. Instantly, the terrified girl snapped her head around, recoiling from the touch. She seemed unaware of what was happening and that worried Dylan.

'She's going to be just fine, aren't you, Isla?' the paramedic said. Dylan nodded his head, but he saw something in the paramedic's eyes, something that betrayed the message of reassurance. He knew she wouldn't be fine, far from it. In fact, nothing would be fine for a long time to come.

Dylan was well aware that being sectioned under the Mental Health Act was not for the faint-hearted, but he had been around long enough to know that once the doctor recommended urgent hospitalisation for an assessment and treatment after a suicide attempt, there was no alternative. From experience, he knew that Isla was already heading down that road.

'I don't want to stay in hospital,' she sobbed. 'Please let me come home with you, Dad,' she pleaded.

With a heart that felt as if it was breaking afresh, Dylan stepped out into the silent corridor, passing rooms occupied by sleeping patients, Isla's desperate screams following him all the way. The sanitary smell hanging in the air made him want to gag. His strides became shorter as he hurried towards the exit. He shook his head, trying to clear Isla's cries from his head. He needed air.

'Don't leave me! I hate you! I wish I were dead!' were the last words he heard before passing through the corridor's double doors into a waiting room. He sat down on a chair and put his head in his hands. When he closed his eyes to try to stave off his headache, all he could see was Isla's frightened, trusting eyes as the nurse had injected her with strong medication to calm her down. *It's for her own safety*, he repeated to himself over and over again. He sat up straight, throwing his head back. *How could he do this to her?* But he knew he there was no alternative if he wanted her to stay alive.

After a few minutes, Dylan sensed someone looking in his direction. The soft patter of footsteps could be heard heading his way.

'Is everything all right?' asked a kindly voice.

Dylan looked up to see an elderly lady with the word 'VOLUNTEER' stitched to her overall.

'Come, let me get you some dry clothes, maybe a hot cup of tea and perhaps some hot food?'

Dylan forced a smile. 'No, I'm okay really. I don't need ... My colleague will be here to collect me soon.'

Not believing a word, the volunteer kept her beady eye on him from her station.

Dylan's mind was still spinning with a multitude of thoughts when PC Cane pulled the Traffic car up outside the house he'd once shared with Kay and Isla. There was a strange car in the driveway and Dylan gave his companion a puzzled look. Cane handed him a set of keys.

'DS Banks told me to give you these, sir, saying you might need them.'

Dylan got out and watched Cane turn the Traffic car in the road to head back to the station. The headlights shone directly into the Anderson's house, and he hoped that it wouldn't wake them and signify his return. He turned to walk up the pathway to the front door and saw that rain was falling again, shimmering down past the street lamp in an orange haze, before splashing onto the paving stones.

He was grateful for the help and foresight of his colleagues. It was all he could do now to put one foot in front of the other; the closer he got to the house, the longer it seemed to take and the more he dreaded going in, but he reached the front door eventually. He put his key in the lock and turned the handle, finally opening the door into the black abyss that had been his home.

His clothes hit the bathroom floor, he turned on the water and stepped into the shower. He allowed the water to cascade over his head and cleanse his fatigued body, but he knew that nothing could cleanse his tired spirit. As he soaped himself, his thoughts went back over the events of the day. He was beaten; but he would not let it show. The water ran down his face, mingling with tears.

He was drying himself when the telephone started to ring. He quickly crossed the room to answer the call.

'Hello,' he said. The line went dead. Cradling the receiver to his face he felt his whiskers, rough and making his face itch. Could it have been Isla? He sat on the bed, watching the phone and silently willing it to ring again, but after a few minutes when it became obvious it wasn't going to, he picked up the receiver and dialled HQ control room to give them the result of the incident.

He was assured by the inspector that the incident log, which had been running since they had first been notified of the person on the bridge, had now been updated. 'I am sorry to hear the news,' the inspector said sincerely.

Dylan was in the bathroom brushing his teeth when the phone rang again. He wasn't in the mood for people messing him around and after the third call he took the phone off the hook. His mobile was on his bedside table should anyone need him.

As he lay down on the wrinkled sheets he wondered if Kay had slept in their bed with Kenny Fisher. Fatigue quickly gave way to merciful sleep and Dylan was spared any further thoughts.

Rudely awoken by the familiar sound of cats fighting, Dylan wondered what time it was. How long he'd slept he'd no idea. He looked at the clock. It was midnight. Launched haplessly back to consciousness, he tried to settle back to sleep, but, try as he might, he found it difficult to clear the chatter in his head. He lay for a while, eyes wide, listening to the silence and watching the flickering glow from the street lamp reflected on the ceiling.

Gradually, he began to take note of the beating of his heart and eventually the thoughts running through his head stilled as he allowed his body to sink into the soft warmth of the bed.

A cool breeze skimmed his cheek but, being neither quite asleep or awake, he didn't question where it came from. He shivered and, annoyed at being disturbed, pummelled the pillow, sank his head back down on to it and turned on his side. He pulled the duvet up tight, under his chin. At first, all was quiet and still and he felt himself relaxing again when, as if from a distance, the sound of Isla's voice exploded into his consciousness.

Dad! Please come, it cried.

Dylan drove to the hospital. It was still raining but it was the fog that made the drive surreal. He felt as though he was driving through time. A flood of memories filled his head, flashing through his mind like an old movie: images of Isla's first day of school, Christmas mornings and bonfire nights. Where had time gone? In his mind he constructed a strongly worded letter to the clinic where she had been a voluntary resident. Anger rose in him. He would demand to know how she'd managed to walk out loaded with the cocktail of drugs they had prescribed, and why they hadn't thought of ringing him immediately to say she had disappeared. Weren't they supposed to have been monitoring her twenty-four seven? Wasn't that the reason for her being there, to be in safe hands?

When morning came, he was still at the side of Isla's bed. She had slept peacefully and appeared calm and serene beneath the starched white sheets. When she woke, she gave him a dreamy smile. He put his hand on her clammy arm, cringing to see that her two front teeth were broken. His eyes left hers and came to rest on a Bible that was on the bedside cabinet beside him.

'We've prepared a room for your daughter so that the doctors can evaluate her further,' said a nurse, as she busied herself checking Isla's vital signs. Another nurse gathered together the little property Isla had with her from the cabinet.

Dylan walked briskly to keep up with the medical team as they wheeled Isla into a lift and down a corridor towards an unknown destination. He was thankful that, with her head bowed down in her drug-induced state, Isla didn't see the signs for the mental health secure unit or feel as pained as he did at all the security measures that had to be taken before people could enter or leave. He looked down at the straps that restrained her. *How had it come to this?* There were so many questions he wanted to ask but he knew he had to bide his time.

When the nurse accompanying them exchanged clipboards with another, Isla was taken off to the left in the wheelchair. Dylan was directed to the right, into a windowless waiting room that was as white, shiny, bright and sterile-looking as the corridor.

'Someone will be out to see you as soon as they've got her settled,' the nurse said. She paused and handed Dylan a clipboard. 'In the meantime, it would help if you could complete this form.' The nurse scurried away before he could say another word.

Dylan sat down. He needed to fill in the form, but first he needed to stop his hands from shaking.

Outside the hospital, he leaned against cold stone, in the space between the entrance and a window, one foot planted firmly against the wall. Hearing his phone ring, he fumbled in his pocket and answered it. He saw that he'd missed several calls.

'Where are you?' Larry's voice sounded desperate.

Dylan smiled a little. Normality was good. 'I'm on my way to the station. I'll catch up with you there.'

'No, wait,' Larry said. 'Don't hang up. We've got calls coming in to say your house is on fire. Good God! I thought you were in there.'

Chapter Twenty-Four

A pall of thick, black smoke lay heavy in the air and, as Dylan approached the scene, he detected the scent of burning peculiar to a house fire: a bitter stench mixing charred dry wood with the odour of burning plastic and smouldering synthetic household fabrics. He parked his car and ran towards the house. At the top of the driveway he stood powerless and immobile. He wanted to run inside the house with gallant intentions, but his spirit was crippled. Faceless people surrounded him: a police officer guarding the scene; a firefighter dragging a heavy hose up the driveway; the obligatory onlookers staring and pointing.

Larry joined him at the same time as his neighbour, Janice Anderson. She touched Dylan's arm lightly. 'Would you two like a drink?' she asked, handing them both a steaming mug of pale liquid. 'My Tony has a friend who is in the fire restoration business,' she said. 'He's on the telephone to him now. Maybe he can help?'

She tottered off in her fluffy pink slippers. Larry gave Dylan a sideways glance. 'Restoration! Is she having a laugh?' Larry said, putting the mug to his lips. He grimaced. The tea tasted like paint thinner.

Seeing the shards of glass, pieces of splintered wood and broken bricks strewn all over the neat patch of garden, Larry whistled through his teeth. 'Who built these houses, the three little pigs?'

'Looks that way doesn't it,' Dylan replied. Outwardly, he appeared to be coping; inside, he cried silently, broken and distraught.

'If this is how bad it is on the outside, I don't hold out much hope for anything inside.'

Dylan could only shake his head in despair.

'What's worse, the whole crime scene is totally soaked in water.' Larry turned to look at Dylan. 'On a positive, we have a witness who saw someone running away, with an arm ablaze: a white male, so at least we have a lead.'

'What twisted bastard would go so far as to try to burn my house down, Larry? Why?'

Inside the house, the stench was overpowering. Dylan's irritated eyes immediately started to water, fumes caught in his throat and he began to cough violently. The firefighter at the door offered him his bottle of water.

'I'll be fine, thanks,' said Dylan. The amount of structural damage surprised him. In his experience, a fire normally tended to consume a room's contents – all the personal items that made the aftermath of a fire such a tragedy for inhabitants – but left the house itself merely scarred. However, as he looked up now he could actually see openings where plaster board had been torn from the ceiling. The staircase itself had all but disappeared: had there been petrol through the letterbox? He could just about make out the remnants of some of the furniture.

Life, as he had known it, was over: dead and buried for ever. All that was left now was to bury Kay and to get Isla well again.

Dylan closed his office door, shutting out the sympathetic looks from the team. He wanted normality; he didn't want their sympathy or pity. He was in the process of unlocking his desk drawer when Larry stuck his head round the door.

'I'll get us a coffee and a slice of toast, shall I?' Dylan's eyes rose to meet his colleague's.

'Don't worry, lad. I'll make sure it's not burnt.'

The door closed behind him and Dylan laughed. What else could he do? It could have been a lot worse; he would have been in bed fast asleep when the fire struck had he not gone to the hospital. He shuddered to think what would have happened then. Isla had saved him.

When the phone rang ten minutes later Dylan paused the CCTV footage he was viewing and picked it up. Barry Thewlis was on his way to see him with updates regarding the accident and Kenny Fisher. Dylan finished his toast and drained his coffee cup just as Thewlis appeared at his door. He invited him in. Thewlis shut the door behind him, his face grave.

'Don't lose it, boss,' he said, 'but Fisher signed himself out of the hospital before we had a chance to speak to him.'

'What?' Dylan cried out, drawing back and throwing his arms up in the air in exasperation. His voice sounded like air escaping from a blacksmith's bellows. His face turned a vivid crimson, deep enough to rival the colour of any red wine.

Thewlis kept his composure. 'Please hear me out. From the outset it was clear to us that the accident wasn't all that it seemed. In fact, we now believe that it wasn't an accident at all.'

The men exchanged a look.

'I'm all ears,' said Dylan.

Thewlis's face remained matter-of-fact when he handed over the rolled-up report to Dylan. 'If you read this, sir, you'll see the lack of tyre marks on the road signifies there was no attempt at all by the driver to brake at any time, a fact which is confirmed by our only witness.'

Dylan nodded eagerly. 'Go on.'

'Neither did the witness report seeing any brake lights until after the car had gone over the edge, something which you'd expect to see if the driver was attempting an emergency stop before the collision with the first bollard, let alone the second and the third ...'

Dylan looked up from the report at the man on the other side of the desk and found his voice again. 'I've been to the scene,' he admitted. 'Not that I don't trust you; I just wanted to see it for myself.'

'Of course you have. I wouldn't expect anything less from you,' Thewlis said, only a slight strain showing in his smile. He inhaled deeply and continued. 'You will see that the passenger seatbelt anchorage point has been deliberately unscrewed. These things, I am assured, don't vibrate loose by themselves.'

In the blink of an eye, Dylan's expression changed. He stared at Thewlis without speaking.

'Also, there is the issue of the passenger airbag not activating.'

Dylan hesitated. 'Surely these faults would have been picked up when the car was serviced?'

Thewlis nodded. 'You'd think so. Which makes me think that any tinkering was done afterwards.'

For a moment Dylan's stomach sank as he imagined the worst. 'A deliberate act?'

'The evidence suggests it. The damage is far greater on the passenger side, which confirms to the experts what our witness says.' Thewlis paused. 'Can I ask, was the vehicle new when you bought it?'

Dylan shook his head. 'No, one careful lady owner; but it was two, nearly three years old. Why?'

'Because it may be that the first owner switched the passenger airbag system off.'

Dylan frowned. 'How would I know?'

'Apparently, the driver is notified by way of a symbol that lights up on the dashboard.'

'Then to my knowledge the passenger airbag was set to "on". I have never seen a light on the dashboard that has signified anything else.' He was thoughtful. 'Saying that, I've not driven the car much lately …' He paused again. 'But I did drive it back from picking Isla up from the university and I would surely have noticed then if there had been anything amiss.'

'All these factors have to be considered by the vehicle examiners.'

'So, let me get this straight. You're saying that whoever disabled the airbag and unscrewed the anchorage point on the seatbelt would have known that, should the car be involved in a collision, the passenger would be thrown through the windscreen, leaving any chance of survival highly doubtful? But the driver of the car would more than likely survive unscathed – seatbelt and airbag still being there to protect them?'

'Exactly! You may recall that the witness to the accident also says in his statement that he got the impression that the collisions were a deliberate act, owing to the fact the driver swerved into all three bollards at speed.'

'Perhaps Fisher misjudged the last bollard or Kay, fearing for her life, managed to drag the wheel from him? My wife would have fought back if she thought for one moment her life was in danger.'

Thewlis's eyebrows rose. 'Or Fisher's airbag activated and he lost control of the vehicle at that point.'

Dylan's eyes narrowed. 'That would make sense. Going down the ravine surely wasn't part of Fisher's plan.'

'I think that is a possibility.'

'Then Fisher was attempting to kill Kay and make it look like it was an accident. But why? Is he mad?'

Dylan was puzzled. 'Is unscrewing the anchorage point on a seatbelt a straightforward procedure?'

Thewlis nodded. 'It is if you know what you're doing.'

'And turning the passenger airbag off?'

'Possibly nothing more than a switch. Again, easy if you know how to do it.' Thewlis looked thoughtful. 'You don't think Fisher was the one who torched your house, do you?'

Dylan looked forlorn. 'Maybe him, maybe Patrick Todd, or maybe some other random idiot whose name hasn't come into the equation yet.' He slumped back in his chair. 'Look, I'll get CID out looking for Fisher and we'll open up this investigation. Another thing I still don't understand is that Kay was not a big drinker, never had been, and yet her bloods showed she was well over the legal limit.'

'That's right, three times over,' said Thewlis.

'So how did that come about? And do you think that points to her being unconscious when the car hit the posts?'

Thewlis's eyes widened. 'Are you thinking that your wife may already have been dead when the accident occurred?'

'Perhaps. But let's not assume anything. We must secure the evidence and let that speak for itself.'

Thewlis stood up. 'In the meantime, we need to find Fisher.'

After Barry Thewlis had left, Dylan called Larry into his office. An incident room needed to be set up and the team required briefing. The priority enquiry was to find Kenny Fisher – and Patrick Todd.

Initially, the office was to be divided into two teams, one to be headed by Dylan, the other by Larry.

'You sure you're up to this?' Larry asked. 'Your priority should be finding a bed for the night.'

Dylan waved his suggestion away as being inconsequential. His red-rimmed eyes offered the hint of a smile. 'When did you become the sensible one?' he asked Larry, looking around the office. 'Anyway, what's wrong with here?'

Dylan was keen to head the team looking for Kenny Fisher, but Larry persuaded him otherwise.

'Think about it. It's highly likely HQ will bring in someone else to head up the enquiry even if you insist on heading it yourself,' he said, meeting Dylan's gaze. 'You know it, I know it. Now if you go looking for Todd, we might just get away without outside interference.' He casually lifted an arm to halt any dissent. 'Don't worry,' he said at the sight of Dylan's disappointment; he allowed himself a little smirk. 'I'll make sure when we do find him that he resists arrest and he gets what's coming to him, you can be assured of that. Mind you, saying that, I don't think for one minute he'll come quietly, do you? Whatever happens, we'll be ready for him.'

The briefing room was well lit. Eight wooden tables with metal legs, surrounded by several rows of folding chairs, all faced in the same direction. A large dry-wipe board was mounted on one wall. The room was without windows and smelt of school dinners.

Dylan's entrance was met by a few raised eyebrows and the odd sympathetic smile. Some faces were familiar, others were not. Standing at the front of the room with Larry, Dylan briefed the team with all the information he had. With all eyes focused on him, he described the suspects.

Detective Constable Ned Granger sloped into the room as quietly as he could, to be met with Dylan's glare. The small, portly figure handed Larry a note then sat down. Larry read the contents and passed it on to Dylan. The room was silent as he also read its contents.

'A witness has come forward in relation to the fire at my home,' he told the assembled gathering. 'The witness says that he saw someone hurrying from my house, frantically beating out flames on his arm. Fortunately for him, the flames were quickly extinguished and he was seen jumping into a dark-coloured Mercedes and driving off. This may or may not be linked to either of the enquiries, but at this stage I think we would be naïve not to think these personal attacks on myself and my family are not linked.' Dylan's eyes found Ned's. 'Have we got a description?' he asked eagerly.

'Yes, the person is described by the witness as of average height and neither fat nor thin.'

Dylan's face fell. 'Fat lot of use that is.' Then his face brightened. 'But we can get confirmation of Fisher's vehicle and the registration details from the company he owns.'

'Exactly,' said Larry. 'And once we have that we will circulate it to all units.'

Dylan looked thoughtful. 'If it was Fisher, then we need to find him quickly to be able to prove that our witness was describing him.'

Ned looked puzzled. 'How do you mean?'

'Think about it. It was dark at the time and without evidence of the burns on his clothing, which I presume he will have ditched by now, and with his recent hospitalisation for burns to his hands in the car accident anyway, the witness could easily be discredited in a court of law by a decent defence solicitor.'

'Another obvious line of enquiry is the hospitals. If someone had a serious injury that required treatment, the port of call for them would be the A&E department, wouldn't it?' said Ned.

Dylan nodded. 'And not just in this county, try over the borders as well.'

When Dylan had finished briefing his team, and all local units were on the lookout for Patrick Todd, he sat down at his desk and contemplated his next move.

His top drawer was open slightly and he was drawn to the copy of the accident file he'd put there earlier. The writing on the front was blurred; the photocopier cartridges needed changing. Dylan removed the photographs and the papers and spread them out on his desk. As he flicked through the pages it dawned on him that Fisher, for whatever reason, appeared to be playing a game with him – a deadly game. Dylan could sense it.

If Fisher was responsible for Kay's death and the firing of his house, he knew he would be gone by now; he was one step ahead of them. They were wasting their time looking in the Harrowfield area. It was this gut reaction that made him suggest to Larry that his team should be making enquiries further afield. If he was heading for the airport in his condition, it would be Leeds/Bradford or Manchester and, if he did need hospital treatment badly, any hospital in between.

Chapter Twenty-Five

The detective inspector's string of bad luck was the topic of conversation throughout the station: everywhere Jen turned they were talking about it. The media, having heard several rumours, were also ringing their contacts at the station for comments, but one thing the police were good at when a fellow officer's chips were down was being supportive. Requests were channelled through the Press Office who presently were giving very little, indeed nothing, away.

Dylan was mindful of the situation but kept his head down and carried on. The hierarchy might think he was too close to the investigation to be impartial, but he was aware that they had no one else available to take over the enquiry at the moment.

'Jack Dylan, off work? You're kidding, aren't you?' said Rita, popping another Pontefract cake into her mouth. She offered one of the small, circular, black liquorice sweets to Jen.

Before Jen could respond, Avril Summerfield-Preston, who had been eavesdropping on their conversation as she passed them, butted in.

'He shouldn't be here,' she said. 'I told the chief superintendent as much this morning. His private life is using up far too much of his energy for him to be able to function properly at work.'

Jen could hardly believe her ears. 'Well, I guess the reality of the police officer's world doesn't always fit into your neat, systematic format,' she said, sharply.

Rita's look told Jen she was impressed by her reaction, and surprised at her defence of Dylan.

Avril gave Jen a dirty look, stuck her nose in the air and flung open the heavy office door. She left with a piece of paper tightly grasped in her hand and the door closed very slowly behind her.

'I wish someone would bloody see her off,' Rita said, offering Jen the sweet packet again.

Jen looked at her out of the corner of her almond-shaped eyes. 'These are moreish! Where did you get them from?' she said, eyeing its embossed image of a castle and an owl.

'Well, you know that officer I was speaking to on the phone the other day, from Pontefract?' she said with a wink.

'He didn't?'

'Oh, yes he did!'

'What're you like?' Jen frowned. 'Does Mr Dylan's job usually mean he's constantly having to look over his shoulder? That must be awful for him and his ...'

'No, does it 'eck. He's just having a run of back luck, that's all. Let's face it, you only need one idiot on your case to cause havoc in any profession.'

Jen looked curious. 'What was his wife like?'

'I didn't know her personally, but I have heard rumours.' Rita eyed her narrowly. 'Still, it's none of my business. Nor yours either.'

A hint of a blush rose in Jen's cheeks. 'No, no, of course it isn't,' she said. 'I've only seen the DI a couple of times.' A cold shiver ran down her spine and goosebumps covered her flesh. 'But I know I certainly wouldn't want to cross him.'

Rita smiled at her friend. 'That's just his detective's mask. He might look hard-faced, but underneath that tough façade he's got a heart of gold. And if ever there's any trouble, everyone knows he's a safe pair of hands. If you had to choose to be on anyone's team, you'd want to be on Team Dylan, any day of the week.'

'Do you think they'll find out who did it?' Jen asked.

Rita laughed out loud. 'It's Jack Dylan we're talking about, Jen. Have no fear, he'll find them, and I'll bet my life on it there'll be no time for a review. Anyway, talking of houses, how are you settling in?'

Jen's smile was wide, but her eyes looked slightly pained. 'I absolutely love it. In fact, I love it so much that I'm worried that if the landlord puts my rent up, I won't be able to afford it any longer.'

'You're a born worrier. We'll cross that bridge when it comes to it.' Rita gave Jen a teasing wink and wrinkled her nose, succeeding in putting a smile on Jen's face. 'Anyway, you've got a spare room, you could always take in a lodger.'

Jen nodded. 'That's definitely a maybe, but at the moment I'm enjoying the peace and quiet.'

'Anything's got to be better than where you were and the psychopath you were living with,' said Rita.

'It's a wonder anyone survived,' Dylan muttered, staring at the mangled wreck of his car.

'Yes indeed,' said the man who suddenly appeared at his shoulder. Lean and willowy and quite a bit older than Dylan, he was wearing saturated blue overalls that reeked of diesel and were tied with thick string at the ankles.

'I was told the anchorage point had been tampered with?' said Dylan.

The mechanic winced, his eyes red-rimmed and sore, no doubt from carelessly rubbing them with his greasy hands. 'Grade 5, 7/16th's fine thread Hex bolt that screws into a locking nut. There is no doubt in my mind it had to have been unscrewed. Like I said to the boss, these things don't come loose on their own.'

Dylan looked thoughtful. 'Not even over time?'

The mechanic shook his head emphatically. 'Nah, and of course if they're not connected the seatbelt is rendered useless on impact.' He pushed a pair of old spectacles, which Dylan noticed had been repaired with sticking plaster, up his nose. 'It's about as much use as a chocolate teapot, as my old mum would say. It's got to have been tampered with.'

The mechanic took out his pen light and pointed its ray of light in the direction of the glove compartment. Dylan couldn't help but notice his scarred grimy knuckles and ragged nails, bitten down to the quick.

'Look, can you see, there? The passenger airbag is switched off.' He looked back at Dylan over his shoulder. 'Someone had to physically do that.'

Dylan paced slowly around the car. It was blatantly obvious to him that the passenger side of the car had received far greater damage than the driver's side, which again confirmed what the witness had described. When he got to the boot, he looked over the roof at the mechanic who'd managed to slip away and make Dylan a mug of tea. Dylan accepted it with a nod.

'I guess it's already been searched?'

'Yes.'

'So where are the contents now?'

'Listed, bagged and tagged and taken away by you lot to be

returned to the owner. Isn't that the usual procedure? Not that they're in a fit state to be of much use to anyone,' he said. 'I can grab hold of a copy of the list of items for you if that'd help.'

'Yes,' Dylan said, 'it might.'

Half an hour later Dylan found himself sitting in the car park at HQ. The list of items found in the car that he'd tossed on the passenger seat before leaving the garage drew his attention and, turning off the car's engine, he sat quietly to read the document. The items were much as he expected: a handbag, a purse, cash, credit cards, store cards, a hairbrush, perfume and make-up, all clearly belonging to Kay, together with a wallet containing credit cards in the name of Kenny Fisher. There was just one item that struck him as odd: a syringe, which had been found in the footwell of the car at the driver's side. What the hell was that doing there?

Dylan burst through the external door and ran through the CID office. He pounded up the steps two at a time. His heart racing, he rushed down the corridor to the Traffic Office. Thewlis and Cane were sitting at their desks, drinking coffee and eating pre-packed sandwiches for their lunch. They both looked startled to see him, especially since he seemed out of breath. If it was the last thing he did, Dylan swore he would get justice for Kay. She might have been an adulteress, but she didn't deserve to have died in such a horrific way.

Cane pulled out a chair for him. 'Here, have a seat. Can I get you a drink?'

Dylan nodded and turned to Thewlis. He steadied himself and cleared his throat. 'I've just read the list of personal items that were recovered from my car,' he began.

'Ah,' said Thewlis. 'Yes, they're in the property store. I was waiting for the right time to return them to you. I thought after the inquest would be best.'

Dylan looked agitated. 'It's my understanding that the inquest will open and close, with nothing more to be done until after the full investigation?'

Thewlis nodded. 'That's right.'

'Look, I told you I wouldn't pry, but I need to know; the syringe that was found in the car ... is Kenny Fisher a junkie or a diabetic?'

Thewlis glanced down at the file that he had obviously been working on and scanned its contents. He shook his head and looked up at Dylan who was sporting a frown. 'We've no reason at all to suspect that he's connected to drugs, but that's not to say he isn't; he may just not have been caught.' He raised his eyebrows. 'As for him being a diabetic ... yes, it seems he was wearing an alert bracelet, so, as the syringe was obviously part of his kit, nothing further was looked at. So, where does that take us, boss?' he asked.

'I need to know what was in the syringe and whether any needle marks were found on Kay's body.'

'On Kay's?' repeated Thewlis.

'Yes,' said Dylan, taking the steaming mug from Cane.

'Why?' asked Thewlis.

Dylan took a sip of his drink. 'Kay wasn't diabetic and she didn't take drugs.' He frowned. 'Well, as far as I know she didn't, although it's becoming increasingly obvious to me that I didn't really know my wife at all.'

Thewlis's eyebrows knitted together in a frown. 'What're you thinking Dylan?'

Dylan's eyes narrowed. 'Kay might have been over the limit, but

I'm wondering whether there could also have been insulin in her body.'

'That I can't answer, either,' said Thewlis.

'I know. I need to see her toxicology results and, also, as the syringe was foreign to the car, I want it swabbed as soon as possible and sent off to the forensic lab to see what it contained. If it turns up insulin, and toxicology also comes back with insulin in Kay's blood, then I think the pathologist needs to have a second look at my wife's body to see if there are any needle marks on it.'

'Don't you think that a needle mark on her skin would have been picked up at her post-mortem?' said Thewlis.

'Perhaps not, due to the severity of her injuries; something which Fisher might have been hoping for.'

Cane's eyes were round. 'I'd never have thought of that,' he said.

'Why would you, unless you'd seen it before?' said Thewlis. 'But he's right, you know. An overdose of insulin can kill and, what's more, a diabetic would know it.'

To Dylan's relief, the recovered items from the accident vehicle had been sealed in individual exhibit bags and the syringe placed in a clear plastic tube.

'Excellent!' he said, gazing at the syringe exhibit as if it was a precious jewel displayed inside a glass case.

Thewlis was frank. 'Because of the number of fatal accidents involving druggies, we're extra careful these days with searches. The last thing anyone wants is a prick from a dirty needle.'

Chris Cane reached for his helmet and leathers. 'I've an appointment with a witness over in Sheffield in an hour. If you sign me the necessary paperwork, I'll drop it off at the lab.'

Dylan's eyes lit up. 'Mark it urgent,' he said, 'and I'll ring to let them know you're bringing it over. Relay the background information and ask them to make it a priority.'

When Cane had left, it felt like a bit of an anticlimax. It was now a waiting game for results. Dylan would need to update Larry and brief the team once the results had been received, but not before. In the meantime, he would update the computer system with the lines of enquiry he had initiated.

'Obviously, it could be that Fisher just used the syringe himself,' he said, only now admitting to himself that the used syringe in the car might not be sinister at all. He understood the delayed reaction: an adrenalin rush could wear off, leaving you depleted and hollow inside. 'But we need to be sure.'

'Yes, I agree,' said Thewlis. 'I must admit I've absolutely no idea what effect injecting insulin into Mrs Dylan, a non-diabetic, would have.' Thewlis cocked an eyebrow. 'But if you ask me a question on braking distances, I might be able to help you.'

Dylan forced a smile. For a moment the conversation sounded strange. For some reason Thewlis had used Kay's full title and he was taken aback. 'Everyone to their own specialism,' he said quietly. He paused for a moment, mulling things over. 'I'm no medic but, dependent on how much was used, I suspect it could have put Kay into a hypoglycaemic coma. With that, regardless of the amount of drink she'd consumed, she'd have been unconscious in the passenger seat, clearly unable to cause Fisher any concerns when he slammed the car into those bollards.'

Dylan returned to the CID Office, the bit now firmly between his teeth. Maybe Fisher had not succeeded in planning the perfect murder after all.

Chapter Twenty-Six

While the hunt was on for Todd and Fisher, Dylan had a funeral to arrange, whether he wanted to or not, and he needed to seek the advice of medical staff at the hospital for guidance on updating Isla with the recent revelation regarding her mother's accident.

Difficult as it was, the task of breaking bad news was a regular occurrence in his role as a police officer. It was something he would never get used to, but also something he had learned how to deal with over the years: a certain degree of emotional detachment was the only way to do the job effectively and efficiently. But, when it was personal, it was different. He was fully aware that, once she heard this latest news, Isla would need additional support, from himself and the medics. There was no way he could hide the facts from his daughter for ever. Undoubtedly, the media would get hold of the story eventually and, although Isla was presently in a secure unit and protected from news of the outside world, if she wanted to attend her mother's funeral – and was deemed fit enough to – there was every chance that unsavoury details might be forthcoming, however unintentionally.

As Dylan sat in the anteroom waiting to speak to the doctor, he felt the knots in his stomach tighten. He contemplated Isla's reaction.

If he knew Isla as well as he thought he did, she would want to know more. She'd always had an inquisitive mind, even as a child. He doubted that had been changed entirely by her present condition. It was important to him that ground rules were laid down between him and the medical staff when it came to responding to any questions she may ask. He wanted guidelines to fall back on when there seemed to be no immediate clues as to what to do next.

The doctor didn't keep him waiting long. When she called him into her office, she offered him a seat next to hers and introduced herself. 'My name is Ande Ankunde but please call me Doctor Ande,' she said, 'everyone does.'

Dylan found the doctor's responses to his questions to be sensitive and down-to-earth. He admired her professional ability to provide comfort, knowing how hard it was to give someone news that they would rather not be hearing.

'After some careful thought, and discussion with the team who are caring for Isla, I think we should tell her the truth.' She appeared a little hesitant as she waited for his reaction. 'But obviously I'll be guided also by you. You know your daughter better than any of us.'

'I thought I did,' Dylan said, 'once upon a time ...' He could tell that Dr Ande was aware of his pain. 'But I agree with you.'

The doctor's smile showed him she was relieved. 'It is considered best practice these days to be as truthful and open as possible. A few decades ago patients were often protected from bad news. In fact, my father published a paper in the 1960s on methods of evasion that could be used in certain circumstances, as it was widely believed that the truth would be damaging to the patient's hope, or motivation to get well.'

Dylan's eyebrows were raised. 'But we now have a different

perspective on human rights … Disclosure is everything in policing these days, too, because of data protection. A person arrested, for instance, even has the right to know what evidence is against them so their defence has time to come up with an alibi before they are put before the court. So I understand where you're coming from.'

'I think each case must be dealt with on its own merits; everyone is different, and has different circumstances. How we go about giving Isla any news is important right now. Her welfare is at the forefront of everyone's minds.'

'I agree. And while I am no stranger to delivering bad news to people, it's different when it's someone close to you. So I really value your opinion and advice on our joint approach.'

'Isla is intelligent and capable of digesting any information we impart to her despite her medication. My suggestion is that you share whatever information you need to in the presence of her daily care nurse, who you have probably met before, and with whom she seems to have struck up a bond. We will of course monitor her reaction, keep a close eye, and take whatever action is required.'

Dylan clenched his fists and took a deep breath. 'I'm going to be reminding her that her mum died in a car accident. Her mother's boss was driving the vehicle and evidence now suggests that not everything is as it first seemed. There is likely to be a court case. I think that is enough for her to take in at the moment.'

Dr Ande's face didn't show any emotion. 'I think the fact that her mum has died will have been the most devastating news for her. In my opinion, how it came about will be secondary to her. I think we need to record on the notes what she is told, so that everyone who cares for her can see exactly what has taken place. Thereafter, we do what we are doing now and continue to monitor her.'

'Thank you for making that more straightforward than it could have been. I agree with you. It's not going to be easy.'

'It certainly isn't, but I'm sure she'll be comforted hearing the news from you, rather than anyone else. I have to tell you she is a very sick young woman, Mr Dylan. She has a long journey ahead of her, which will require a lot of co-operation on her part if she is to get better.'

Dylan's eyes were downcast as he nodded.

'But, be assured, we are doing everything we can for her.'

Dr Ande made a move to stand. 'Shall we get this over with, if you are ready? I don't think any time is going to be a good time, do you?'

Dylan nodded. 'Yes, and thank you for your time,' he said, offering her his hand.

'Not a problem. We are all here for Isla.'

When he entered her room, Dylan was shocked to see Isla lying so still on her bed, with tubes running out of her arms into the monitors. But she seemed to receive his news with a certain amount of resolve. He was encouraged to leave her when she was brought her afternoon tea, which consisted of soup, sandwiches, jelly and ice cream.

Isla waved him off with a limp hand and a weak smile. She licked her lips and blew him a kiss. 'Love you,' she said quietly.

'I love you more,' he replied, as he always did.

When he was gone, she pushed the tray of food away and closed her eyes.

Dr Ande walked with Dylan to the end of the corridor. 'I am meeting with the rest of the team looking after Isla this afternoon to discuss the way forward,' she said.

'Please keep me updated. You can get hold of me anytime on my mobile,' Dylan replied.

The news that Dylan couldn't attend Kay's post-mortem was expected: protocol did not allow it, which he knew was the case. With Larry occupied on the hunt for Fisher, Sergeant Thewlis and DC John Benjamin were the nominated officers and he knew they would glean what they could to enable him to have the best possible chance to get justice for Kay.

Delays in the release of Kay's body for her funeral were inevitable now that a second post-mortem was required, and its time and date were dependent on the availability of the pathologists who would re-examine the body.

Dylan's house had been released from its crime-scene status, however, so he had arranged to meet the insurance personnel at what was left of the property.

Josh Ferrell, the loss adjuster, was a tall, thin man with a long, narrow face and a neatly trimmed, auburn goatee beard. A smile lifted the corners of the young man's mouth as he extended his hand in greeting, but his gaze went straight beyond Dylan, down the path towards the charred ruins of the house. As if reading Dylan's thoughts, he asked if it was okay to go 'inside'. His voice was soft and sympathetic. Dylan nodded his approval and followed behind him.

Ferrell moved around the house in silence, taking notes and ticking boxes. Several times he stopped and hummed and hawed, lightly stroking his beard and looking from Dylan's charred lot to his clipboard and back again. Sensibly, he'd worn knee-high green Wellington boots.

The inside of the house was a blackened, soggy mess. Wet debris stuck to the bottom of Dylan's shoes and when Josh Ferrell stopped to ask him the mandatory questions, it suddenly hit him: his past no longer existed. He was consumed by an unfamiliar sense of hopelessness.

As they wandered through the remains, Dylan stopped now and then to pick up a shard of glass, or piece of pot that could potentially cause harm to anyone cleaning up – why, he didn't know. There were far too many for him to remove on his own. The pace of the viewing was dictated by the other man and was extremely slow. Hands stuffed into his pockets, Dylan hung his head, shuffled his feet and kicked the toes of his shoes around in the dirt. There was nothing for him to do but stew in his powerlessness. When spoken to, he lifted his head and scanned the debris and tried his best to seek answers to the questions being asked of him.

Acting on the insurance company's orders, several workmen were already present and in the process of erecting secure fencing around the property. Of course, Dylan would have a key to the gated access, he was told, so that he could salvage any personal belongings – if there were any left, which he sincerely doubted.

The ruins still bore a strong smell of petrol fumes, which didn't go unnoticed by Ferrell. Before he left the house, he informed Dylan he would be in touch with a report and a possible settlement figure as soon as possible. Dylan believed him when he promised he wouldn't 'drag his feet'.

'Do you have somewhere to stay?' asked Ferrell. Dylan was taken aback. He looked down at his stained wax jacket, the frayed bottoms of his heavily creased suit trousers and realised he must look a right state. 'I'll be fine. I've requested a place at Heartbreak Hotel …'

Ferrell gave him a quizzical look.

'The police-owned flats,' said Dylan. 'Believe it or not, they've actually got a waiting list!'

'Oh, I believe it, all right,' Ferrell said. 'My sister was briefly married to a copper.'

235

Dylan sat in his car with his head in his hands; he felt numb. He owned nothing, not the car he sat in, not a wardrobe of clothes, not even a place to lay his head down at night, and he had nowhere to bring Isla home to when she was released from hospital. But at least, for now, he'd done what he needed to do and he could concentrate on getting justice for Kay, which was also the only thing he could proactively do for Isla.

He was angry and he wanted revenge. He had a lot of issues to resolve, but he knew that, if he worked through them systematically, he would eventually succeed.

Dylan's priority remained to trace both Todd and Fisher. He knew in his heart that one, if not both, of these men had brought disaster to his door.

When he returned to the office, he found it hard to concentrate. Images of Kay continued to hover in his mind, both as his wife and as her lover's mistress. He was aware that some of his colleagues would think him overzealous in his enquiries. Was he clutching at straws, because it was his wife that had died in the accident? He believed otherwise. He was merely being thorough. He'd been to enough crime scenes over the years to realise that nothing should be overlooked; ignore an 'action' at your peril, as his mentor, Inspector Peter Reginald Stonestreet had taught him.

Jen headed to the supermarket in her lunch break to buy a few fresh vegetables. As she strolled around the store, her thoughts were mainly about Max waiting for her at home, and of the lovely, peaceful walks in the countryside that were waiting for them both to enjoy. 'God's own country' she'd heard Yorkshire called. Now that she was settled, and free, she could concentrate on getting to know it.

She'd loved *Wuthering Heights* at school. Now she couldn't wait to see where the author had lived and been inspired. She found herself silently reciting one of her favourite Emily Brontë quotes as she made her way through the store, basket in hand: *I have dreamed in my life, dreams that have stayed with me ever after, and changed my ideas; they have gone through and through me, like wine through water, and altered the colour of my mind.* She was excited about discovering more.

One way of avoiding boredom while waiting in the queue for the checkout was to people watch. Jen was fascinated by the hotchpotch of human life that would never usually be brought together. It was probably why people queued in relative silence, she decided.

Jen turned when a lady some way behind her shouted to her obese husband who was leaning on the trolley in front.

'D'ya want some Diet Coke?' Their child, obviously tired, screamed over her father's reply. Two minutes after the father had silenced the child by putting a hand over her mouth, he yelled back. 'What d'ya say?'

Feeling a little embarrassed, Jen looked elsewhere, and unexpectedly caught sight of Jack Dylan standing at the entrance to the store. The hair on the back of her neck stood on end as their eyes met. She smiled nervously.

'Next!' the cashier said to Jen in an irritated manner.

Distracted, Jen unloaded her basket. As she packed her bags, she realised Dylan was no longer standing there and she was filled with disappointment. Scanning the entrance, she looked everywhere and at everyone, to no avail.

Dylan's eyes flashed a hint of excitement as he listened eagerly to what Larry had to say. He put his half-eaten pork pie back in its paper bag and drained his coffee cup.

'The hospital staff at Burnley have alerted us to a patient in A&E requiring treatment for burns to his arm. He's using the name Kevin Fisher. On questioning, we were told that Fisher also has previous burn injuries, which he told staff he received in a road accident. He won't elaborate on his recent injury, other than that it happened at work. Trouble is they have no way of detaining him, so we've got to get there ASAP.'

'I'm coming with you,' Dylan said.

'No, you're not!' Larry snapped. 'Your target is Todd. Remember? We discussed this.'

So shocked was Dylan by the authoritative tone, that Larry had disappeared out of the office before he had time to argue.

Larry was right and Dylan knew it. As he stood at his office window, he saw two CID vehicles tearing out of the metal station gates, en route to Burnley, Lancashire and he willed them with every ounce of his being to bring Fisher back to face the music.

Kenny Fisher lost his balance and fell face forward onto the stone flags. One arm in bandages, he had clocked the police team at exactly the same time as they had seen him emerging from the revolving doors at Burnley hospital's entrance. When he'd attempted to run away, four officers, out of the traps like whippets at the local greyhound track, were immediately in hot pursuit.

Fisher swayed as DC Andy Wormald lifted him unceremoniously off the ground by grabbing hold of the collar on his jacket.

Getting into a police vehicle was difficult for Fisher with his hands cuffed behind his back. Not only that, they twisted against the bone on his wrists – he'd cried out several times in pain as they were put on. The officers were unsympathetic. A quick search had revealed a sheath knife tucked in his right boot together with a set of car keys, a wallet and his passport in his coat pocket. Besides being clearly prepared to do a runner, Larry had every reason to believe he would have used the knife against the officers if he'd been given the opportunity.

Larry spun his prisoner around so that his back was facing the open door of the car, put a hand roughly upon Fisher's forehead and pushed downwards to thrust him towards the vehicle. 'Mind your head,' he said in a casual way as Fisher fell into the back seat, hitting his head. 'By the way, you're nicked!'

Larry and the team were on their way back to Harrowfield with Fisher well and truly collared. Putting in the call to Dylan to say he had Fisher in custody was highly satisfying.

Detective Constable Wormald used the keys they had found in Fisher's possession to locate a Mercedes parked in the disabled bay of the hospital car park – a quick getaway had obviously been part of Fisher's plan.

The three vehicles were driven in a convoy down the motorway. Larry sat next to Fisher who was prone on the back seat of the first car, shivering. When he caught the detective sergeant looking down at him his lips curled into a mocking smile.

'Something amusing you?' said Larry, his eyes darkening. He wondered if it might have been Fisher's voice that he'd heard talking to Kay the night he had called with Dylan's coat, but the few words he'd muttered so far hadn't allowed him to be certain.

Fisher didn't respond to the DS, whose anger steadily rose inside him, radiating heat throughout his body.

From his office, Dylan watched the vehicles creep into the police station yard. His mobile rang. He took a deep breath, took two steps towards his desk and reached over to pick it up. 'Dylan,' he snapped.

'The syringe tested positive for insulin and your wife's toxicology results also show an abnormal amount of insulin in her blood,' said Thewlis.

'Bastard,' Dylan growled, as he watched Larry grab Fisher by the shoulders and drag him out of the car and onto the ground.

'And now we wait for the coroner's officer to get in touch with a date for the second PM,' said Thewlis. 'I'll keep you briefed.'

Dylan's office phone started ringing, but his mind was focused on one thing only, and that was seeing Kenny Fisher, the man who'd murdered his wife. Purposefully, he walked past the desks in the CID office. Such was his concentration that Ned Granger had to stand, lean over and grab his arm to gain his attention. 'Boss,' he said urgently. 'We've had a definite sighting of Patrick Todd, in Pearson's bookies on the high street in Brelland.'

Patrick Todd paced his cell, small though it was, with one hand placed over his swollen eye and the other holding up his trousers because they had taken his belt away. There was no reason why Jack Dylan had had to hit him so hard – he would be having a word about that with the duty solicitor when he saw him. His head was pounding. Resisting arrest, they'd said. Of course he had! But Dylan running at him like a stampeding bull, fists flying, and landing a punch that should have been kept for the boxing ring, was way over the top in any arrest. For God's sake, he'd just been sitting minding his own business on a stool in the bookies, still inebriated from the dinner time session at the Old Cock.

Todd slid onto the small, plastic mattress that lay upon the bunk secured to the cell wall and curled up, sore, angry and bewildered. Blood still ran from his crumpled nose, and his burst lip felt crusty to the sweep of his tongue. He wiped it on the blanket they had given him, then smeared the whole bloody mess on to the shiny magnolia-painted cell wall.

'If only detectives carried batons,' Dylan said to the custody officer as he stood at the custody suite counter.

'It's a bloody good job they don't, Dylan,' said Larry. 'Otherwise we would have a murder on our hands. Whether it was self-defence or not!'

Dylan was never without his mobile these days and always kept it charged. He had taken to holding it in his hand as though it was a lifeline, hoping he would get a call with good news from the hospital and fearing, with equal intensity, that if news came it would be bad. When the phone eventually rang it was Isla's doctor and Dylan listened with his heart in his mouth.

'I'm afraid the team here think we need to act now. Isla is not eating enough to sustain her. We are worried about major organ failure if we don't intervene.'

Dylan mumbled through numbed limps. 'I'm on my way.' His voice was calm; his hands trembled.

White knuckles gripped the steering wheel. Waiting for the traffic lights to change, he forced his fingers to relax.

People moved about the hospital with a lazy afternoon casualness, migrating from one building to another. In the face of coming rain, the air felt heavy and still as grey clouds gathered overhead.

With his head down, Dylan walked to the ticket machine as the rain started to fall lightly. There was a queue to pay for the parking and he stood, waiting, one part of him anxious to get to Isla's bedside, another wanting to run away to happier times.

Chapter Twenty-Seven

Isla was curled up foetus-like beneath the sheets, her bed framed by stainless steel metal guards. A machine to her left displayed cryptic results. It hummed, breaking what otherwise would have been an unbearable silence. Dylan could hardly bear to see the image before him. Her tiny skeletal frame was severely out of proportion: her head made barely an indent in the soft pillow, yet seemed way too big for her body. She had never been a big girl, but twenty-nine kilos was what they said she weighed now. Where had the red, chubby cheeks of his beautiful, adorable angel gone? He bent his head and kissed her thin-boned hand, webbed by almost translucent skin, that lay so delicately, limp in the palm of his.

He sat beside her through the night watching, waiting, hoping, praying for a miracle. The slow rising and lowering of her chest showed him that she was comfortable and calm.

To the right on her bedside cabinet sat a book and beside it her childhood teddy. Uncomfortable under the unblinking gaze of the soft toy, Dylan picked Teddy up and cuddled him. Something pricked his finger, drawing blood. Shaking his hand, briefly convinced he had been stung, he pulled a tissue from its box and wrapped it around his finger, watching as the blood was absorbed quickly, forming a slender thread on the paper. He checked the bear over. Inside one arm he found the blade of a pencil sharpener, which Isla must have concealed within.

Tears welled up in his tired eyes. 'Why Isla? Why?' he asked, as he threw the blade in the bin and put Teddy back in its rightful place, watching over her.

Shaking, he took a deep, ragged breath, leaned back into the chair and gazed again on his daughter, not for the first time questioning her sanity and seeking within him an answer as to what he should – could possibly – do. There was no policy to guide him, no training for this unexpected role. He looked up and he prayed, but the stark white ceiling merely stared back and he berated himself. If there was a God then why would he allow this to happen? His eyes turned to the clock on the wall. It was seven minutes past seven. Suddenly, he felt drawn to Isla's book. He reached up and pulled it from the shelf. He stared at it, willing it to give him a sign, some sort of guidance, but instead it sat heavy in his hands, silent and self-contained.

He opened the cover and he saw she had signed her name on the inside. Running his fingers over her writing, he felt closer to her. He flicked through the pages, one by one, and on the seventh page found a folded piece of writing paper. With his heart beating fast, he opened it.

Dear Dad,

I wish I could make you understand.

I wish you knew what it was really like for me but, then again, I hope you never know.

I cannot fight any more than I have done.

I want you to understand, I've tried so very hard, but it's beaten me.

Please don't let them try to keep me alive.

I wanted to have a life, but I don't have one.

Don't cry for me.

If I could give you one thing, I would give you the ability to see yourself through my eyes.

Then you would realise how special you are to me.

I want you to be happy.

I will always love you.

Isla xx

Dylan reached for Isla's hand and as it lay in his he felt a slight tremor – did she know? 'Please, Isla, don't leave me,' he begged her.

When there was no answer, he composed himself, stood, looked about him and pushed the piece of paper deep into his pocket. He bent down and kissed Isla briefly on the cheek. Quickly, he turned on his heel and walked away, not daring to look back, for fear he would crumble.

Dylan looked up, closed his eyes and offered a silent thank you as he twisted his wedding ring round his finger. Kenny Fisher was behind one of these cell doors, but which one? His eyes locked with the custody sergeant for a brief moment before he tore his away, reluctant to heed the officer's warning not to jeopardise Fisher's trial.

'Don't you worry, we're taking good care of him, sir,' the officer said, with a nod of his head and a wink.

Dylan forced his lips to turn up at the corners, though he felt nothing like smiling. What he didn't know was that Detective Sergeant Larry Banks had already warned the staff that Dylan must be prevented from seeing Fisher at all costs, if they didn't want a death in police custody on their hands.

Dylan's stomach had tightened in anticipation and, with all his senses on high alert, his right hand instinctively tightened into a fist as he tried unsuccessfully to remain calm. The cell area was warm compared with the office and he guessed that a prisoner had complained of the cold, so the heating had been adjusted accordingly, as per Home Office guidelines.

The custody sergeant watched him stop at Fisher's cell door. Dylan put his hand to his temples and swayed a little before resuming on course to his destination: the exit. Shoulders back, he pushed the double doors wide open, to an onlooker appearing cool and confident.

But Dylan's head felt fuzzy and, feeling disorientated, he headed towards the toilets. A thin sheen of perspiration covered his forehead, so he cupped his hands together and splashed cold water on his face to revive himself. Glancing in the mirror as he dried his hands on the rough paper towel he'd grabbed from the machine on the wall, he realised how much he'd let his appearance slip lately. His hair looked wild and windswept, not from the weather, but from him dragging his hands though his hair; his face was aged by anxiety and his eyes shadowed by fatigue.

Back in the CID office he began to feel slightly better, mostly owing to the banter of his colleagues, teasing him about him using a knock-out punch on Patrick Todd. His hand still throbbed and he fervently hoped that Todd's nose was hurting just as much. Alone in his office, he slid open his desk drawer and took out two paracetamols, heading to the kitchenette for a glass of water. The tablets might not help his mood, but they would help to dull the pain somewhat.

As he put the glass to his lips he heard the door swing open and Jennifer Jones came in. He couldn't help looking at her. Her blonde hair was tied back in a neat ponytail; the colour and cut of her dress made her look elegantly feminine. Despite the confined space, she took no notice of him standing at the window as she put the tray full of mugs down beside the sink, turned on the tap and squirted washing-up liquid into the bowl. Suddenly, he was aware of the tension within him as, mesmerised, he watched her slowly and carefully put one mug after the other into the soapy water. It gave him a sense of normality, observing a picture of domesticity, and he was grateful for the moment of tranquillity it brought him. Dylan added to her pile of washing-up with his empty glass and she looked up at him and smiled warmly. He picked up a tea towel.

'Gosh, that looks sore!' she said, her expression sympathetic. 'You don't need to ...' she said, as she nodded her head at his swollen red knuckles, the tea towel and the pot he had lifted out to dry.

Dylan took a deep breath and straightened up. 'I want to ...' he said, with a faint-hearted smile, 'really I do.'

'How did you do it? Or shouldn't I ask?' Jen grimaced.

'It's no secret. I was defending myself.' He raised an eyebrow.

Was that a glint of mischief she could see in his eyes?

'We located the man who recently put me in hospital and I didn't fancy any more stitches in my head, so I hit him, wham, straight on the nose.'

'I guess he's locked up now?'

Dylan nodded.

Jen listened patiently to the details. Her concern was genuine and she smiled back at him reassuringly, showing just the amount of support and care he needed. Her eyes were wide and he assumed it was out of curiosity. It was lovely to be listened to so appreciatively. He could hear his voice becoming emotional as he talked and he choked back the tears.

'Why are people such idiots?' she said. Her eyes were on Dylan with a mixture of interest and understanding and he didn't want their conversation to end.

Jen put the kettle on and he stood and watched her reach for the coffee jar, tussle with the teabags and scoop sugar into the mugs. He brought her the milk from the fridge.

'Would you like a drink?' she asked, holding up a steaming mug. When he took it from her he flinched at their contact.

'How're things with you?' he asked to cover up his embarrassment. 'I understand your partner threatened you?'

Jen busied herself and, when she turned with the tray in her hands, he saw she was blushing. Saying nothing for a moment, she waited for him to open the door. When she did speak her voice was calm and somewhat guarded. 'News travels fast round here,' she said, a smile tugging at the corner of her mouth.

'Oh, I'm sorry,' Dylan said, his hand on the door knob. 'I didn't mean to …'

She rested the heavy tray on the work surface again.

'The only reason I know about it is that I was the on-call negotiator and I got a copy of the Log through, for the negotiators' database. I was stood down about two miles away from the house when uniform informed Control that they had sorted him.'

Jen could barely speak. 'Thank you.' She looked up at him. 'He's now my ex, of course. I hadn't known him long. The relationship was a huge mistake. Brought about by loneliness, I guess.' Her face broke out in a shy smile. 'I should have listened to my dog, Max. He's a better judge of character than me, it appears.'

'What sort of dog have you got?'

'A golden retriever.'

'Give me dogs before people any day of the week.' Dylan's eyes clouded over. 'I'd quite like a dog myself.'

'Why don't you get one?'

Dylan sipped his coffee. 'I'm never at home; it wouldn't be fair.' He stopped and looked thoughtful. 'Come to think of it, I don't even have a home to be at!'

'I'm sorry. I heard.' It was Jen's turn to look uncomfortable. 'I don't know how you're coping with everything ...' She paused. 'And work too.'

'Work gives me a focus, a reason to get up every morning, if that makes sense. Turns out my wife had been cheating on me for some time. Although I wouldn't have wished her dead, they do say things happen for a reason. I'm still waiting to see what that reason is, but she paid for her bit of excitement with her life.'

'I've just moved into a rented property with my dog, Max. It feels like a fresh start for me. I was extremely lucky Rita in admin knew about a little cottage that was coming up for rent. Have you any idea who burnt down your house?' she asked.

Dylan nodded. 'Yeah, the same bloke who was seeing my wife. He's been locked up this morning.'

'I thought she died in a road accident?'

'It appears that the accident wasn't an accident at all.'

Jen raised her eyebrows. 'And I thought I had problems. Mine don't even scratch the surface compared with yours.'

Dylan sighed deeply. 'I guess it can only get better, although for now I'm probably going to have to move into Heartbreak Hotel until things get sorted.'

Jen frowned. 'Is that a real place?'

Dylan laughed out loud, seeing the serious expression on her face.

'No, its police flats that are mostly used for officers who are in some kind of crisis.'

'It doesn't sound like a happy place.'

'No, but at least I'll have a roof over my head instead of sleeping in the office.'

'You're not?'

Dylan nodded. 'Don't tell Beaky,' he said in a whisper. 'If she finds out she'll hit the roof.'

'I won't.' Jen shook her head. 'And, on that note, I'd better get these drinks back to admin, otherwise I'll be out on my ear.'

Sitting back at his desk, Dylan felt a sense of control returning and, being a control freak, he welcomed the feeling. Even when he was informed there were no rooms free at Heartbreak Hotel for the foreseeable future and instead he was to be given a hospitality suite at Bishopgarth Training School in Wakefield, he wasn't upset. The housing arrangement was open-ended, so he could come and go as he pleased.

His thoughts were interrupted when Larry Banks put his head around his office door and, seeing Dylan sitting in his chair, walked straight in, brandishing an angry fist.

'I wanted to pummel his fucking face for you.' Larry threw the interview notes on the desk.

Dylan's hopeful thoughts began to drain away as he struggled for composure. Instead he swore silently under his breath. 'I'm all ears.'

Larry sat on the edge of his seat looking increasingly agitated. 'He's happy to talk, much to the disgust of his expensive barrister. According to him, he started seeing Kay just after she started working for him.'

'Nearly two years ago?' said Dylan, in amazement. 'Then why this now?'

'He says, after spending time with her while you were away, he'd asked her to leave you, thinking she'd jump at the chance. But she refused. So he decided that if he couldn't have her, then no one else was going to.'

Dylan looked up at the ceiling, leaned back and locked his hands behind his head. 'What a cliché! I wish I had a pound for every time I've heard that line said by a murderer!'

'Classic isn't it? Apparently, he thought seriously about dispensing with you instead. If you didn't exist, he was sure she'd turn to him, but when he discussed it with her she told him otherwise.'

Dylan stared at Larry. 'She *knew* he was thinking of killing me?'

'Yes, according to him. While they were having a romantic meal together on the night of the crash, he'd given her one last chance to say she'd leave you, and when she flatly refused he made an excuse of needing to make a private phone call, went out to the car, and swiftly switched off the airbag. Apparently, he'd already disengaged the seatbelt anchorage bolts having done the research in his bid to see you off, understanding from Kay that she usually drove the car and that you regularly travelled in the passenger seat.'

Dylan sucked in his breath. 'He could have killed Isla!'

Larry nodded emphatically. 'He said he plied Kay with vodka that night, sneaking it into her Diet Coke. Apparently, she was none the wiser and got quickly drunk. I guess, considering she didn't normally drink much, that's not surprising, is it? I let him talk. I'd no intention of stopping him before the forty-five minute tape ran out.'

Dylan sat forward, his elbows on his desk. 'His plan was flawed. The car left the road.'

'His airbag activated, as we suspected,' Larry said matter-of-factly.

Dylan gave a low moan and briefly he buried his head in his hands. 'If she had agreed to leave me, then she'd still be alive.'

There was silence.

'God, I wish she had ...' he said in a whisper.

Larry gave a non-committal grunt. 'He couldn't face rejection. Apparently, he was used to getting what he wanted – nobody says no to Kenny Fisher, not his family, not his friends, not his staff: no one.'

Dylan looked shocked. 'He has family?'

'Estranged, not surprisingly.' Larry's words hung in the air.

'Tell me, did he mention the insulin?' Dylan asked. He was curious.

Larry shook his head. 'No, and we didn't mention the fact that we'd found the syringe or the results of the blood tests.'

'I want his car searched for a spanner or any kind of tool that would render a seatbelt anchorage point useless. He might be talking, but he's not telling us the whole story yet. But that doesn't matter; we will prove beyond doubt that he did it for the CPS and the courts.'

'Well, he's had every opportunity, so he must have a reason for not telling us everything. Once we have the results from the pathologist at the second PM, we'll drop that bit of information on his toes and see what his reaction is.'

Dylan's phone interrupted them.

'It was Derek Booth,' said Dylan, as he put the receiver back down. 'They're going to re-examine Kay's body this evening. I'll inform Thewlis and Benjamin and notify SOCO to attend to take the necessary photographs and samples,' he said, with a mixture of sickening curiosity and heartbreak. He needed to know that the investigation would be as thorough as in any suspicious death and, even though he wasn't in charge, he would be damned if he didn't oversee it.

'Did he say why he torched the house?'

Larry's gaze fastened on Dylan's ashen face. 'He blames you. Firing the house was obvious to him, but he wanted you in it.'

Dylan's eyes were wide, his expression blank. 'The silent calls on the night of the fire?'

'Yes, those calls. He told us he'd rung you to ensure you were home before setting off to drop a petrol bomb through the letter box.'

'But I couldn't sleep so I went to see Isla at the hospital.' Dylan could feel his body going cold at the thought of what might have happened.

'Did I really ever know Kay?' he said, wiping his hand across his face to disguise the tears welling up inside. 'How on earth did she get involved with this madman? Do you think she's ever been unfaithful before?'

Chapter Twenty-Eight

'Todd's nose is broken.'

'Tell someone who cares, Larry.'

It was obvious to Dylan the DS had no intention of leaving his office. Larry yawned loudly. Dylan lifted his head up to look at him, opened his mouth as if to speak, then closed it again and returned to his reading. Larry took a seat as he sipped a much-needed energy drink.

Dylan's head remained down as he pored over the documents that were spread out on the desk in front of him. He allowed himself a self-satisfied smile.

'They've christened you "Basher" in the cells,' Larry said.

'I told you, it was self-defence,' muttered Dylan.

Larry laughed, a throaty laugh. 'Keep telling 'em that, and eventually CPS will have no choice but to believe you.'

Dylan looked Larry in the eye. 'I'm waiting to see what he says in interview.'

'On a positive, you're still here to tell the tale and a good job too. I've told the team you'll be in the bar tonight. I think you need a break and I also think they deserve a drink for a job well done, don't you?'

Dylan gave a slight smile before responding. 'I guess that means I'm paying?'

Larry grinned. 'Yeah, well, you'll be getting a nice insurance payout ... Actually, you'll be needing a new car,' Larry lowered his voice, and leaned towards Dylan, 'and it just happens I've a mate who can help you out ...' Dylan gave him a dismissive twist of his lips. 'There's a lot of things I need before I buy a flash car ...'

The DS had the good grace to look shamefaced. 'Let me know when you find out the results of the second PM, then we can arrange for another interview – and charge Fisher with Kay's murder.' He rose from his chair and walked lethargically to the door. With his hand on the handle, he turned to face his colleague. 'So, it's the bar later then?'

Dylan nodded. 'If it'll make you feel better.' It was the last thing that he wanted to do but it wasn't as if he had a home to go to.

The office door was ajar. 'Penny for them?' Jennifer Jones said, popping her head inside. Dylan looked up. She walked in and picked up the empty cup from the corner of his desk, where it had been placed to avoid him spilling the contents on his paperwork. 'Are you ready for another?'

His eyelids were heavy, but he felt calmer than he had done since the accident. It was a welcome feeling. 'Yes, thank you.'

'How are you?' Her smile was engaging.

'Strangely enough, knowing that Kay had been cheating on me for some time has helped me to deal with her death. I've accepted that what she did was her choice and I realise now that I couldn't have changed what happened.'

'Good. One day at a time,' she said softly.

'The team's having a drink in the bar tonight, would you like to join us?' Dylan said.

In the interview room, DC John Benjamin and PC Vicky Hardacre lowered themselves into the chairs opposite Patrick Todd and his solicitor. A table sat between them and the accused. Dylan could see via the link to his office that Todd was sitting on his hands, in case his body language gave him away – he was no stranger to being interviewed and had already shown that he had no respect for the law. There was no way he was going to come easy.

'I didn't know if fucking Sherlock had clocked me or not, did I? I was as high as a fucking kite and off m'head on coke. In fact,' Todd said with a laugh, 'I didn't even know if he were real, or a figment of my fucking imagination.' Todd squirmed in his chair.

Dylan was listening intently to the conversation when a slight tap came at his door. The door opened and in walked Jen with his coffee. He motioned her over and she stood beside him watching the screen, so close he could hear her breathing – and he hoped she couldn't hear the rapid beating of his heart. The smell of her perfume was intoxicating and he found himself involuntarily distracted by her presence.

'What did you hit Detective Inspector Dylan with?' John asked Todd, leaning towards him, his eyes boring into the prisoner's, intent on an answer.

For a moment, Todd faltered. 'A wooden bar off a broken trolley in t'station yard.'

Jen drew in a breath and held it for a second. 'He's admitted hitting you?' she asked.

'Not up until now, he hasn't, but John has just reeled him in like a moth to a flame.' Dylan's smile was wide at hearing the confession.

'That's what you call good interview technique.' Dylan switched the screen off and Jen took a quick step back as Ned Granger walked through the door.

'They'll charge him with section eighteen wounding now and then he'll be going home.'

'Going home?' said Jen, confused.

'Back to prison where he belongs,' said Ned.

Kay Dylan's funeral at the crematorium would be a quiet affair. She had a few old, distant relatives and some close friends and colleagues he only knew from her talking about them. How many of them were real, or merely an alibi for her lies, he could only guess. Apart from that, there were just the neighbours.

He was informed that Kenny Fisher had made a formal request to attend the service. It had been refused. The good news was that, although it had taken some finding, the pathologist had eventually located a needle mark on the right side of Kay's neck, not easily visible due to the injuries she had sustained.

Dylan was pleased for two reasons. One: he now knew that Kay would have known nothing about the accident. Two: it showed him and the CPS and the courts just how determined and premeditated Fisher had been in his planning of her death. There would be no accepting a manslaughter plea from Fisher's defence team.

The more Dylan tried to rationalise his situation, the more surreal it felt. Sitting at his desk, bleary-eyed with leaden tiredness, he found it hard to concentrate on the file he was reading. He couldn't identify words from the string of letters in front of him. He desperately wanted to lie down and sleep, but he knew from experience that if he did, hell would come chasing him.

Rubbing the pain from the crick in his neck, Dylan lifted his head and attempted to blink away the tiredness from his eyes. Frustration made him push the paperwork to one side and with bone-aching lethargy he pulled himself to his feet and left the office with the intention of making himself a large, strong coffee.

On his way through the CID office Larry stopped him. His hand reached into a large brown envelope containing some forms for Dylan to sign. 'I'm just about to charge Fisher,' he said. 'The remand file will be ready for tomorrow morning's magistrates court.'

Alone once again in his office, Dylan shut the door behind him and looked down at the clothes hanging from his body, his belt fastened as tight as it could be so that his trousers wouldn't fall down. He had lost weight. Was it any wonder? His fingers went automatically to the stubble on his chin as he took a step towards his desk; his hand wandered around his neck to the long straggly clumps of hair. He put his coffee mug down and, with the intention of going for a wash and a shave, turned to open the small wardrobe bought to hang his uniform in, where he'd put a towel, a razor and the mug that contained his toothbrush and toothpaste. Instinctively, his tongue ran around his teeth and swollen gums, already bleeding in places, owing to the lack of regular cleaning, he guessed.

He rummaged through the cupboard, panic overwhelming him as he realised that the socks, underclothes and shirts he had bought from the supermarket had all been worn and were now screwed up at the bottom of the wardrobe. He gathered them in his arms and put them in a carrier bag, wrinkling his nose at the smell of body odour. Lifting the bag and tying its handles, he dropped it in his bin. After all, he had nowhere to wash them and couldn't face a night, nor spare the time, to sit in the launderette. He'd call and get some more ... but when? The thought filled him with despair – whenever was he going to find time, for as soon as he could get away from the office, he wanted to go straight to the hospital to spend time with Isla.

As he slumped into his chair again, there was a knock at the door and Jen appeared, carrying two large bags, her perfume wafting towards him like a breath of fresh air. 'I thought you might need these,' she said, at his quizzical look. Holding the bags up she gave him a kittenish smile. 'You'll need to look smart in that Heartbreak Hotel.'

Gratitude overwhelmed him. He wondered, with all that had happened to her recently, how she could possibly have it in her to think about him? Then it hit him. Of course, she was happy now, he could see how content she was by just looking at her face.

His own depression seemed to engulf him like a heavy coat, behind which he was unable to disguise his despair. He sighed heavily and choked back a lump that rose in his throat. 'Sadly, there is no room for me at Heartbreak Hotel,' he said. Finding her face, he gave her a forced smile.

Jen could see the strain and the tiredness that he tried to hide from her and she briefly closed her eyes. Seeing the unintentional distress the revelation had caused her, he felt terrible.

'But they've offered me a room at Training School,' he said in a voice that was as upbeat as he could muster.

'Is that not good?' she asked. 'You sound disappointed.'

He screwed up his nose. 'It's busy, noisy and twenty miles further away from Isla, but beggars can't be choosers. I don't have an option if I want a roof over my head.'

There was an odd moment in which neither of them spoke. Dylan opened the carrier bags. He looked inside. After a few moments his eyes found hers again and they were smiling.

'How on earth did you know what I needed?'

'I knew how I felt when I had to leave quickly, with few belongings. I can't begin to imagine what it must be like to have nothing,' she said. 'And then, there's the funeral … You'll need something smart for that.'

The room filled with a powerful silence as he looked at her. It was Jen who broke it.

'Why not move in with me and Max?' she blurted out. 'For a few days anyway … Or at least until there is room at Heartbreak Hotel?' Her face blushed bright red as she realised what she had just said and at Dylan's silence. 'If you can stand lodging with a strange woman and her dog, that is.' Her heart was pounding as she waited for his response.

Dylan was speechless. His eyes glazed over. The effort to hold himself together, not just fall apart right there and then, was almost too much. Swallowing down the lump that had risen again in his throat, he just said, 'Really?'

Jen didn't know what she was doing. She focused in on him. She attempted to keep her voice gentle and her tone light, but he could hear the tightness creeping in as she spoke. 'I understand if you're worried what others might think.' She threw her head in the direction of Ned loitering outside in the main office.

Dylan's face broke out into a wide smile. 'No. Oh God, no,' he said, with a brief, gruff chortle. 'I got past worrying about what people thought of me years ago, when I became a police officer. It's the strange woman bit I'm worried about,' he teased, although his eyes showed deep gratitude. Taking a deep breath, he tried to steady himself.

She chuckled. Her eyes were bright. 'Look, I've got to go and walk Max, then I'm due at aerobics in the gym, so I'll get you the spare key and write down the address. You can stay as long as you like. I won't tell, if you won't.'

As Jen walked out of Dylan's office, Larry walked into her path. 'You going to aerobics tonight?' he asked. Jen smiled at him pleasantly, but avoided giving him an answer.

Dylan's emotions switched swiftly. His normal posture took over.

'Like a drink on a stick that one,' Larry said to Dylan, his eyes still on the door that she had just walked through. 'I'll be off then, boss, and set up a tab in your name.'

'Yes, well don't go getting blathered before I get there. I'm going to see Isla first,' Dylan warned him.

Larry shook his head. 'Would I, boss?'

'Don't call me wood eye,' they said in unison.

Chapter Twenty-Nine

Hell shouldn't feel so comfortable, Dylan thought guiltily when he woke up the next day.

He was warm and he felt a sense of belonging, silly as that seemed when it was his first night in a strange bed, in a near stranger's home. For the first time in a very long time, he could once again hear the birds singing. The spring sunlight appeared unduly bright through the bright yellow bedroom curtains, also welcoming him, it seemed. The house was peaceful, and as he lay there wallowing in comfort that he had not felt for so long, he allowed himself to drift in and out of a dreamless sleep. It was Sunday morning and bells rang from the village church, as if reminding him so. For the first time in days, even weeks, as exhausted and beyond tired as he was, he felt that opening his eyes might be worth the effort.

Throwing off the duvet, he got dressed and surveyed his room in daylight for the first time. The carpet was a mottled brown that matched the easy chair which looked out over the garden. Over the arm, Jen had laid soft towels, and a towelling dressing gown hung behind the door.

When he pulled back the curtains, he closed his eyes to the sun's brightness and remained statue-like for a moment to bask in its warmth before he opened the window to smell the fresh air. He saw washing hanging out on the line and watched it dancing in the light breeze; he was comforted by the normality of everyday home life that didn't include suspicion, lies and the anticipation of something inexplicably bad clouding the atmosphere, which he'd been living with for so long. He embraced the feeling with open arms.

Even the clothes in the wardrobe spoke of a fresh start, few as they were. He felt very smart; he had nothing to be ashamed of. He could hold his head up high. For all those that were aware of what had gone on, and the others that speculated, he knew he had done nothing wrong.

Jen was in the kitchen when he went downstairs. Her blonde hair was tied back in a ponytail that hung down her back. It seemed longer, somehow, and the style suited her. Her face was devoid of make-up and it made her look younger. Dylan had worried that there would be awkwardness between them. But such was his relief at the simple comforts, and gratitude for her help, that he felt he could be completely natural.

Max hopped from foot to foot at Jen's booted feet as, with his lead in her hand, she opened the back door to let him out. Her lips curved up into a slight smile and her blue eyes shone with affection.

'I'll be back shortly,' she said. 'I'll cook breakfast for us, shall I?'

Dylan smiled warmly. 'Much as I'd love that, I'll have to take a rain check,' he said, looking at his watch. 'I've a briefing in an hour.'

Did he see disappointment in her eyes. And she in his?

'I'm cooking a roast for tea, about six,' she continued, above Max's bark, demanding her attention. 'You're more than welcome to join us?'

When she'd gone, he took a cup from the drainer, a spoon from the drawer, sought coffee from the glass jar on the kitchen worktop and milk from the fridge. If he was in hell, then this was indeed a cruel trick. He looked around him. There was no splendour, no extravagance, just homely comfort in abundance. Could this new opening in life be no more than a dream, a cruel taunt, reminding him of what he could have had, but what he'd never be worthy of?

As he drove to work, he reflected on how his thoughts of Kay and Kenny Fisher had begun to diminish since he'd met Jen. Was he being disloyal to Kay's memory and to their marriage, to think of Jen now, so soon? He enjoyed her company; was that wrong too? She was gentle, she was open, she was kind. Each time he looked into her eyes, he felt a thrill. He'd asked her about her previous relationships and she'd been truthful about Shaun, her childhood sweetheart, and her reason for travelling north. She must have been very much in love with him to move three hundred miles and leave her family and friends behind, to try to get over him. He guessed that her unfortunate affair with Martin had come about through terrible loneliness and a need to be accepted.

But, of course, he was also aware that her heartache for her first love could not have worn off straight away. If she held him up as a high standard, finding someone to take his place in her life – and trusting them – might be hard. Of course, some women loved only once, but not someone as openly kind as Jen, surely?

He smiled as he thought of her welcoming face and her warmth and stopped to allow some churchgoers to cross the road in front of him and caught the eye of the vicar standing at the gates of the church. He immediately looked away in shame. Well, the magic had definitely worn off in his marriage some time ago, but he had loved Kay once, and fiercely. It saddened him that he had had to accept she'd never felt the same, but she no longer existed. He had to get over his guilty feeling that he could have done more to save their marriage if he had tried. It was too late now; she was gone.

Ned's smile didn't reach his eyes when he entered Dylan's office. The briefing was over and, sensing he wanted to speak to Dylan, the others had excused themselves and left. When they'd gone, Ned shut the door.

'Have you had your phone off, boss?'

Dylan looked down at his mobile and saw the missed calls.

'The hospital needs you to go right away,' he said. 'It's Isla.' He threw Dylan his keys. 'The firm's car is at the door.'

As the nurses and doctors brushed past Dylan in Isla's room, he kept a level gaze, but inside he felt scared. Sitting at her bedside, he clenched and unclenched his hands helplessly. He looked up at the drips and tubes that were keeping her alive. His hand instinctively went to his pocket and he felt her note there. 'I'm sorry, Isla ... I couldn't do it,' he whispered.

At the nurses' station Dylan helped himself to a coffee while they attended to Isla. Dr Ande saw him and went over to him, helping herself to a hot drink. She invited him into her office and closed the door behind him.

'It's nobody's fault, you know. It's a chemical imbalance, an illness. Just because you can't see it, it doesn't mean it's not there.'

'Perhaps not, but it doesn't make it any easier,' he said. Dylan saw a look in the doctor's eyes that told him that there was worse to come. Feeling numb, he nodded. 'Go on.'

'I'm sorry,' she said. Her eyes hooded over. 'Isla's organs are failing. I think it's too late.'

'Too late?'

'There is nothing more we can do but make her comfortable.'

Dylan sat down beside Isla's bed. 'Keep fighting, little one,' he said, as he gently stroked her on the forehead and kissed her cheek. 'I love you. I need you to stay with me. Please, please,' he begged.

He had never felt so utterly powerless.

Isla was asleep. He sat for an hour or longer and dozed in the big chair until he heard her stir and he woke as she did. He took her hand in his. A faint smile, as though worked up by enormous effort of will, moved across Isla's lips. She mumbled unintelligibly for a moment or two and Dylan held his breath, turning an ear to try to interpret what she whispered.

Then, suddenly, she stopped, opened her eyes and looked up into the corner of the room. For more than a minute she was silent, with her eyes focused only on one single spot. Dylan looked over his shoulder to see what she was looking at. There was nothing there. He heard the nurse's soft footsteps behind him as she entered the room. She too turned and looked up and he knew then it wouldn't be long.

'I'm coming, Mum,' Isla breathed, as Dylan felt her squeeze his hand ever so gently; and when she released it her eyes closed slowly for the final time. He rose to gather her in his arms, as if in a dream, needing to hold on to her so tightly that he might never let her go. He'd rather he went with her.

Silently, the nurse padded towards the window and opened it wide. The cool breeze that floated in was welcome, but he shivered; goosebumps ran down his spine.

'Why did you do that?' Dylan asked, as sipped the strong, hot tea that the nurse brought him.

'To let her spirit go free,' she said calmly.

'Thank you,' said Dylan.

Physically and mentally, he was wiped out. His footsteps were heavy and they echoed on the linoleum flooring in the corridor. Every step he took away from Isla's bedside felt like walking in treacle. When he reached the revolving doors that led to the outside, he welcomed the cold breeze that ruffled his hair. He hurried across the car park.

The gravel crunched under his feet and, as he breathed in the cool, fresh air, he hoped and prayed that Isla was now at peace, with Kay. But any sense of peace was not to last long; under his windscreen wipers fluttered a penalty notice. Dylan mouthed a sharp curse to the sky and stuffed the paperwork in his pocket, biting his lip. He wanted to pinch himself – was he dreaming? Surely, this hell he was living could only be a nightmare?

He might have been on a railroad train, looking out the window and watching the scenery, as he drove to the funeral home in a trance, to make the arrangements to turn Kay's ceremony into a joint one with Isla's. An only child, his own parents dead, the burden – even if he had wanted it to be – could not be shared.

In his heart he berated himself yet again, wishing that had he known she would get her wish, he could have eased Isla's suffering more effectively. The death watch had been so difficult to endure. There were days when he had seen her only briefly, not because he didn't love her, but because it tore him apart. And now she was gone.

Chapter Thirty

He parked his car outside the funeral home – he was early for the appointment. Automatically, and without thinking, he picked up the messages on his answerphone.

In an unemotional tone, Dawn Farren's message told him that the head of Field Colt Children's Home, Peter Donaldson, had been found dead in his car. It was thought to be suicide. The staff had been given a date of closure of the home. Nick Fowley and Tanya King had retracted their statements. Dawn suspected they were too afraid of the consequences to speak out. But when she spoke of getting the youngsters justice her voice changed. She assured him that no matter how many months or years it took, she would have her day in court with those responsible for the child sex abuse.

A result? He should have cared. He felt numb.

The next message was from Larry, who advised him that Fisher and Todd had been remanded in custody. He anticipated they would both enter guilty pleas eventually, but Dylan knew there were no guarantees once a defence solicitor saw the colour of money that came with a not-guilty trial.

Patrick Todd was looking at possibly twelve years behind bars and Kenny Fisher at life imprisonment with a recommendation he served a minimum of thirty years for murder and for arson with intent to endanger life.

Dylan briefly wondered if they would speak to each other in prison, himself being the common denominator. Not that it mattered. What did matter was that they wouldn't be lurking loose in the shadows waiting for him, or anyone else that they chose to focus their anger on.

Death, Dylan was more than aware, had a strange effect on people, and his own former belief in the hereafter had been called into question. Once he had finished at the funeral home, he could not, after all, face returning to the police station and, instead, he drove to his new temporary home.

Max, surprised and obviously pleased to see someone walking through the front door in the middle of the day, didn't bark, but instead proffered a low, guttural growl that rumbled from his throat. When Dylan tickled him under his chin, his big brown eyes looked up at him trustingly and he pressed his firm, soft head under Dylan's hand. He leaned closer, his flank against the side of Dylan's leg, as if sensing his mood. It felt natural to Dylan to respond by bending down to ruffle the retriever behind his ears and offer him a few softly spoken words.

Max followed him upstairs and lay in the bedroom doorway, watching him dress. His eyes were narrowed and focused tightly on Dylan, until his eyelids became heavy and almost, but not quite, closed. When Dylan had changed out of his work clothes, Max followed him to the door, his tail wagging expectantly and Dylan didn't want to disappoint him by leaving him behind. He left a note for Jen, just in case she should drop by and wonder where the dog was, opened the back door of the car to allow Max to jump in, and once again got behind the steering wheel. He headed towards the Haworth moors.

Max soon settled on the back seat and Dylan found himself reaching for the radio. Seldom had he felt the need for music as much as he had done lately. Immediately, 'Angels' by Robbie Williams burst over the airwaves. He had been a favourite of Isla's and she'd loved this song. Instead of turning the volume down as he usually did, with a scowl, he turned it up. He listened to the words as if Isla was sitting in the car singing them. Tears ran down his cheeks, unchecked. He pulled to the side of the road to catch his breath.

Then it was time for the news and, as he listened to the newsreader talking about man's inhumanity to man, he composed himself and drove on. After the news he did a double take as Gareth Gates came on, pouring his heart out with 'Unchained Melody'. And, finally, as he pulled up on the moors, the heartrending 'Hero' by Enrique … Isla had picked the songs for her mum's funeral – if there was ever a time that Dylan should feel that Isla was with him, it was now. It really felt as if she was speaking to him from beyond the grave.

It was fiercely cold and the terrain on the moors was unforgiving, but as he struggled against the wind, Dylan felt his veins tingle and his strength gradually being reinforced. He found himself laughing at Max's antics and was in awe of his power, watching him running downwind just as fast as he ran up the hills. When he reached the pinnacle of the rocks, which commanded a wide-reaching view of the county for miles, he sat for a moment or two and Max came and sat in solidarity by his side. He stroked the animal's head and felt a sense of comfort he'd never experienced before. No wonder Jen thought the world of Max.

It was half past six when Dylan arrived back at Jen's. When he opened the door, he was met with the wonderful aroma of dinner cooking. The table was carefully set, with knives, forks and spoons on linen napkins. There were two wine glasses and lit candles, which were dripping wax on the silver candleholders. Flowers adorned the cottage's stone mantle and there was a real fire in the hearth – it gave him hope and the promise of what a real home could be.

Max was the first in the kitchen and when Dylan put his head around the door he saw the dog's head in a large bowl of kibble and Jen peering into the oven. She stood up, picked up an oven mitt and put the oven dish on top of the stove. 'Dinner will be ready in five minutes,' she said. When he didn't answer she looked up at him. 'You okay?' she asked, gently. 'I hope you don't mind me assuming you'd want to eat with me?' Her eyes were wary, but full of hope. 'I just thought you might be hungry.'

Dylan stared at her for a long moment. 'Thank you,' he said, swallowing hard.

The day he had been dreading was finally upon him and Dylan suddenly found himself sitting in the front row of the crematorium at the funeral. He sat on his own near the aisle, alone but where he was expected to sit: closest to his loved ones – nearest the coffins.

He attempted to listen to the soothing classical music he had randomly chosen, along with the songs chosen by Isla for her mum, but found he couldn't concentrate. Standing with his back to the others, he was the focus of their attention: the grieving widower; the grieving dad.

He knew others were in attendance because he could hear them shuffling into their seats and the faint rustling of their coats as they removed them. It was warm in the crematorium. He was vaguely aware of whisperings echoing around the room, but the others there, they were nothing to him.

The music stopped and he heard the brushes at the bottom of the big doors at the back of the room as they slowly closed. There was the sound of footsteps coming down the aisle and a hand gently grabbed his shoulder from behind. He felt a kiss on his cheek and he instinctively he knew it was Dawn and Larry, who sat down behind him, and he felt extremely grateful for their support.

The Humanist celebrant talked about Kay and Isla, and gave the account of their lives that Dylan had related to her. She talked about Kay's first husband, Isla's father, and how he had been taken away from them. She didn't mention God or say that Kay would go to heaven. Kay hadn't believed in God unless it suited her, but Dylan prayed that, if there was a god and an afterlife, his wife and daughter would be there together.

The service was short and the heavy, crimson curtains in front of the coffins closed. He heard the crying and tears of the congregation and yet his own eyes remained dry. He was a realist; it wasn't Isla and Kay in the boxes before him but merely their shells, the remains of the bodies they had lived in.

When he got back into his car and listened to his messages the first words he heard were from Jen. In her soft, gentle way she told him if he needed anything to let her know and that she was thinking of him. Now, blinded by tears, he could hardly believe his luck. What had he done to deserve her friendship and kindness? He wasn't sure, but whatever it was, he was officially grateful he had done it.

'I'm going to take Kay's and Isla's ashes to Haworth and scatter them together,' he said later that night. 'I think they'd both like that.'

He knew a chapter of his life was over, and the memories would leave deep scars, but he had to put it behind him. It would never be forgotten, but he needed to look forward, not back, for his own sanity and survival.

And who knew what this relationship with Jen would bring? After all the recent turmoil in his life, for now it was the brief respite he needed, based on friendship. They would keep the fact they were living under the same roof as much of a secret as possible, for as long as possible. The last thing he wanted was to bring his enemies to her door: as he'd recently discovered, he had many.

'*Carpe diem*,' was his toast to Jen.

Maybe Miss Jones was his end of the rainbow?

One thing he now knew for sure: tomorrow was never promised, but it wouldn't stop him living for today.